CERBERUS

JOHN FILCHER

ISBN: 978-1-60414-706-3

Published by

Fideli Publishing, Inc.
119 W. Morgan St.
Martinsville, IN 46151

www.FideliPublishing.com

CERBERUS

Characters

Mark Toft, Capt. – Captain of the *Ike*

Christine Hansen, Cmdr. – XO of the *Ike*

William Bryce, Lt. Cmdr. – Engineering, *Ike*

Amy Baker, Specialist – Engineering, *Ike*

Felipe Mendez, Lt. – Helm, *Ike*

Gene Corbyn, Lt. – Science, *Ike*

Ashley Diving Hawk, Ensign –
  Communications, *Ike*

Travis Harris, Lt. – Assault shuttle pilot, *Ike*

Juan Sanchez, Gy.Sgt. – Marine, *Ike*

Ralph Tennyson – Marine Alpha team

Devin Rodman – Marine Alpha team

Sean Colton – Marine Alpha team

Davy Hallard – Marine Alpha team

Jerry Gee – Marine Charlie team

Henry Lee – Marine Charlie team

John Kowalski – Marine Charlie team

Dan Ronin, Capt. – Captain of *Cerberus* and prior
  Captain of the *Ike*

Diane Mueller, Cmdr. – XO of *Cerberus*

Elvis Lazarus, Lt. Cmdr. – Chief engineer, *Cerberus*

Pierre Delacroix, Lt. – Sensors, *Cerberus*

Kristoff Alphonso, Lt. – Fabrication, *Cerberus*

Matt LeCroy, Lt. – Tactical, *Ike* and *Cerberus*

Marcy Anzio, Lt. – Weapons, *Ike* and *Cerberus*

Maria Delgado, Lt. – Communications, *Cerberus*

Hirohito Taketa, Lt. – Medical, *Cerberus*

Antonio Perez, Lt. – Helm, *Cerberus*

Kelvin Sunderland, Lt. – Commander Air Group
  (CAG), *Cerberus*

Adam Taylor, Deck Chief – Flight Deck, *Cerberus*

Erin Johnson, Pilot Officer – Bulldog 1 pilot

Hal Patterson, Chief – Bulldog 1 rear-seater

Helmut Meyer, Pilot Officer – Bulldog 2 pilot

Sophie Schmidt, Chief – Bulldog 2 rear-seater

Antonio Russo, Pilot Officer – Bulldog 3 pilot.

Michael Jonsey, Chief – Bulldog 3 rear-seater

Reggie Parsons, Pilot Officer – Bulldog 4 pilot

Terry Gellin, Chief – Bulldog 4 rear-seater

Gary Chanson, Pilot Officer – Bulldog 5 pilot

Akira Nakamura, Chief – Bulldog 5 rear-seater

Greg Lowridge, Pilot Officer – Bulldog 7 pilot

Paul Drayson, Chief – Bulldog 7 rear-seater

Brett Mackey – Marine Bravo team

Ed Wilson – Marine Bravo team

Carlos Guthrey – Marine Bravo team, Force
  Omega

Terry Allison – Marine Bravo team

Steve Cupper – Marine Bravo team

Ty Jeffries – Marine Bravo team

Toshi Kanagawa – Marine Echo team

Adrian Longman – Marine Echo team, Force
  Omega

Rhee Lee – Marine Echo team

Han Pak – Marine Echo team, Force Omega

David Danfries – Marine Echo team

Julio Gonzales – Marine Echo team, Force Omega

Nancy Dos – Marine Echo team

Brett Blackwater – Marine Gamma team

Jefferson Langley – Marine Gamma team

Louis Caron – Marine Gamma team

Victor Berger – Marine Gamma team, Force
  Omega

David Addington – Marine Gamma team

Juan Diaz – Marine Gamma team

Aldo Pena – Marine Gamma team

Jason Priest, – Marine, *Cygnus*, Force Omega

Dale Dannon, – Marine, *Cygnus*, Force Omega

Reggy Smith, Capt. – Argo Station

Hu Nagun, Capt. – Captain of the *Kitty Hawk*

Steve Fisher, Cmdr. – XO of the *Kitty Hawk*

Mary Benton, Tactical Officer – *Kitty Hawk*

Ned Thatcher, Helmsman – *Kitty Hawk*

Michelle Rodgers, Capt. – Captain of *Ceres*

Tom Chastain, Cmdr. – XO of *Ceres*

Terry Ignatius, Tactical Officer – *Ceres*

Alfred Jurgenson, Capt. – Captain of *Cygnus*

Jessup Rodding, Adm. – Admiral, Wayside Station

Hobson, Col. – Fleet Intelligence

Wellington Harrison – Confederation President

CHAPTER 1

SOL SYSTEM ΛSTEROID BELT

The sudden heeling over of his ship unceremoniously dumped Capt. Dan Ronin off the small bunk in his ready room and woke him from an exhausted sleep. He heard the combat alarm sounding loudly over the intercom.

"Action stations, action stations, said the ship's tactical officer Lt. Matt LeCroy over the repeating blare. "This is no drill! Set Alert One throughout the ship."

Captain Ronin noticed the time as he scrambled to his feet and scooted out the door onto the bridge. He'd only slept for two hours since he cycled off the bridge to get some rest. *I need to have a word with the management of this joint. A guy just can't get any decent shut-eye around here,* he said to himself.

"Captain on the bridge," announced Cmdr. Mark Toft, glancing over from where he sat on the Captain's chair. He stood to make way for Ronin. Toft had been Ronin's second in command for the past three years of combat. By now, the two trusted each other implicitly.

"Sitrep." Ronin said, asking for a situation report as he quickly took his seat. He hoped the dark circles under his eyes didn't look too bad. "Did they try to sneak another missile up our pipes?"

"Yes, sir," Toft said, nodding. "Point defenses got it before impact, but it was still close enough to feel that little love tap anyway. We're still trying to nail down where they are."

Ronin looked at the readouts on his screens, which maddeningly showed little progress since he last glanced at them two hours ago. The ship's sensors continued reporting the same dense clutter of the asteroid belt into which they had chased their quarry before losing them. The ship of the Asiatic Collective fled the earlier fight at Tango Four Two Two, after the enemy formation fell prey to an ambush led by Ronin, which destroyed four out of five ships. They had been hiding in the belt, waiting for the AC formation.

"Ironically, the same belt that gave us ambush cover now hides the surviving, but still unidentified, AC frigate," Ronin noted aloud to Toft.

Toft nodded, too tired from days of chasing to waste energy on unnecessary speech. The dark circles under his eyes, which matched his hair color, were just as dark as Ronin's.

"LeCroy, have long range sensors unfuzzed yet?" Ronin asked his tactical officer.

"No, sir, it's still hashed out from all the junk floating around out there. This extra dusty cloud isn't helping either," said LeCroy, speaking over his shoulder from his station in front and to the left of Ronin's Captain's chair.

Commander Toft frowned, his brown eyes narrowing at the unchanging situation after days of pursuit. "Maybe we should change tactics and make them think we lost 'em?"

"Exactly what I'm thinking, Commander Toft," said Ronin, his green eyes and sandy hair reflecting small glints of the instrument lighting. "Launch some sensor drones and set the *Ike* to run silent."

"Aye, aye, sir," responded Toft. "Tactical, let's launch a flight of drones. Helm, engage silent running."

The *Ike* shuddered while the drones launched, then the ship began to drift forward as the engines were cut, along with most of the ship's systems powering down. Ronin looked at LeCroy and said, "I don't expect much of anything to occur for a few hours. We should keep resting before the show starts. You want the first watch?"

"Yeah, I'll take first watch," LeCroy replied. "I can't sleep after that last missile. We'll shake you awake if anything starts to happen."

Ronin half-smiled. "Can you do it gently instead of having enemy ordinance do it instead?"

"Getting finicky with your wake up calls in your old age?" Toft said, laughing.

Ronin just raised his eyebrows and laughed softly with a "ha" before they both rose to leave the bridge.

"Set Alert Two and keep the point defense crews in their nests," Ronin said to LeCroy, walking out past his station while LeCroy assumed the Captain's chair.

Ronin's return trip to his bunk was blissfully short. He walked into his ready room to continue his nap in the small bunk that folded out of the wall next to his desk. *I'll just take a short nap. Two more hours sounds awfully sweet about now,* he told himself.

"AI, wake me in two hours," Ronin said aloud.

"Acknowledged. Wake-up call in two hours," responded the ship's AI, right before Ronin fell asleep.

After days of pursuit on top of an eight-hour shift, Ronin started the fight feeling exhausted, and he knew as well as anyone that rest was required to remain sharp. Leading a ship as complicated as the *Ike* required full command of the crew's senses. Ronin was no exception.

The *Ike* was an older warship. Even though she was twenty years old, extensive refits had automated more of the ship and reduced the needed crew to 1,100. But, there was only so much refitting and automation available for a twenty-year-old war bird that stretched over 600 feet in length, and which had more than 20 decks.

* * *

The lights in his ready room suddenly snapped on. "Captain Ronin, it is time to wake up. Captain Ronin, it is time to wake up," announced the ship AI, rousting Ronin from a deep sleep.

Bleary-eyed, Ronin thought for a second, *it has to be a mistake. I just went to sleep minutes ago.* Or so he thought, until he asked what time it was.

"Ship's time is 0300 hours," said the AI.

The time stunned Ronin into alertness. "Wait, it can't be 3 am! It was 1900 hours when I laid down for a two-hour nap. Why didn't you wake me at 2100 hours like I asked?"

The AI promptly replied. "Just before 2100 hours, Commander Toft decided you were too tired and reset the alarm for eight hours as long as all remained quiet. He said to revive you if the drones or sensors detected anything. There have been no contacts since drone launch."

Ronin's eyebrows shot up over that response, but he appreciated the update and extra rest.

"AI, is Commander Toft back on the bridge?" asked Ronin.

"Affirmative, he was unable to sleep and returned to the bridge. Sensors indicate his medical readings show it is past time for him to rest," said the AI.

"OK. Inform him I will return momentarily. I just need a quick shower and change of uniform."

Ronin rubbed his face with his hands while he sat on the edge of his bed as he tried to wake up. As he did so, it reminded him this was a habit he'd had since he was a child in Green Bay, Wisconsin. He'd seen his father do the same thing before getting up for the day. That memory now came back to him as it often did in the first moments upon waking.

Those were happy days. Ronin enjoyed walking to school on the crisp fall mornings. He had excelled in his coursework and was popular among the other students. There was always something exciting to do in the city, as well as in the surrounding area, which was known for its forested beauty, beaches, and lakes. As an adventurous young man, Ronin was equally at ease fishing and hiking on the Door Peninsula as he was bumping elbows among the busy downtown area and its massive skyscrapers that were home to millions.

Ronin's sleepy mind continued to wander. At the time of The Fall of Civilization, also known as World War III (WWIII), Green Bay was the center of a mid-sized metro. The war resulted in the collapse of civilization around the world, and the few cities that survived took centuries to fully recover. Green Bay, having managed to avoid total destruction during The Fall, was one of the epicenters of the recovery. Like many of the larger pre-WWIII cities, the ruins of the former large cities were distant memories that were still largely avoided. After graduating from Naval Academy in Green Bay, Ronin had been off-world much of the time since and he still missed the sights of the modern city he loved so much.

Feeling refreshed, Ronin returned to the bridge and approached his chair to relieve Toft. "Thanks for the extra shut-eye. Maybe you should go get some now," he said to Toft.

Toft yawned as he nodded and replied, "Oh, I plan to grab a few hours now that you're back in the saddle. See you in a few," he said, leaving the bridge to return to his quarters.

Ronin settled in and looked over the latest scan reports. Nothing but dust and rocks. *They can't have gone far. To disappear like they did would require killing their engines and coasting to avoid detection.* He sipped his coffee. *Ah, Kona coffee! Wish they could synthesize the beans so I wouldn't have to drop so much coin on my own stash.* Like most navies in history, the Confederate Navy ran on coffee.

Ronin resolved to let Toft and the primary bridge crew rest for as long as things remained quiet. That resolution did not end when Toft returned to the bridge by 1000 hours, but Dan knew it would be futile to order Toft to go back keep resting.

"Looks like all is still quiet," commented Toft.

"Yup," said Ronin, "Since that last missile, we haven't come across anything more threatening than boredom."

"Any ideas, skipper?"

Ronin's eyes narrowed a bit. "Since they can't have gone far due to the need to go dark and disappear, we have a few things we can try, mainly along the lines of outlasting or outwitting them. I'm tired of trying to outlast them, so maybe we can stir things up a bit. See what shakes out."

Ronin had Toft's full attention now. "What are you thinking? Launch all our drones to flush them out?"

Ronin shook his head and said, "Our scans show the dust surrounding this area of the field is heavily concentrated with iron. I was thinking we modify a nuke to create an EMP magnetic resonance field out of it so we can track magnetized iron particle movement, and look for particles getting pushed or pulled by their hull ionization."

Toft's eyebrows knitted together as he looked at Ronin like Ronin had lost his mind. "Um, what?! Even out in space, the Treaty of Midway forbids touching off a nuke. We do that, and we're likely to get jailed or blown out of the sky by both the Collective and our own fleet."

Ronin, eyebrows raised as he looked up at Toft and shook his head. "No, there wouldn't be any fission detonation. I try not to be as stupid as I look. I'm thinking we have a barely controlled reaction to release a large amount of energy in the form of magnetic charge. That requires providing power for a sufficiently long duration to give the particles a charge, while not sending out an explosive shock wave that would just foul the sensors. Let's get Lieutenant Corbyn over here and run this idea past him if you're not opposed to looking into this."

After a few quiet moments to consider the proposed scheme, Toft said, "Well, in that case, I'm game. Could be another first for the *Ike* if it works."

"Lieutenant Corbyn? Come over here, please," said Ronin.

"Yes, sir, what can I help with?" asked Lt. Gene Corbyn, the science officer. After hearing Ronin's idea, Corbyn nodded and said, "I read about that in the bulletin from the fleet science department. It's just a theory they had toyed with during a war college debate, but our scientists thought it might be something to look into if the need arises. There hasn't been time or resources to give it a whirl yet, but the basic theory and mechanics were more straightforward than expected."

Toft looked at Corbyn and asked, "How long do you think it would take to set this up?"

Corbyn responded, "A few hours. We have the plutonium and necessary parts onboard, and we just happen to have a huge iron dust cloud handy. I just some time to run simulations and cobble the programming instructions together to control the reaction."

Ronin nodded and told Corbyn to get started immediately. He turned to Toft and said, "Why don't you take the bridge while I go take care of some paperwork in my quarters?"

Toft nodded, and replied loudly for the bridge crew to hear that Toft is assuming control of the ship, "Roger that. I have assumed command."

Ronin finally returned to his quarters. He hadn't been back there in several days since he left to begin the chase. While the Captain's small ready room was by necessity next to the bridge for quick access, his larger quarters were several levels below it. As he sat at his desk and completed some neglected reports, Ronin's mind began to wander as he mentally replayed Toft's warning about nuking iron dust.

Ronin wasn't surprised by Toft's strong reaction to lighting off a nuke. In fact, Ronin mused, it was typical among the postwar society that rose from the ashes of WWIII over seven centuries ago.

Commander Toft was a tall, lanky product of Sioux Falls, South Dakota, a once rural state that later became a major population center after The Fall of Civilization. Like Green Bay, the now major city of Sioux Falls also benefited greatly by its distance from the twin devastations caused by plague and nuclear destruction that wiped out most large metros that existed before the war. After The Fall, the two became city-states that later joined with other surviving city-states in North America to build civilization anew.

Few historical records from prior to The Fall were in existence because of the ravages of time and the extent of the destruction from the war. Accordingly, the history of what happened had been pieced together from scraps that remained, but they suggested humanity at the time generally belonged to either an Eastern or Western alliance. The Collectivist East was poor, heavily polluted, and its people were merely servants of the Collective. The Democratic West coalition and its citizens were a different animal. The West's rich economy left the Eastern alliance's economy in the dust and made the rulers of the East terribly envious and fearful, especially after the West established colonies.

The Fall began like many so wars began. One side thought they could take something they wanted from the other, and grossly misjudged the situation. Legend says the East wanted the wealth and colonies of the West, but the East couldn't win a straight-up battle.

In a diabolical assault, the East determined the most effective strategy was to leverage the trade and tourism that existed between the alliances as a pathway for releasing a bat flu among its own open-air markets in a free trade zone. Significant numbers of citizens traveling to Europe and the Americas entered that free trade zone and would spread the virus across the planet. From the perspective of the East's leadership, another not-insignificant advantage of secretly releasing the virus was that it would cull its own overpopulated herd of people while simultaneously cutting down the numbers in the West.

As a result of the East's efforts, 400,000 humans were infected and unknowingly served as virus incubators and delivery systems, but the West almost immediately detected the nefarious scheme and swiftly reacted by shutting down their economies and travel. Initially their quick response successfully confined the spread of the virus and limited casualties to about a million. The virus containment did not hold, however, and it began to spread uncontrollably.

The West's defense strategy was to respond to an unconventional biological attack with a nuclear counter strike. When containment failed and millions more had become infected, the West launched nuclear missiles in a retaliatory strike. The forces of the West overpowered the East's air defenses and as a result most Collective cities were laid waste. Soon, billions were dead and cities on both sides were reduced to radioactive or biological ruins.

Ronin knew the old records got pretty sketchy about which side first sought to formally end the war, but he figured it didn't really matter. The war ended with the signing of the Treaty of Midway on the small island where the Americans once defeated the Japanese navy during a WWII battle in 1942. Midway was chosen as the location of the treaty signing because its remote yet mutually accessible location was relatively sheltered from nuclear fallout and the virus.

Even though WWIII was formally over, the remains of both civilizations effectively collapsed anyway because of the widespread planetary devastation and nuclear and biological horrors faced by the dwindling number of survivors. The Dark Ages had returned to Earth.

Old legends and myths spoke of space travel by the West before the war. Moon landings, man-made satellites, asteroid mining, and eventually the discovery of a jump gate leading to habitable planets. As a kid in the old American state of Wisconsin, Ronin had been captivated by the old legends about the colonies that had been lost because of The Fall.

A few old records uncovered at a place once called the Johnson Space Center in the radioactive ruins of Houston, Texas, mentioned colonies in some area called the Baidam Constellation, but there was no further information to help locate any such constellation. Those records either had been destroyed or, as Ronin thought was much more likely, never existed. In the 150 years after the record fragments had been found, nothing else had turned up to substantiate them.

Space colonies don't exist, Ronin snorted to himself as he caught his tired mind wandering. *Even if those myths turned out to once have been real, they were probably wiped out in the war. They wouldn't have thrived once cut off by The Fall if they hadn't had time to sufficiently establish themselves. Too many technical details to overcome, and space is too hostile. Childish fantasies,* he told himself.

CHAPTER 2

MAGNETO BOMB

Corbyn turned to face Ronin and Toft on the Ike's bridge, saying, "We're ready. I ended up using some fuel from the ship's fusion drive instead as it is significantly more refined, which makes it easier to control the reaction."

Ronin nodded and replied, "Excellent. Lieutenant, make it happen."

"Right away, sir," Corbyn responded, turning to his station to begin the reaction.

Corbyn opened a ship-wide commlink and announced, "This is Lieutenant Corbyn, prepare for electro-magnetic pulsing. Reaction begins in sixty seconds." At the one-minute mark, Corbyn initiated the pulse reaction.

Toft and Ronin looked at each other several minutes later. Toft softly asked him, "How do we know the reaction began? Isn't there supposed to be some sign?"

Ronin shrugged and was about to ask Corbyn for an update when Corbyn announced from his science station, "Sensors indicate field charge is building significantly. The iron dust is becoming magnetized and is starting to shift around. Scanning for pattern anomalies now."

Several more minutes passed quietly. As Ronin was reading the scans on his screen, Lt. Marcy Anzio, the weapons officer, broke the silence. "Scans of the dust show a pattern disturbance 70,000 miles out. Vectoring the nearest drones to investigate. One hour until they reach the area," she announced loudly.

The *Ike* continued scanning and watching the dust. After 50 minutes elapsed, Corbyn reported, "Captain, only the one pattern anomaly is showing up on long range scans as a likely target. The others are just pattern eddies. I'm going to run a high-power search focused on that location to see what turns up."

Ronin nodded and said, "Go ahead. It'll light us up like a Christmas tree even from that far away, but making ourselves visible at a distance might help flush them out if they think we've seen them."

Corbyn entered the commands to focus the powerful sensors on the anomaly. At this distance, the return of the information was near immediate. "Captain, sensors pinged a hull with iron composition right where the anomaly is!" said Corbyn excitedly.

Just then, Anzio loudly said, "They see us! We have launch detection. Eleven warheads inbound. No fighters launched. Tactical prediction is a shoot and scoot for evasion. Range to target, 70,000 miles and closing."

"Return fire and get us moving behind those rocks floating to our port side. We'll hide from the incoming ordinance there and let the existing drone screen guide our birds," ordered Ronin. The *Ike's* powerful fusion engines quickly pushed the ship into position.

"Launch countermeasures and more drones. I want eyes on what's happening on the other side of these rocks so we know what's going on," said Ronin. The *Ike* shuddered with multiple decoy and drone launches. "Rig for silent running. Time to make like a hole in space," he added.

The Ike went dark again, with only power for life support and weapons systems. Minutes passed, when Anzio reported, "Inbounds time to target, two minutes. They're locked on to our decoys because we disappeared behind the rocks. Drone screen telemetry says our missiles are tracking the enemy even though they're running. Drone optics shows her to be a Type 054A frigate. Our AI reports we have positive ID of the ship. It's the *Shanwei!*"

Ronin nodded in satisfaction. The *Shanwei* would be a good prize.

Crewed by over 500, the sizable AC frigate was a worthy and able opponent for a powerful destroyer like the Ike.

Weighing in at 20,000 tons, the Ike was still swift and deadly despite being long in the tooth. She could achieve .20 lights (1/5 of light speed) using her newer model fusion drives, and launch 20 Tomcat fighters along with dozens of anti-ship missiles from her magazines. Those new fusion drives also enabled the ship to carry several turrets of light and heavy rail guns now attached to her hull plating as a result of a refit five years ago.

There were newer, more powerful ships in the Confederation fleet, but Ronin was very proud of the Ike. During the current dust up between the Collective and the Confederation out here in the solar system, the Ike had demolished nearly a dozen frigates and one destroyer while largely avoiding being damaged in return. After five years of combat, the Ike had developed a reputation for being a tough, lucky, and well-run ship under Ronin's command. *Time to get lucky again,* thought Ronin.

Anzio reported, "Enemy missiles spent themselves on the decoys. No more inbounds. Telemetry reports our birds had no trouble locking on to the *Shanwei* as the drone optics and sensors have her in line of sight and her engines are flaring out all kinds of energy as she tries to run."

Another minute passed. "Impact! Drone optics confirms multiple warhead impacts on *Shanwei*. She's drifting and venting gases. One bird impacted near her drive system. Target isn't going anywhere," said Anzio.

"Excellent work everyone. Move the drones in close and have them scan for threats they can before we arrive. Helm, bring the Ike down to Alert Two status and move us in to the *Shanwei*," ordered Ronin.

CHAPTER 3

THE SHANWEI

Six hours later, after heavily scanning the area to look for possible traps, the Ike closed with the heavily damaged *Shanwei*.

"She sure took a beating," noted Corbyn. "Hull is holed just ahead of the engines and amidships. We're not reading any power signatures over there. She's dark and cold, Captain."

Ronin nodded and used the half moon shaped node attached to his collar to open a commlink to Toft, who was standing by down in the launch bay. "OK, Toft, did you hear that? *Shanwei* is still dark and cold. You're a go for the away team boarding."

Toft immediately responded, "Roger that, Captain. We'll launch immediately."

Toft turned to the Marine pilot officer. "All right, lieutenant, let's launch and get this party started."

"Launch in three, two, one. Launch!" responded Lt. Travis Harris, increasing power with the throttle. Minutes later the shuttle was passing over the hull of the *Shanwei*. "Ever get this close to an enemy frigate sir?" asked Harris.

"No, this is incredible. Captain Ronin would like to claim her as a war prize if possible. No one has captured an intact frigate before. We could learn a lot about their weaknesses by studying one," replied Toft.

"Over there. See that? Looks like a landing bay, and it's not too damaged," said Harris.

"Bring us over and let's take a look," replied Toft.

"Back at the Marine Academy in Bismarck, we studied advanced boarding tactics and had some vague guesses on what they believed AC ship layouts would be," noted Harris. "But since space combat typically resulted in most enemy ships being completely destroyed, there weren't any surviving ship hulls to guide our instructors so they focused more on improvisation tactics using what we might be likely to encounter. There haven't been any boardings for the same reason."

"Velocity tends to make a mess of targets, doesn't it?" Toft responded. "I saw one AC frigate get erased from a single rail gun round. It was akin to seeing a meteor strike on a planet. Boom! No more ship or even any parts of one. Just dusted it."

"Sir, I think there's enough clearance for us to squeeze in next to that wreckage on the right," Harris suggested as they inspected the landing bay. "You want to give it a whirl?"

Toft indicated to proceed with a nod.

Harris slowly guided the shuttle into the hangar. Other than a slight metallic scraping sound along the side of the hull, the landing was uneventful.

"By squeeze, you meant push stuff out of the way to make room, Harris?" said Toft.

Harris responded with a small laugh and smile. *Commander Toft wasn't as uptight as he thought. You never knew with naval officers.* "Pretty much, sir. Seemed easier to try that than to try to stick the landing onto an exterior airlock somewhere."

Toft laughed and turned to the Marine landing party. "Alright, Gunnery Sergeant Sanchez, let's do this."

Gy.Sgt. Juan Sanchez nodded and began issuing orders to the boarders. "We're in! Complete your exosuit checks and let's stay sharp out there. Sensors show dark, airless, zero G conditions out there, but there's no guaranty someone didn't survive in a spacesuit. Keep your heads on a swivel and stay ready in case we find an ambush or any survivors. Toft and Harris will keep watch from the command shuttle."

The Marines responded with a variety of grunts, ooh-rahs, and roger thats. Marine exosuits are a marvel of engineering. Essentially an armored, environmentally self-contained motorized power suit with guns and a small fusion engine, Marines could live in them for weeks before running out of fuel or food paste. The screens on the inside of exosuit helmets could display Tacnet data, or infrared and starlight vision as needed. Command exosuits even had adaptable AIs who developed personalities that mesh closely with the team leader. Perhaps the most startling innovation in an exosuit was its ability to intercept the nervous system impulses before they reached the muscles due to the bio-circuitry imprinted below a Marine's skin. This early interception meant there was no lag time when a Marine decided to move, so it immediately feels natural to the occupant.

"If you apes were actually able to read and write in something more advanced than crayons, I wouldn't have to go through this again," Sanchez said after the suit checks were completed. "Alpha team, look for a bridge. Bravo Team, head aft and secure the engine room. We assume it's in the center of the ship, but no guarantees. Charlie Team, you have life support, so go aft with Bravo and see what you find."

"How do we know when we find Engineering, Sergeant?" said Cpl. Brett Mackey, doing a reasonably good job at sounding serious.

"I don't know, Corporal Mackey. Look for the big things that go vroom vroom or something!" yelled Sanchez. "Move out!"

ALPHA TEAM

Alpha team jumped off first. Using their suit jets and lamps, they quickly oriented and began moving to the forward section of the hangar bay where they spotted a closed airlock door.

"Alpha 3, can you open the door?" asked Corporal Ralph Tennyson, whose own call sign was Alpha 1.

"Trying now Alpha 1. Knock knock," said Private Devin Rodman (call sign Alpha 3), turning the locking handle and pushing it inwards. "There's a bunch of junk floating around in a passageway Alpha 1. Multiple bodies included. Parts of them, anyway."

Alpha moved single file into the dark passageway. It wasn't pretty. It didn't matter none of the crewmen in this section had environment suits on when the life support died, as this section suffered some violent shaking that pasted their remains all over the surfaces and set various parts of them floating about.

"There's a service tube we can use to get further down into the ship. Let's take it," said Tennyson.

Rodman acknowledged, and started floating down the service tube since he didn't need to bother with the ladder while the gravity was out. "Reminds me of those dark scary tunnels we trained in at Camp Dakota, don't you think, Colton?" said Rodman to Pvt. Sean Colton (Alpha 2) who was coming down the tube behind Rodman.

"Quiet! Alpha 3, we don't care about the good old boot camp days in the Bismarck right now," hissed Tennyson. "Keep your head in the game."

The team went down a few levels, encountering little debris along their route. At each level, they silently stopped and look around. They came to a landing where they could see several passages intersecting outside a sealed double-width hatchway.

Rodman radioed Tennyson, who was still down the ladder. "Alpha 1, I see a double hatchway that's important enough to have several passages intersecting just outside. The configuration matches the predicted command and control indications we're supposed to keep watch for when scouting enemy ships. Permission to proceed beyond the hatchway?"

"Any signs of enemy troops or damage we need to avoid?" Tennyson asked.

Rodman waited a few moments before replying, "No, Alpha 1. Empty of enemy personnel in all directions, and only small bits of debris floating about."

"Proceed, Alpha 3," Tennyson said. "Alpha 2, Position your men to repel potential intruders from those passages."

Colton responded with a double click indicating message received.

Once the boarding party was in place, Rodman went to work trying to manually open the hatches. They were twisted slightly from the force of the missile impacts and unwilling to open. Grunting, Rodman tried using his powered exosuit to force them open but the doors did not budge.

"Alpha 10, use the breaching jaws on the hatches," ordered Tennyson.

Pvt. Davy Hallard, a young, heavy-built redhead from Oklahoma, acknowledged and glided over to the hatches with his breaching jaws and found some leverage for both him and the jaws before announcing, "Ready. Alpha 3, can you pull on the door while the jaws do their thing?"

"Sure thing," said Rodman, as he got a firm purchase on the walls with his feet and a good grip on the handle of the door with his hands. *It's a good thing sound does not travel in space, because the breaching jaws would have created an ear-splitting screech as they brute-forced the hatches open and tore the hinges off in the process*, thought Rodman.

"Alpha 2, go!" roared Tennyson, which prompted Colton to spring from his ready crouch into the darkened beyond with his weapon pointed ahead.

Looking around, Colton's sensors revealed a dark, lifeless room with a large forward view screen, several work stations situated in a circle around a central command chair in what appeared to be a fairly conventionally arranged warship bridge. They also clearly identified enemy personnel, none of whom would be threatening anyone anytime soon. "Alpha 1, looks like we found the bridge and the remains of the command crew," said Colton. "It's as dark as your girlfriend's soul in here. Looks like the bridge is not in terrible condition, though."

"Commander Toft, this is Alpha 1. We appear to have found the bridge. Other than corpses or some of their parts, no enemy contact."

"Roger that," acknowledged Toft. "Secure the area and wait for Bravo and Charlie."

Tennyson, who had already positioned the team to secure the bridge and its connected passageways, responded, "Acknowledged. Floor is secure. Awaiting Bravo and Charlie progress report."

BRAVO TEAM

Bravo team moved aft quickly, deducing that Engineering is logically in close proximity to the engines visible on the rear of the *Shanwei*. Two closed hatchways appeared to lead to the rear of the vessel. Bravo 1, Cpl. Brett Mackey, a tall black man from Alabama, ordered his team to take the right side passage, according to the team's current orientation facing the hatch.

"Bravo 5, take us in the port side hatch."

Pvt. Terry Allison (Bravo 5), also from Alabama, acknowledged: "Roger that, Bravo 1." The hatch refused to open. "No joy on open. Bravo 6, bring your breaching jaws," he added.

Pvt. Steve Cupper (Bravo 6) immediately moved into position with the jaws and quickly wrenched open the hatch, which had been stuck due to the slightly twisted hinges and misshapen hatchway after the missile impacts. "Breach completed," he reported as Bravo 5 moved into the dark passageway with his weapon pointed forward.

Seeing the long access with other connections to distant parts of the ship provided by the other side of the breach, Mackey had chosen wisely. "Jackpot, Bravo 1. Looks like we scored a long passageway," reported Bravo 5 as he quickly floated aft down the spine of the ship. "We've got some obstructive debris about 300 feet in. Doesn't look like we can clear it," he added. "I'm going to take the ladder tube way near my position down a few levels. See if we can find another route."

Two clicks from Bravo 1 acknowledged the report. Allison began egress down the tube way. The first two level exits also revealed blocked passageways. "Must've been a helluva strike," muttered Allison. As he looked around the exit hole on the third level, he could see some debris floating around but it still seemed passable. "Bravo 1, Bravo 5. Egress on the third level. Looks passable. Beware of floating debris."

Mackey replied, "Roger that Bravo 5. Egress on third level down, watch for debris. Bravo team, follow Bravo 5." Clicks confirmed receipt of the orders.

Allison moved slowly down the third level passage, cautiously watching for enemy activity and navigating the debris field in the dark all at the same time. He could hear his breathing and pounding heart in his ears, and his tension had skyrocketed.

"Sweet cripes!" screamed Allison when he moved a floating obstruction to reveal a ghostly dead face behind it.

"He's dead, for heaven's sake!" said Cupper.

"Stop being so jumpy, Bravo 5," said Mackey.

"Been watching too many scary horror movies," muttered Allison to himself. "Gotta stop that," he concluded.

They came to a wide hatchway roughly 50 yards further on, about two times the size of a normal passage. "We've got a double size hatchway down here, marked with what I swear looks like a pair of tool symbols that appear to be a screwdriver and a wrench."

Mackey smiled in his suit helmet. "Jackpot. Fleet Intel reports suggested enemy Engineering uses those symbols. I have to presume a double sized hatchway suggests this is our destination. Bravo 5 and 6, breach the hatch. Bravo 7 and 3, entry position with weapons hot."

Clicks acknowledged the orders.

Allison positioned himself with good traction to pull the hatch wide as Cupper got the breaching jaws set up. With a round of nods to each other and to 7 and 3, Cupper engaged the jaws. For the first thirty seconds, there didn't seem to be much happening until suddenly the hatch metal on the outside of the jaws bent slightly and the hatch grudgingly opened wide enough to admit the Marines if they entered single file. Bravo 7 and 3 obligingly did so, and they were followed by most of Bravo team. There were dozens of frozen corpses floating around in the cold, Zero G of Engineering.

"Bravo 1, if this isn't Engineering, I don't know what it would be," said Cupper, speaking over the radio.

"Agreed, Bravo 6. This has to be it. We're not reading any power signs even from in here."

After circumnavigating the area, Allison reported, "Bravo 1, other than the starboard engine, this room doesn't appear heavily damaged. Reactors are cold though. Sensor reading suggests the fuel core was ejected just after impact to prevent catastrophic overload."

Mackey looked towards Allison for a moment, and then ordered, "Secure Engineering. Bravo 5, take three and scout for survivors or threats. Keep in contact."

Mackey opened a link to Toft. "Commander, Bravo 1. Engineering is secure. Minimal visible damage in the compartment, but some passageway obstructions avoided en route. Sending route map now."

Toft replied from the shuttle in the hangar, "Acknowledged. Alpha reports bridge secure. Hold position and await Charlie."

CHARLIE TEAM

"Charlie 1, Charlie 3. No joy in here. I can't tell what this section is supposed to be, but I can tell what it's not and that's Life Support. There ain't no machinery on the other side of the hatches," said Pvt. Henry Lee, the big, blue-eyed and raven-haired private from the mountains of Virginia, in his slight southern accent.

"Roger that, Charlie 3. Backtrack to the access tube way about 50 feet behind you and let's try another level," ordered Charlie 1, also known as Cpl. Jerry Gee from Arizona.

Lee clicked acknowledgment and retreated to the tube way. "At the tube way. Heading down now," he reported as Charlie team reformed behind him.

Lee floated down six more levels before finding an exit that wasn't obstructed by wreckage. "Level six, egress clear. No tangos. Moving down passage," he reported. Lee shone his headlamp down the dark hall as he moved, scanning each hatchway for something that might suggest it's the Life Support section. *Why the heck don't they use intelligible symbols for stuff? Can't make heads or tails out of this gibberish.* He stopped when he came to a hatch marked with what Lee thought looked like a symbol for blowing wind. *Either this is the farting room, or it's Life Support*, he thought, prying open the hatch.

He peered into the darkened room. A few corpses were tethered to their work chairs, arms floating in the zero gravity. Lee could see some large shapes and several control consoles, so he motioned to Charlie 4, Pvt. John Kowalski from Kansas, who was holding his weapon just out of sight of the hatchway.

Using hand signals, Lee indicated he was going in and Kowalski, who was a close quarter's combat specialist with multiple black belts in various martial arts disciplines, needed to have his back. Kowalski nodded silently, holding his submachine gun at the ready while Lee entered the room.

As Charlie team secured the area while the room was investigated, Lee was startled to recognize Mandarin writing that translated to English meant "Air Control System." *Who knew your goofing off minor in Man-*

darin would turn out to be handy some day? Other consoles marked in legible Mandarin indicated buttons for "Power," "Flow Control," "Vent Control," and so on.

"Charlie 1, Charlie 3. I think we've found it. I can make out Mandarin writing for flow and venting controls, and a whole console marked 'Air Control System.'"

Gee responded instantly, "Roger that Charlie 3. Um, how is it you think you can read and recognize Mandarin writing?" he asked, joining Lee in the Life Support section.

"Long story, Charlie 1. You'd get bored without any pictures to help you understand it," said Lee, who was trying to avoid disclosing the reason he could read Mandarin.

Gee turned to look at Lee and said with a poorly hidden smirking sound in his voice, "Oh, I think there might be a story there our team might enjoy. No way would a big gorilla like you learn something more complicated than making mud pies without a good reason."

A roar of laughter flooded the open radio group commlink from Charlie team. "Charlie 3, what was her name? She must have been a babe for you to go through that!" Charlie 4 quipped.

Lee sighed and looked up in exasperation before replying, "I really hate you guys. Her name was Maryanne." Lee's hopes that would quell his comrades died a quick death as the commlink was filled with wolf whistles, whoops, and requests for inappropriately intimate relationship details.

"All right, you animals, pipe down and get your heads in the game and secure this area," yelled Corporal Gee before switching over to the command commlink.

"Commander, Charlie 1. Life Support is secure. No visible compartment damage. Sending route map now."

Toft replied from the shuttle in the hangar, "Acknowledged. Alpha and Bravo have secured their objections. Wait a moment while I bring in the other team 1s."

Moments later, Alpha 1 and Bravo 1 confirmed they were conferenced in before Toft continued. "Dispatch scout teams to finish sweeping the ship while you maintain security over your objectives. Once the ship is secure, engineering teams from the Ike want to poke around."

The leaders of Alpha, Bravo and Charlie teams confirmed and dropped the conference to cascade Toft's orders.

CHAPTER 4

WAR PRIZE

our days later, Captain Ronin walked into the Ike's situation room with Toft and Lt. Cmdr. William Bryce, who grew up in Vermillion, South Dakota, where he also studied engineering at the University of South Dakota before joining the fleet. Bryce strode to the holograph projection of the *Shanwei* that was floating in the center of the room. He looked at Ronin while pointing to the port side rear quarter of the spacecraft in the holo.

"Captain, we think we can jury rig the port power plant of the *Shanwei* and get the reactor back online to power the remaining engine on that half of the ship. Survey teams report very little damage to the port side of the ship, and since the reactor core was ejected to prevent a chain reaction overload, all we need to do is feed it some of our fuel to get it back online."

Ronin nodded slowly, unconsciously biting his inside cheek as he did so. "Would our fuel even work?" he asked.

"Yes, sir. Our fuel is actually far more refined than the stuff the *Shanwei* normally eats, so it's much safer without all the contaminants that are present in their normal fuel," responded Bryce.

With a slight smile, Ronin cocked an eyebrow at Bryce and said, "Well, thanks for putting it in plain English so even I could understand it. Toft, let's back the Ike off to a safe distance and retain an absolute minimum to crew the *Shanwei* while they try to breathe some life back into her."

Toft and Bryce both nodded to Ronin and responded in unison, "Aye, aye, captain."

Bryce then brought another part of the *Shanwei* to their attention by pointing to the center of the ship on the projection. "Here's what I wanted to show you: this hanger amidships. Best we can tell, there's some sort of command and control shuttle in here."

Bryce motioned with his hand to zoom in to the hangar to show the shuttle. "The initial boarding party couldn't see it when they first arrived, but once they secured the ship they made note of a large oblong object in their reports. If we can crack the commlink encryption between this shuttle and the *Shanwei*, it could give our side a significant advantage by listening in on enemy communications. I recommend we remove this shuttle and tow it from the Ike just in case we have a catastrophic restart of the *Shanwei*."

Ronin nodded slightly and said, "Agreed. Get a flight crew over there to tow her while you and your team get ready to restart the reactors."

Two days passed while crews from the Ike prepped the *Shanwei* for reactor restart. "Captain, we're as ready as we'll ever be. We were able to reduce the prize crew to a half dozen volunteers for purposes of the restart," said Bryce.

Ronin listened to Bryce's message, looked over at Toft, who nodded and said, "The Ike and the *Shanwei* shuttle are ready sir. We are standing by at a range of 25,000 miles."

Ronin nodded and spoke into the commlink node on his collar, "*Ike* and shuttle report ready. Initiate restart."

Bryce acknowledged and commlinked the Ike's reactor specialist using the node at his workstation, Amy Baker, who had volunteered to come aboard *Shanwei*. "Specialist Baker, start the reactor."

"Aye, aye, sir." acknowledged Baker, in her New England accent. The medium-height redhead then looked down at the *Shanwei* engineering station where she had parked herself. "Here goes nothing," she muttered, fingers crossed in her left hand while her right index finger hovered over a red glowing, touch screen button in a station powered by portable generators from the Ike. Her finger tapped the screen and the button began flashing, followed by a slight jolt. Had there been oxygen in the room, she would have heard a loud clanging sound that would have accompanied the jolt. Minutes passed while the reactor began to spin up and screen indicators on Baker's screen reflected slowly rising power output.

"Power at 50 percent and rising," announced Baker over the commlink. "Power output at 75 percent, and holding steady. No fluctuations," she observed. Overhead lights blinked on, and her suit sensors showed rising air levels in the room. "Reactor at 85 percent as planned. Helm, can you begin port engine restart?" she asked.

"Aye, port engine ready to accept feed. Beginning ignition," reported Lt. Felipe Mendez, the Ike's helmsman who was now on the *Shanwei's* bridge. A soft thrumming began that could be felt throughout *Shanwei*. "If our translation software is accurate here, port engine board is green. Looks like our repairs are holding," announced Mendez over the commlink.

Bryce rapidly scanned through *Shanwei's* systems as they were linked to the *Ike's* computers "Command data links established. *Ike's* AI (Artificial Intelligence) is muscling its way into *Shanwei's* computing core through the portals we hacked. Bypassing security protocols. We're in! We have complete control of *Shanwei*," stated Bryce triumphantly.

Ronin smiled in satisfaction. "Excellent. Confirmed if *Shanwei* makes way using the port drive at 85% power as we discussed?" he asked.

Bryce had continued absorbing the hacked data as it flowed in and was collated for review by Ike's AI, and was about to answer Ronin when Ike's AI responded first.

"Affirmative, Capt. *Shanwei's* port drive is functional enough to safely propel the ship to most destinations. The temporary repairs by the engineering crews are allowing the ship to move under its own power again although if any of the prize crew attempt to travel between Engineering and either Life Support or the Bridge they'll have to wear an environment suit due to the lack of life support in the heavily damaged areas between Engineering and the rest of the ship."

Upon seeing Bryce's annoyed look at having his report co-opted by Ike's AI, Ronin half-smiled at Bryce and said, "Well, in fairness, I failed to specify to whom that question was addressed!"

Bryce raised his eyebrows in response, and muttered "Aye, sir. Anyway, where would you like to drive that crate over there?"

Ronin looked down at his chair screen, and typed in a series of coordinates before announcing, "Our destination is classified. Accordingly, I've entered our destination directly into Ike's navigation system. Security protocols are engaged, which will prevent any of the crew from being able to access nav systems or identify where we're heading unless they're quite good at dead reckoning without the aid of computers."

Toft's head, and everyone else's, turned in surprise at Ronin's response. "Classified? There's a classified destination? No wonder you kept it to yourself," noted Toft.

CHAPTER 5

POINT NINER-TWO-NINER

ive weeks later, the small convoy led by the Ike approached the rendezvous coordinates known only as Point Niner Two Niner. Hidden in the system's asteroid belt far from Earth, they were far from prying eyes or scopes due to distance and a heavy concentration of dust obscuring visual or sensor contact.

Ronin looked up from his scope and glanced over to Ensign Diving Hawk, who was sitting at the main commlink station for the ship. Ashley Diving Hawk was very young and from northern Montana, where her ancestors were among the few survivors of WWII. While their former reservation had not been nuked or even suffered much from nuclear winter, the bat flu from China had nearly wiped out the tribe of her ancestors. After centuries of intermingling with other survivors, Diving Hawk's name was the most tribal aspect of her.

"Ensign, send a directional hail to the coordinates I sent to your screen, and stand by. Let's see who's out there," said Ronin.

"Transmission sent, Captain," responded Diving Hawk.

Seconds later her station beeped with an incoming reply. "We have a response already?" asked Toft. "There must have been someone camped out on the frequency," he continued.

"Send the response to my screen, Ensign," ordered Ronin, who began reading his screen intently. "Fleet ships are arriving soon, ETA two hours," stated Ronin. "We're to hold position."

Two hours crawled by with sensors still fuzzed from all the interference, then Diving Hawk's commlink system beeped with a new message. "Incoming message from the Kitty Hawk, Captain. They have us in sight and are pulling along side. Visual link established," she said.

"Put it on the main screen," said Ronin, recalling that the Kitty Hawk was a newer Corvette in the fleet. A sleek and fast escort vessel for ships like the Ike, the Kitty Hawk packed quite a punch.

The bridge's forward screen opened to reveal a grinning image of Hu Nagun, captain of the Kitty Hawk. Nagun, a product of Oregon and a die-hard Oregon Ducks fan, was descended from a Vietnamese family that had immigrated to the United States before WWII.

"Hello, old friend. Long trip just to bring that fifty bucks you still owe me," he noted wryly with a crooked smile and raised eyebrow.

Ronin smiled and laughed before responding "Nagun! You old pirate. I guess they'll let anybody captain a ship these days! And as I recall, it's you who still owes me because you stole my date that night and stuck me with the bar tab."

Nagun roared with laughter and said, "She was a monster! I did you a huge favor by swiping her, buddy. She made life miserable until I could ship out and leave her behind. Best fifty bucks you ever spent. You OWE me! She made my life miserable for three long weeks!"

By now the crews of both bridges were trying very hard to suppress smiles at the banter between the ship captains.

"Hmmm. You might be right after all," said Ronin with a huge grin. "I suppose you're going to tell us what the scoop is now?" he asked.

His face turning serious, Nagun thoughtfully looked at his old Academy roommate and said, "Ronin, all I can tell you is Ike has hauled your new toys far enough. Leave them with me, and we'll make like Santa by delivering them to the good little girls and boys who aren't on the naughty list this year."

Ronin snorted and replied with a raised eyebrow, "With pleasure. You want I should just drop them where they are?"

"Yep. We brought everything we need for this pleasure cruise, and we even brought some party favors for the Ike. Stuff a guy like you'll be inappropriately excited about, like munitions and food and stuff so you can keep skulking about, causing trouble," said Nagun.

"We're not returning to a base?" said Ronin in a surprised voice. "We've been out patrolling for six months already."

Nagun nodded, and said, "Long patrol, what can I say? Maybe you can bag some more game before you return to the nest. Your orders are onboard the containers that your crews will bring back to your hanger."

CHAPTER 6

WAYSIDE STATION

Six months of ambushes and combat later, the Ike was coming in from a record-setting long patrol: six enemy frigates, a handful of shuttles, and a captured war prize frigate, plus a year out in the wild without leave. Ronin was proud of his tired ship and crew. They were finally coming home to Wayside Station, which earned its name because the monstrous space station was mobile.

Wayside dwarfed the Ike, which never failed to impress Ronin whenever he had the opportunity to watch as they approached. One hundred and fifty decks tall and weighing in at a massive 300,000 long tons, Wayside was a combination command and control station as well as a shipyard, crewed by 11,000 fleet personnel, including a large number of engineers.

He had been ordered to report immediately to the Admiralty. *I wonder what's the hurry,* he said to himself as he entered Wayside. *I've been gone forever and they know we're exhausted. Ike needs a refit and repairs, and we should be up for extended leaves. I have a lot to do without getting caught up in someone's bureaucratic time-wasting.*

Minutes later, Ronin reached the offices of Adm. Jessup Rodding, and he was surprised at how quickly he was rushed through security by the guards and orderly.

"Admiral is waiting for you now, Captain. Would you like some coffee before you go in? The Admiral thought you probably could use a slug of the real thing when you arrived," said the orderly.

"Yes, thank you," responded Ronin, gratefully taking a sip of the wondrous black liquid and straightening his dark gray uniform. He sighed as he tilted his head back, eyes closed for a moment to enjoy the taste.

His cache of coffee hadn't been refilled as part of the resupply six months ago, which in his opinion is a serious oversight by the Fleet. He knocked on the Admiral's wooden door and heard "Enter!" from behind the door. *Admirals and their little luxuries,* thought Ronin as he opened the door.

Admiral Rodding stood up and walked over to greet Ronin.

"Dan! I know you're tired from an outstanding patrol, but this is top priority and things are moving fast," he said, shaking hands with Ronin before he had a chance to salute. "Grab a seat at the table over there and we'll get started," said Rodding in his soft West Virginia accent.

Once seated, the Admiral quickly poured himself a cup of coffee and looked at Ronin. "Captain, this discussion is Top Secret, understand?" he asked Ronin.

Ronin nodded that he did.

"What do you know of jump gates?"

Ronin's eyebrows shot up at the totally unexpected question. "Not much. They're little more than old legends from before The Fall. Some sort of drive tech that accessed a jump gate which instantly lead to another jump gate elsewhere. Only we don't know what that tech was, or where these gates might supposedly have been, or how to find them. And beyond a few old references, we've never found anything to substantiate that they ever existed," said Ronin.

Admiral Rodding nodded thoughtfully, before responding. "Yeah, about what everyone knows and thinks. Fairy tales," he said. "What if I told you there's now more to it than a few old myths?"

Despite his weariness and it being the middle of the night on his ship's time, Ronin sat up straighter, looking intently at Rodding. "Sir? I don't understand," he said.

Rodding had a small smile quirking up the right side of his face as he watched Ronin's visible surprise and confusion at being told there may be more to the myths and legends than was generally believed.

"All right, well, I'm not here just to pique your interest. That's not all, Ronin. Effective immediately Captain Ronin, you are relieved of command of the Ike."

Ronin's face failed to hide his disappointment at the stunning news. "Sir! Am I being charged with something I did wrong? I, I don't know what it would be. Are you sure? That's career ending," stuttered Ronin.

Rodding smiled fully this time. "Relax, Dan, you're not being demoted, or prosecuted, or any of that crap. In fact, both those announcements are related and intersect with you in the middle. You ready to follow me?"

Ronin, utterly confused and far too tired to figure out the games being played here, simply nodded.

"OK. Let's wander over to Fleet Intelligence. They're waiting to brief you on what's up," said Rodding as he stood up. "Bring your coffee though. Looks like you'll need it."

Ronin grabbed his mug as he stood to follow the Admiral, who was already headed out the door.

"And brace yourself for a review of your record," he added mysteriously.

The two of them walked down the station's white outer corridor in silence until they reached the secure area for Fleet Intelligence. Two quick retinal scans, then armed guards in black Fleet Intelligence Security uniforms escorted them to the area's briefing room. A large conference table with a holoprojector in the middle dominated the room. It was projecting a holo of a region of space Ronin did not recognize. He gazed at the holo for several moments before realizing he was quietly being scrutinized by the intelligence officer who was seated at the table.

Ronin quickly saluted, while Admiral Rodding was already walking over to the other officer. "Ready when you are, Colonel Hobson," he said, approaching the tall officer in a black uniform at the table. Colonel Hobson rose, nodded and extended to shake Ronin's hand.

"Glad to meet you at last, Captain Ronin. We have quite a show for you this evening," he said in a smooth Indian-British accent. "If you're ready, please have a chair and we'll get started. Please confirm for the recorders your understanding that everything discussed here is classified Top Secret."

Ronin responded, "I confirm my understanding everything discussed here is Top Secret." A beep sounded, indicating Ronin's understanding was logged into the security system.

Ronin was now fully alert, as being brought to a meeting with any-one from Fleet Intelligence will make even the most placid officers expe-rience a bout of anxiety. He felt like the rug had cruelly been pulled from under his feet due to having Ike taken away from him, and his gut was sending all sorts of warning signs about Colonel Hobson's upcoming news.

Hobson sat down and looked at Ronin, his black eyes and dark skin showing a moment of thoughtfulness on how to begin before he began reading a summary memorandum on his screen. "Ronin, Dan J., Cap-tain of the Confederate destroyer Ike the past seven years. Prior to that, first officer for three years on the Delphi class frigate, the Frisco. Highly decorated, numerous successful tours of duty interdicting smugglers before successfully transitioning to combat against AC ships when the current hostilities commenced five years ago when AC fired upon Con-federacy ships in the Lagrange Point Incident.

"Since then, you've become more of a pioneer in single-ship hit-and-run tactics than any other Captain in the fleet. Accordingly, your command has been detached to do just that, and is tasked with making mischief and keeping the enemy off balance while most of the rest of the fleet operates in combat formations. It is a valuable role, which you've excelled at.

"Born and raised in Green Bay, Wisconsin. Attended the Naval Academy there. Parents are Robert and Julia Ronin, who still reside there. Widowed when the Frisco was hit during an engagement, your two children, Sarah and Edward, are in the care of Robert and Julia while you work to make their world safe again. Correct so far, Captain?"

Ronin, hiding his impatience at having his time wasted on a quick recital of his own background, merely nodded.

"Captain, do you know why your last patrol was extended without warning?" asked Hobson.

Saying nothing besides "No sir," Ronin merely shook his head and waiting for Hobson to continue.

"There were several reasons. One of which is the operational tempo has accelerated due to enemy activity the past two years and you captain a destroyer, of which there are never enough to go around. The second reason was to keep you and the Ike occupied for a while because of information from the *Shanwei* which the Ike's AI sent to Fleet Intelligence," said Hobson.

Ronin's eyebrows shot up in surprised and he blurted out, "Sir, I didn't authorize the AI to make any transmissions to anybody. We were keeping communications to the initial burst to mask our location and prevent intercepts for operational security."

Hobson nodded and responded, "I know Captain. Ike's AI was following the Hades Ordinance, which is a subsystem hard wired into each ship's computer. Like the mythological Hades, which is the underworld of the dead, this ordinance looks for pre-Fall information. When a fleet AI encounters anything linked to a predetermined data set of pre-WWIII information, the AI encodes it for priority burst transmission to fleet intelligence. No record of the transmission is retained and to maintain maximum operational security, no one on that ship is made aware of the transmission."

Ronin nodded and said, "I presume you're telling me now because I have a need to know?"

Hobson cocked an eyebrow as he nodded, "Correct, Captain. *Shanwei*'s main computer yielded a bounty of information thanks to you and your ship regarding their fleet, encryption protocols, tactical capabilities and the like; however, we deem a piece of intel *Shanwei* was carrying of top priority. It seems our old friends in the Collective have found jump gate records in the old Russian Baikonur Cosmodrome in Kazakhstan."

Startled despite himself, Ronin asked, "What were they doing in Kazakhstan? It was a No Man's Land due to the bat flu pestilence that depopulated the entire region during The Fall."

Rodding leaned forward and noted, "Dan, the Collective has been treasure hunting for old technology in their old installations from prior to The Fall for quite some time. Same as the Confederation, although neither side wants to draw attention to that fact.

"As you know, due to the passage of time and the widespread destruction that occurred due to The Fall, we found ourselves in the situation where we possessed more advanced technological information than historical. That technological advantage allowed the Confederation to rebuild in a fraction of the time it would otherwise have taken, but we still don't know anywhere near as much about the time before The Fall as we would like."

Ronin thought back to his history classes as a schoolboy. Civilization fell into barbarism, but there were some smaller (at the time) cities that survived due to different combinations of leadership and residual technical data, which they managed to pass on to future generations. Those cities held on to become city-states at first, and then eventually they banded together to reform a new nation as civilization re-emerged from the ashes.

Hobson looked away from Admiral Rodding and back to Ronin. He picked up where Rodding left off and answered the disbelief written on Ronin's face. "All of that is true, Captain. And there's a lot more. *Shanwei* was carrying a coordinate to this system's possible jump gate location. It was the coordinate we happened to be missing. Our spies inside the Collective are pretty clear they may need more coordinates to find where the old gate may have been, but with the information from *Shanwei* and other data recovered from the pre-Fall base on Ganymede, we now have a set we think could lead us there. You will take a fleet ship there to investigate."

Ronin looked at both Rodding and Hobson for a moment before asking the obvious first question they all knew would be next: "Sirs, since I've just been relieved of command of the Ike, what's my next ride?"

Rodding smiled. "I thought you'd never ask, Dan. Your next ride, as you called it is a new, top secret ship called Cerberus."

He looked down and pressed a screen button next to him. The holo projector replaced the current image with an image of Cerberus. "She's nothing like anything the fleet has elsewhere. For purposes of figuring out the scale here, the old Ike is 20,000 long tons, 605 feet long, 60 feet wide, and crewed by 1,100 with a main propulsion drive of two fusion engines. Cerberus is an entirely different animal. Weighing in at 100,000 tons, Cerberus is 2,000 feet long, 500 feet wide, crewed by 2,500, and powered from two different drives. You'll have three sub light drives for propulsion up to .3 lights, and jump drives for FTL mobility. Cerberus also carries two full squadrons of Tomcat fighters and half a dozen FTL capable Bulldogs for scouting and reconnaissance as well as combat control missions."

The onslaught of information completely floored Ronin. "Wait, sirs! This is coming at me too fast here. Gravity jump drives? FTL is...even possible? What old base on Ganymede? Ah," Ronin stammered before being interrupted by a smiling Rodding.

"All right, son, relax. I can see we need to give you a baseline for all this. Yes, Faster-Than-Light is now a reality although no one knows yet, and it's an FTL jump system that doesn't need a gate. You're limited to jumps of 20 light years under our current navigation, technological and power systems. Your FTL capability has an outer limit of 100 light years due to fuel constraints.

"Yes, the technical FTL knowledge was greatly aided by our secret discovery of an ancient Western base that had been hidden on Ganymede centuries ago. It was a scientific outpost when The Fall occurred, and before the scientists there passed away, they saved their data so it could be recovered far in to the future. They had figured out Mankind wouldn't be back for quite some time based on information that had been beamed to them while civilization crumbled. Ganymede Station also had one of the missing coordinates for the Sol jump gate. And as for Cerberus, you'll soon be on your way to see her."

That last comment sounded mysterious enough to prompt Ronin to ask, "On my way? Cerberus isn't here in Wayside's shipyard?"

Colonel Hobson shook his head slightly and said, "Welcome to the world of secrets and misdirection. One of the other reasons why Ike was kept patrolling is simply because we don't have enough large ships out there. The Confederation hasn't been making enough of them while the shipyard that built Cerberus was itself being constructed for Project Argo. That temporarily diverted an enormous amount of resources from new ship construction, which necessarily meant ships like yours had to stay out longer."

Admiral Rodding nodded and continued on where Hobson left off. "Now that Project Argo is operational, the Argo shipyard will build more warships like Cerberus, as well as other classes of vessels. To help protect Argo, the shipyard is both mobile and self-sustaining with extensive mining and food production facilities. Because you've been brought in on this as the new captain of Cerberus, you'll leave directly from here for the shipyard under strict operational secrecy. Commander Toft will captain the Ike going forward, and you'll get to select some crew from Ike to come along if they're willing to follow you with no questions asked and no prospect of the leave they have coming."

With that, Rodding and Hobson both stood and, mirroring their movement, Ronin stood up as well. As they shook hands, Hobson told Ronin further orders await him upon his arrival on Cerberus.

CHAPTER 7

PROJECT ARGO

After the unexpected excitement of boarding a new transport bound for an undisclosed location followed by a hurried launch and full power flight, the trip settled down into a routine for the selected Ike crew who accompanied Ronin. When Dan had received permission to poach some of his crew from the Ike, he quietly spoke with some of his officers and crew members who he thought would be open or able to make the transition to Cerberus with him even though there was little he could tell them at the time. Over a hundred chose to join him on Cerberus on that basis. Although he resorted to enticing some officers to follow him by sweetening the deal with promotions, Dan was pretty satisfied with those of his people that he kept. He even brought along the entire Marine Bravo Team and lieutenants Matt LeCroy and Marcy Anzio. Bravo would be joining the other two Marine teams already stationed aboard Cerberus.

They spent the three-month transit productively getting up to speed on their new, top secret ship. To maintain mission secrecy, they were kept away from all the other passengers in a secure section of the transport and not allowed to interact with anyone from beyond that security zone.

Ronin waited for a few minutes outside the simulation machine while LeCroy completed the simulation. Finally, it ended and LeCroy emerged from the unit.

"Thoughts?" Ronin simply said. Since LeCroy was the only former Ike crewmember who had prior experience in testing and designing simulations, he was the natural choice to test this one first.

"The sims are too basic and fail to incorporate the type of new tactics which our hardware makes possible. It's like some tech guy programmed his notion of tactics into the system, but he didn't know what he didn't know," said LeCroy.

"Agreed," said Ronin. "Let's grab Lieutenant Anzio and talk about what we'd like to see in a sim over lunch. I was pretty underwhelmed by my first few runs through the system, too. Jump systems not being used to their potential, over reliance on perfunctory and unimaginative fleet tactics, and orthodox command and control based on outdated tactics and capabilities. Cerberus isn't even going on a mission like that," Ronin continued.

Ronin, LeCroy and Anzio sat in the empty crew's mess and discussed changing the sims.

"First thing that came to mind was the lack of jump bombs," Anzio noted. "I'm pretty sure we can rig up something for short range jumps that goes *boom*."

LeCroy nodded, stating, "That would be great. Tactically speaking, only a few light seconds would be needed to be tactically relevant. The sims also didn't factor in our gravity lenses. They're intended to help drive the ship for jumps, but the field they make can be calibrated into a highly effective, long range sensor suite that can pinpoint objects and movement based on how they affect the field harmonics."

"Good," Ronin said. "I was hoping they were feasible. Have the AI incorporate those variables into the sim. I'd also like it to incorporate a stealth mode based on using the grav lenses to bend light around the ship. It won't reduce certain emissions like engine and power signatures, but it certainly makes sense to have the ability to cloak the ship so we can sneak up on enemy vessels, or conduct surveillance unmolested by anybody. And I also want more lone wolf tactics in the sims. Right now, they were made for conventional fleet movements, but Cerberus isn't attached to any other fleet ships for the time being. We may have to do a lot more hit and runs as well as sneak and peeks."

"Lone wolfing it," Marcy responded. "This will be a different world, all right. No more large-scale fleet tactics. LeCroy and I will get started with the AI, and call you with the new sims are ready."

With that, the team finished their lunch and Ronin headed to his quarters to continue reading up on Cerberus technical data while Anzio and LeCroy returned to the simulation room.

It's going to be a totally different mindset to reverse the the new crew members' former emphasis on large scale, fleet formation tactics and start focusing on lone wolfing it, thought Ronin as he walked.

***

"Captain Ronin to the bridge. Captain Ronin to the bridge," came the announcement from Ronin's regulation, half-moon-shaped commlink node attached to his uniform's neck collar.

"Acknowledged," responded Ronin, quickly leaving the simulation room and jogging down the main passageway to the transport's bridge. As he walked, he again thought how odd it was to spend months on a top-secret transport of a design unknown to him and his crewmembers coming from the Ike. They had spent the entire trip locked away in a secure area of the vessel, and now he would exit that area for the first time during the entire trip.

He stopped at the closed airlock and thumbed the screen reader next to it. As he was expected, the hatchway quietly opened and Ronin quickly walked through to the black uniformed Fleet Intelligence Security guard who was waiting on the other side.

"Sir, if you would follow me to the bridge," said the guard, but more as a command than a request. They quickly traversed the secured section of the ship until reaching the command bridge.

"Welcome to the bridge, Captain Ronin," said the transport's commanding officer.

"Colonel Hobson, why am I not surprised to see you?" remarked Ronin, recognizing the now-familiar colonel sitting in the command chair. "I'm a little surprised to see someone with an infantry rank in command of a naval vessel, though."

Without taking his eyes from the front view screen, Hobson tilted his head towards Ronin as Ronin walked towards the command chair. "I'm full of surprises, Captain," said Hobson. "Names, ranks, and so on.

It's like I was never there. And Fleet Intelligence tends to do things their own way. Suits me just fine."

Ronin noted Hobson never identified the name of their transport, which seemed to not exist as far as the fleet was concerned. Hobson looked at him for a moment.

"Captain, you never asked me or Admiral Rodding why you were selected to command Cerberus. I presume you've figured it out and didn't need to. Yes?"

Ronin nodded. "It seemed like the obvious choice for a deep space mission beyond all chance of help if trouble was encountered was to take the captain of the ship whose role most closely resembled that mission profile. Ike spent long periods of time hunting the enemy on its own. That requires a very different mindset and tactics than formation warfare."

Hobson nodded slowly, before responding, "Indeed it does, captain. It also requires independent thinking, a willingness to conjure up innovative solutions, and tenacity unmatched by more conventional ship captains. Your record is replete with those characteristics.

"We especially liked your use of the Magneto Bomb solution to flush out *Shanwei* from its hide. Most commanders would have given up the chase long before then and been satisfied with an already highly successful mission. You topped that by using a science experiment to find, outgun, and capture an enemy ship that became a treasure trove of valuable information. Your new command will require all that and more."

Ronin's attention was drawn to the view screen and the strange looking structure that it showed.

"Argo Station. Current location classified, but as you can plainly see from the image of nearby Europa, it's currently hidden among the Jovian moons. Next time we show up, who knows?" said Hobson touching his console to magnify the image for Ronin.

Suddenly Argo Station loomed large in the view screen. Looking it over, Ronin was impressed. The station was enormous, and appeared to be a central cylindrical core extending several hundred levels in length and tapering at the ends, surrounded by three separate wings of massive superstructure that were able to move and wrap themselves around vessels parked within them.

As they approached closer, Ronin was able to see two structures inside the nearest superstructure wings on the side of their approach. One was obviously Cerberus, with her large, armored hull lit up. Cerberus had a sleek appearance despite her size, with a tapered prow in front and huge drive engines in the rear. Twin landing bays located along her length on opposite sides of the outer hull of the ship lent the appearance of a top and bottom of the ship when such concepts were normally meaningless in spacecraft. Both landing bays connected to the large hangar bay, which bisected Cerberus amidships. Weapons and sensor pods were currently secured in their resting positions that hugged the hull. As his attention moved to the next visible wing, Ronin couldn't identify the other object as it appeared to be a partially completed cylinder of enormous size.

Noticing Ronin's attention to the under-construction cylinder, Colonel Hobson stated, "It's another Argo Station under construction in that other wing. Fleet AI determined the first few stations can replicate themselves a few times before they begin to churn out four vessels at a time. For now, it's a station plus three ships.

"By the way, the other two vessels under construction are the sister ships of Cerberus, code named Ship Hulls 402 and 403. Construction won't be complete for several months yet," said Hobson.

"Can Argo Station perform an emergency jump while it's building other vessels?" Ronin asked, breaking his silence.

Hobson shrugged. "I don't know, Captain. It hasn't been gamed out by the boffins that I'm aware of."

When Ronin glanced at him in response, Hobson shrugged again and said, "No, I really don't know. If *Argo* can jump fully loaded, its information that's on a need to know basis and I apparently didn't have a need to know.

"We're about to dock with the station. I assumed you wanted to be present to get a look at the station while we did so. Orders have arrived for you, Bravo team, and lieutenants LeCroy and Anzio to immediately proceed to Cerberus. As you can imagine, there's a lot to do before you can get the ship underway."

"Yes, it's overwhelming, really," Ronin responded. "And we've got a few things we'd like to fabricate before leaving the station. Hopefully Argo Station can spare a few hands to help us make that happen."

"Oh, you'd be surprised," Hobson replied. "There are 43,000 crew working aboard *Argo*, plus thousands of AI controlled construction machines and fabrication printers."

Soon, docking with Argo Station was completed. As Ronin and his former Ike crewmembers approached the airlock doorway, it opened and a black uniformed Fleet Intelligence Security team was there to meet them.

"Captain, please have your crew follow us." said the security team leader in a commanding tone. It wasn't articulated as a request. The leader did not identify himself, which seems to be a common trait among the black uniformed security teams. He was a tall, heavily built man, with vaguely Hispanic features and an Argentinian accent.

"Lead the way, please," responded Ronin, nodding.

The group walked down a short hallway that turned and opened into a maglev tube.

"We'll ride the tubes in style, Captain. Otherwise, it's a really long walk," commented their tall, dark and enigmatic guide as everyone began boarding the tubecars.

Once they began to move, the magnetic propulsion tubecars were like missiles. "Wow! A thirty-minute tubecar! This station must be unbelievably huge," Lieutenant Anzio commented upon their arrival at Cerberus, prompting grunts of agreement from the other crewmembers.

If you only knew, thought Ronin. Since the others hadn't seen *Argo* from the outside like Ronin had, nor had he informed them, they really didn't know.

Their guide escorted them to the Cerberus boarding hatchway, which was down a docking tube connecting to the hatch. "Cerberus is a real beauty, Captain. None of us has ever seen a ship like her in the fleet. Is she a new type of vessel?" asked the guide.

Ronin responded as they glanced at each other. "Operational security rules prevent me from discussing that. Sorry, I can't tell you more than that," said Ronin.

"Understood, Captain," replied the guide. "I even know better than to ask, but curiosity was killing us."

Ronin smiled at his reply. As the hatchway opened into Cerberus, it occurred to him that his guard was obliged to ask as a test to see if Ronin would observe the top-secret nature of the projects.

As the former Ike officers and Marines walked into Cerberus, the white hallway was lined with the officers of Cerberus in their gray fleet uniforms and Ronin was piped aboard by the ship's boatswain with a traditional naval ceremony.

"Cerberus Actual, arriving," announced Cmdr. Diane Mueller, the tall, blonde executive officer, in German-accented English. In response to the announcement, the assembled crew and officers saluted.

"Permission to come aboard, Commander Mueller?" said Ronin, returning the salute.

"Oh, yes, sir!" Mueller smiled and shook Ronin's outstretched hand. "We've been awaiting your arrival for six months as we finished fitting out Cerberus and getting her ready. We have several options of things ready for you to choose from to do upon your arrival, but we weren't able to take your temperature in advance about what you'd want to do because we're operating under radio silence orders."

"Is a ship tour on the menu?" asked Ronin with a raised eyebrow as they walked behind the dismissed crewmembers returning to their stations.

"Yes, sir, that was the top option. We have a lot for you to see," Mueller responded.

Hours later, Ronin was sitting at the small desk in the office section of his small quarters, reviewing personnel files and making a few duty adjustments. His primary bridge crew consisted of some very qualified personnel, although the international composition of the crew wasn't something any of them had previously experienced.

Traditionally, crews originating from the same nation manned Confederation warships. As a 43-year-old Captain from Wisconsin, Ronin had only commanded crews of American origin in his past two postings, He re-reviewed the crewmembers' files after having met them today to compare his mental notes to what he had read.

Cmdr. Diane Mueller was a tall, blonde-haired, blue-eyed, thirty-two-year old from Rothenberg, Germany. Her husband, Karl, was a highly qualified civilian scientist attached to Cerberus. Since they had both volunteered for the duty so they could be together for Diane's tour of duty for once, they were permitted to bring their three children along for the duration of the Cerberus mission. Few families were permitted aboard combat vessels unless exceptional circumstances involving both parents justified it. Mueller was a very experienced XO, but she lacked a background in the type of hit-and-run combat missions Ronin specialized in. Ronin thought she would soon have her own command when he studied her file, but some concern about her background nagged at him. *Based on very limited information given to them, Commander Mueller and her husband volunteered for a very different mission profile than she has previously experienced. Unless she is very quick to adapt to a completely different mindset, there might be a rude awakening in their future,* he thought.

A thirty-year-old Israeli with the highly unusual name of Elvis Lazarus was the ship's chief engineer. His parents were big fans of an ancient singer who apparently had been known only by his first name. They discovered a scratchy recording of the singer's music in an archaeological dig they had been conducting in the ruins of a city once called "Nashville." Although raised in New Tel Aviv, Lieutenant Commander Lazarus was born a few months after the discovery, while the expedition was still on site, which had made him the first human born in Nashville since the plague wiped it out centuries ago.

Lt. Matt LeCroy would again handle Tactical on the bridge. He was twenty-seven years old, and had been born and raised in Laverne, Minnesota, before going to college at the University of North Dakota. About six feet tall with brown hair and hazel eyes, LeCroy was already on his third tour of duty with Ronin.

Ronin relied on LeCroy's sound judgments and had come to trust his lieutenant with his life. He was very pleased LeCroy chose to accompany him to the Cerberus.

The same held true for Lt. Marcy Anzio, who once again would run the ship's weapons. Anzio and LeCroy had to function together as a team that unified weapons and tactics into a smoothly functioning unit on the ship. The twenty-six-year-old Anzio was on her second tour of duty with Ronin, but had integrated with LeCroy so swiftly and smoothly that Ronin knew they had to be a package deal to bring them to Cerberus. Born and raised in Russellton, near the ruins of Pittsburgh, Pennsylvania, the 5'2" Anzio was dark-haired with olive skin and dark eyes.

Scans were a new department for Ronin. On the Ike, Scans were integrated into Tactical, but on Cerberus the scanning was so much more powerful that the flood of information required a standalone bridge function. Lt. Pierre Delacroix would run the station. He was a tall, raven-haired, blue-eyed, twenty-nine-year-old combat engineer and scanning specialist from the Bordeaux region of France, with prior combat tours on the Confederate frigate *Achéron*. Interestingly, there was a personal file note from the captain of *Achéron* to beware Delacroix's poker skills unless you'd like to become bankrupt before you knew what happened. Ronin's late wife, Marie, having heard Ronin's stories of legendary poker players in the fleet Marines, had forbid him from ever playing a hand, so that their family wouldn't starve. Ronin consented and to this day he wasn't tempted, especially having been forewarned about Delacroix's skills. Another completely new function to Ronin was Fabrication. Not only did the existence of the unit tell Ronin a lot about where Cerberus might find itself someday, the large size of the area and huge population of AI 'bots operating in Fabrication suggested to him the ship was expected to handle long deployments far from where it could call for assistance.

Fabrication was under the leadership of thirty-year-old Lt. Kristoff Alphonso, who came from the Greek island of Mykonos, part of the Cyclades. On his first tour of duty, Alphonso triple majored in college with a combination of Computer Design, Mechanical Engineering, and Robotics. Clearly, he was a genius at designing and building.

Communications was run by Lt. Maria Delgado, a thirty-two-year-old combat veteran from Brazil on her fourth tour. She had graduated from university at the age of nineteen, then set off on three successive combat tours on other ships before helping devise new communication protocols to strengthen fleet commlink security.

Medical was under Lt. Hirohito Taketa, who hailed from Kyoto, Japan, where he had obtained advanced medical degrees in surgery, robotic surgery, and medicinal synthesis. The experienced fifty-year-old Ship's Doctor had served several tours on a combat vessel, aboard a space station, and in an Earth-side naval hospital in Green Bay.

The ship's helmsman and navigator was Antonio Perez, from the South American nation of Chile. Just twenty-four years old, he was already on his second tour, having joined the fleet at sixteen. His prior duty station was on the destroyer Chacabuco, a newer, more powerful class of destroyer than the Ike. Perez was transferred to Cerberus because of his familiarity with the Cerberus navigation system, which was nearly identical to the system aboard Chacabuco.

Ronin's review of the crew files was interrupted by a soft intercom chime indicating a call from Colonel Hobson on Argo Station.

"Captain Ronin, would you and Commander Mueller be available to come over to Fleet Intelligence at 1400 hours tomorrow for a briefing? I know it's kind of a big ask so soon after you arrived on Cerberus, but the Admiralty wants to bring you up to speed on the latest aspects to your mission as quickly as we can."

"Sure, we'll meet you there, sir," responded Ronin. After the link was closed, Ronin wondered what was so urgent that they were being rushed through a new vessel commissioning. He didn't like the possible answers he came up with.

CHAPTER 8

SHAKEDOWN

At 1400 hours, Ronin and Commander Mueller arrived at Fleet Intelligence on Argo Station. The black uniformed security guards were expecting them, and they quickly were escorted into a briefing room where Colonel Hobson was waiting.

"Captain, Commander, thank you for coming. If you would be seated, we can get started so you can return to Cerberus. I took the liberty of having coffee and snacks delivered, so I hope you'll find them agreeable," said Hobson.

"Thank you, Colonel, that sounds wonderful," said Ronin as the two of them sat at the conference table.

Hobson touched a screen button. Behind him, a white wall with a portrait of the Confederation President suddenly changed into a tactical screen display of the Sol system. Hobson stood and turned to face the screen.

"All right, as you both can see, this represents the current tactical situation in this system. Because of the Treaty of Midway, there is no combat on Earth between the Asiatic Collective, aka AC, and the Confederation, so all combat officially takes place off planet. The Belt remains a confused mix of independent Belters, AC-occupied rocks and ships, and Confederation rocks and ships. Earth's Moon is nominally under mixed Confederation and Collective management, even though there aren't any bases on it that we know of. Mars is solely ruled by the Confederation. The moons of Saturn and Jupiter out here are unclaimed, at least officially. Does that square with your understanding of the current strategic situation in Sol system?" asked Hobson.

Both of them nodded, and Mueller asked the same question Ronin was about to ask. "I thought there was some activity around Ganymede? The map doesn't suggest anything there."

Colonel Hobson smiled, noting "Very perceptive of both of you. Correct. Now let me show you the real situation in this system," he said, reaching over to press another screen button.

The display changed. Now there were blue markings indicating Confederate control of Ganymede, several more asteroids in the Belt, the Jovian moons of Europa and Io, and Titan, the huge moon around Saturn. Red markers appeared as well, indicating AC control of a swath of the Belt, the small Jovian moon Pandia, and the moon designated Saturn IV, which is sometimes called Dione, although no one knew why.

"So, it would seem the Confederation and the AC both control larger portions of the system than is publicly known," commented Ronin. "Are the locations selected because of resources, or some other reason?"

"Both. Let me explain," added Hobson, clasping his hands. "The majority of both sides' early acquisitions were primarily because of resources. Could be a mix of minerals, other times a convenient resupply location not unlike the space version of old train depots that eventually lead to colonization around them. Or depots that were eventually abandoned when new technology rendered them obsolete and there were no other compelling reasons to keep them."

Ronin and Mueller nodded in understanding.

"In the past two years, that pattern was changed somewhat by history. In this case, I mean the ancient history from before The Fall," continued Hobson.

The Fall again. Why does that suddenly keep coming up in mission briefings, wondered Ronin.

"Remember the old observation about how long engineering specifications live?" asked Hobson.

Ronin nodded and responded, "That's the story told by the ancients about how the width of two horses eventually influenced the dimensions of the old American space shuttles because the railroads had been built to accommodate horse-drawn wagons."

"Correct, Captain," Hobson stated. "While sometimes separating facts from myths can be difficult, in this instance, the popular story has been confirmed. I'll walk you both through this so we can move on.

"The booster rockets of the space shuttle were constructed for transport by rail. American railroads were an unusual width of 4 feet, 8 1/2 inches. They had been built by the British, who had matched the U.S. railroads to the size of pre-railroad tramways in Europe.

"As we continue back in time, we learn that the people who built the first tramways in Europe used the same tools used for building wagons. They matched the width of the tramways to the spacing of the wagon wheels, so they could align with the ruts in the roads of the time and avoid breaking wagon wheels.

"Imperial Rome built those roads thousands of years ago for the benefit of their legions and the roads have been in use ever since. The wheels of Roman war chariots made the original ruts in those ancient roads. Those chariots were built just wide enough to accommodate the back ends of two war-horses," said Hobson. "So, how does the life expectancy of engineering specifications impact Cerberus today?" he asked rhetorically.

"Because at the pre-Fall base on Ganymede, which we've been exploring, the Confederacy has located information strongly suggesting the old jump gates and interstellar colonies are real and, combined with information captured by you from *Shanwei*, indicate where they may be located," Hobson said, answering himself.

"What?" exclaimed Mueller.

"I still thought those weren't real!" said Ronin at nearly the same time.

Ignoring their outbursts, Colonel Hobson pressed another screen button and the wall display changed again. "As I was saying, the old carry-forward specifications included a description of the dimensions of the jump gates, which influenced the design and dimensions of Cerberus, in the hopes she could one day fit through a gate, assuming they ever existed. After you complete the commissioning of Cerberus and her shakedown cruise, the Admiralty has ordered Cerberus to jump out to the anticipated coordinates of the old jump gates to investigate," he announced.

"Cerberus has been under extended testing and AI controlled construction, but we anticipate there will still be some of the usual birthing pains of a new ship, with new tech and also a radically new class. How long do you estimate before the shakedown cruise may begin?" Hobson asked.

"Best guess at this point is two, maybe three weeks," responded Mueller. "Mechanically, it appears most of the systems are operating as designed and they have been extensively tested and stress-tested prior to our arrival. Crew sims are already underway, and we have implemented new sims of our own design as well," she concluded.

"Excellent. Is there anything we can do here to help prepare for your mission?" asked Hobson.

"Yes, there is. We'd like to discuss our ideas for a new weapons system and several other tweaks to the ship's systems with the engineers from Wayside," said Ronin.

"OK. Expect them to come aboard to discuss them within the hour," said Hobson, concluding the meeting with a few more pleasantries and handshakes.

After Dan and Diane returned to Dan's ready room on Cerberus, Diane mentioned something Dan hadn't thought of. "Captain, did you know we have no records of a Colonel Hobson in the Confederation databases? He doesn't exist."

Dan's eyebrows shot up. "Really? And yet he has all kinds of access to everything. Even the Admiral defers to Hobson's authority. And yet, we don't even know his first name."

Diane nodded. "Who he is, and where he has that kind of access and authority is quite a mystery. I doubt we'll ever find out the truth."

* * *

Twenty-five days later, Ronin sat in his command chair. Both he and Mueller had dark rings under their eyes from too much work and not enough sleep from winding up Cerberus' readiness for a shakedown. Now that the engines were certified as fully operational, the ship hummed with power.

"Helm, prepare to take us out. Standard launching speed, please," Ronin ordered.

"Aye, aye, Captain. Standard departure speed," Lieutenant Perez replied, pressing the screen buttons to execute the command. As Cerberus pulled out of the shipyard superstructure, the ship's exterior camera's focused on space suited construction personnel waiving to the ship excitedly. They tied into a camera feed from a drone that was positioned to film the beautiful ship leaving the shipyard.

"Steady as she goes, Captain," said Perez.

Despite their exhaustion, the bridge crew fairly shook with energy due to the excitement of finally driving their vessel under her own power. Her hull plating, which was unlike anything Ronin had ever seen before, gave her a relatively smooth 1500-foot exterior in the front, broken by a hangar bay bisecting the lateral spine of the ship in the middle. The drives in the rear of the ship were both higher and wider than the main body. Get close enough to her, and you could also see the various sensor blisters and turrets of rail guns or missile launchers. Cerberus cleared the shipyard superstructure and headed out for her shakedown cruise. There was nothing quite like taking a new ship for an inaugural drive.

CHAPTER 9

JUMP GATES

A month later, Cerberus completed her shakedown cruise and returned to Argo Shipyard to finish her fitting out. After docking, Colonel Hobson boarded the ship to meet with Ronin and Mueller in Ronin's ready room adjacent to the bridge near the center of the ship.

"We were successful in creating jump bombs according to your specifications, Captain. One of our more creative techs dubbed them Grasshoppers because of their jumping abilities. Two dozen of them are being loaded into the ship's magazines and the shipyard is making the changes to the ship that you've ordered," said Hobson.

"That's great! Thank you, Colonel. Have there been any change to our deployment orders?" asked Ronin.

"Yes, there is," said Hobson. "Our spies have reported the AC ordered a war bird to the same coordinates where they suspect the old jump gate to be located. It left port fourteen months ago under heavy acceleration. Be advised to expect potential hostilities upon your arrival. Report your findings after you complete your survey of the area and expect further orders."

After the colonel's departure, Mueller looked at Ronin and said, "It still doesn't seem possible we're actually being sent out to ascertain whether the jump gates to the colonies were real."

Ronin nodded and responded, "Agreed. We're chasing ancient fairy tales. Maybe the fleet will have us look for some of the other wonders of the ancient world on our next mission. Feel like trying to find the Hanging Gardens of Babylon, Commander?"

Mueller laughed softly with a small smile. "Why not? Maybe we'll become the most famous archaeological spacecraft in history?" she said.

* * *

The next few weeks passed swiftly as they made the final changes to Cerberus that were needed to make the ship operational. Finally, the ship and crew were ready to depart from the Argo once more.

"Argo reports all docking connections severed, Captain," reported Perez.

"Excellent, Perez. Standard docking speed, take us out," responded Ronin while looking at the forward view screen. Slowly, Cerberus left the shipyard, and continued on into space.

"Perez, set course for the system's outer rim to the coordinates I sent to your station. It's time to make a ship-wide announcement of our mission," said Ronin.

Ronin thumbed the intercom and spoke to the crew. "Attention all hands, this is the Captain. These past few months you have incredible accomplishments to be proud of. No one has commissioned a new class of warship as quickly as you have, and no crew has ever served aboard a ship quite like Cerberus. She is a very special, one of a kind vessel that will become legendary. Now we have a mission that is hopefully one fitting for such a special ship.

"Our first mission is to proceed to a point in space beyond Sol system to investigate an old legend. Fleet Intelligence believes our destination may have been a possible location for jump gates that lead to the mythical Colonies of Earth. Cerberus is to proceed to the coordinates and investigate the area. Stay alert and prepare for FTL jump momentarily. That is all," said Ronin, turning to look at the very surprised face of Lieutenant Perez.

"Lieutenant, initiate jump 1," Ronin said to Perez.

"Aye, aye, Captain, initiating jump 1," responded Perez.

Cerberus disappeared before reappearing elsewhere in a small flash of light, called a jump flare. Perez, monitoring his boards, announced,

"Jump 1 complete. Taking navigation position reading now." Moments later he added, "Captain, we have arrived at the designated coordinates."

"Conducting broad sensor sweep now, Captain," said Lieutenant Delacroix at the Scans station.

"Early threat assessment reports one bogey, now designating as Bogey A. Time horizon, approximately one week until our image reaches them. Constant bearing, decreasing range. They're headed our way," LeCroy announced from Tactical.

Ronin nodded, then announced, "All right, we just skipped over fifteen months of sub light travel time, so we have some time to do a more thorough evaluation of this location. Let's do a deep dive and see what we come up with." Delacroix and LeCroy quickly got busy with their equipment after Ronin's announcement.

"I recommend we launch some drones towards the bogey in case it turns out to be the AC hostile we believe it is. They could give us some advanced warning of any inbound ordinance," said Mueller.

"Agreed," said Ronin.

Hours later, Mueller and Ronin were tired from reviewing poor quality scans that radiation kept interfering with.

"Other than the patch of high-density radiation blocking our view forward and the bogey approaching from Earth, there just isn't much to see this far out here," said Mueller, standing up to stretch out the kinks while the two were in Ronin's ready room. "I don't see many options other than to jump and greet our AC visitor even though they're too far away for us to ID the ship and possibly cause a confrontation, or jump further out to see what's beyond the radiation using optics because the radiation hot spot in front of us is so intense our sensors are fuzzed from it," she concluded.

"Agreed. Since our orders didn't send us here to pick a fight, let's have Perez plot a jump path around the hot spot and we'll take a peek behind the curtain. Have our rear cover drone screen go dark for now and we can collect or reactivate them later," ordered Ronin.

As Mueller returned to the bridge to give the orders and prepare the ship, Ronin pondered the obvious. *What could possibly have caused a radiation hot spot of that magnitude out here in the middle of nowhere.*

The only answer he knew was thermonuclear detonations on a large scale. Could be numerous blasts, or one huge one. He hoped there was another answer out there instead.

Ronin walked over to the restroom attached to the ready room and splashed cold water on his face. *Going to have to stand down soon and make way for the second watch. Can't wear everyone down on the first day.*

After drying his face, he looked at himself in the mirror and thought of Sarah and Edward. Other than video messages, he hadn't been able to visit them since his last leave on Earth, over a year ago. In that time, growing dangers seemed to lurk everywhere. *How tall they must be getting. I've got to get some time off with them.*

A chime interrupted his reverie. He heard Mueller's voice saying, "Captain to the bridge."

Ronin quickly left the ready room and returned to the bridge. "Status?" he inquired.

"Course plotted, and Cerberus is ready to make way again," said Mueller as Ronin replaced her in the command chair.

"Perez, execute jump," said Ronin.

"Aye, aye, Captain. Executing jump," responded Perez, pushing the button to send the ship elsewhere.

"Jump 2 complete," said Perez moments later as the ship jumped sideways by three million miles past the outer edge of the hot spot. Seconds later, he followed up with, "Executing Jump 3," which moved Cerberus forward beyond the diffuse hot spot barrier by twenty million miles.

"Weak gravity well located ahead," announced Delacroix. "No visual of what's causing it," he noted.

"Put it on view screen," commanded Ronin. The bridge crew stared ahead, trying to see what could cause gravity out here.

"Reduce magnification by factor of ten," said Mueller. The picture appeared to leap backward in time as the AI complied with the order. "Is it a black hole?" Mueller wondered aloud after the change in visual perspective revealed what appeared to be a dark eclipse in space.

By now, Delacroix's sensor suite had some time to provide additional data readings. "Commander, our sensors are still a bit fuzzed from our proximity to the hot spot but so far the readings suggest that's a dark planet out there," he responded.

Mueller and Ronin glanced at each other while Anzio vocalized what everyone was thinking. "A ninth planet?" she asked, shocked. "We're so far away from Sol, we're practically in outer space!" continued Anzio.

"Distance to Planet Nine approximately three months at current cruising speed," noted Lieutenant Delacroix, unconsciously giving a name to the dark planet as he did so.

While the bridge crew grappled with the concept of an unknown planet floating behind a radioactive hot spot that blocked the ship's advanced scanners, Ronin made a decision. "Helm, jump us to a spot halfway between the hot spot and Planet Nine, as Lieutenant Delacroix called it. Launch a drone screen when we arrive and let's run a thorough scan from there."

"Aye, aye, Captain," responded Perez, beginning the process of calculating the jump and preparing to execute the order. "Jump calculated. Destination appears clear of obstructions. Ready to execute," he added a few minutes later.

"Execute jump, Mr. Perez," said Ronin. In a pair of jump flares, Cerberus reappeared at the halfway point.

"Contact! Metallic objects. One, possibly more bogeys. Distance, 4 billion miles. Speed, nominal. Constant bearing, increasing range," announced Lieutenant LeCroy.

"Assuming they're looking this way, it'll be about five hours until they see our arrival flare," said Mueller.

"All right, if they see us, it'll be quite some time until they could get here, assuming they can change bearing that quickly. Realistically, it is likely even longer. Said Ronin. "Cerberus will be long gone by then if need be. Let's check out the neighborhood. Call in your seconds from second shift, and everyone get some rest. It's been a long day."

Once second shift was in place, Ronin and Mueller returned to his ready room. "Preliminary scan results indicate the bogeys are traveling somewhat slowly. Too slow for an effective patrol, and they aren't following the same course so they are pulling apart without any course deviations noted," said Mueller.

"Light refraction even suggests one hull is tumbling. We can't get a clear read on the other," Ronin nodded tiredly. "I'm guessing these might be ghost ships, or remnants of them. AI agrees with that assessment. If they've been traveling at the same velocity all along, it would seem they've been out here for hundreds of years," added Ronin.

"Correct, Captain. Using the assumptions of constant bearing, velocity and origination near the hot spot, they have been traveling for approximately 753 years," responded the female-sounding AI of Cerberus. "This time horizon is consistent with the Science Department's measurements of hot spot radioactive decay since our arrival," added the AI.

Ronin and Mueller looked at one another for a few seconds before Ronin spoke. "Given the extreme intensity of the radiation in the hot spot, I can only imagine how bad it was 753 years ago."

Mueller nodded. "Science Department believes it was some sort of massive nuclear event, or a series of them, to cause that level of radiation. Legend holds even the intense radiation in the ruins of old Washington, D.C., had decayed to match ambient surrounding levels a century after The Fall," she commented.

Ronin yawned and stretched for a few moments. "Let's grab some rack time and sleep on it while the sensors work up a more complete report," he said.

"Good idea," responded Mueller. "It's been a long day, and we need to stay sharp."

Ronin nodded. "OK, let's regroup at 1200 hours and figure out our next steps based on what data we have. See you tomorrow, Diane."

Mueller returned to her quarters, feeling like she had been away for a week. *I wonder if it will be hard to get to sleep. Too much excitement, and I feel like an overtired kid before holiday.* The door to her quarters swished open to reveal her husband and children tucked up under his arms as he read a bedtime book to them.

"Mommy!" cried her twin daughters, Sonya and Sophia, springing up to hug her.

"We missed you!" said Sophia, as Sonya simply buried her face into Mueller's neck. The seven-year-old twins were blonde, blue-eyed mirror images of their pretty mother.

Her husband, Karl, stood and simply waited with a knowing smile while the girls hugged Mueller for a few moments. "Well, well, look who decided to join us in time for bedtime stories," said Karl, his blue eyes twinkling.

"It feels like I haven't seen you three for a week," said Mueller tiredly. "What a long day!" she continued. "Come on girls, let Mommy get you tucked into bed," she said as the girls followed her into their bedroom.

A few minutes later Mueller entered the bedroom she shared with Karl. She got ready for sleep and fell into bed as he handed her a glass of water and crawled in beside her.

"I saw the report concluding the radiation hot spot is unnatural in origin, but I don't understand the science behind your area's conclusion," Mueller said to Karl, curling up in his arms. "Can you walk me through the simple version of it?" she asked.

Karl sighed contentedly for a moment as he thought about how to summarize the science at a high level. "It basically was a series of logical deductions. There is no detectable mass at the gates; therefore, there is nothing that could produce energy or radiation byproduct. Coupled with observations that the radiation seems to slowly be reducing in intensity and the trajectories of multiple objects our visual scanners picked up and tracked back to the vicinity of the hot spot leads us to conclude there was some sort of energy event at the hot spot."

Mueller listened with her eyes closed, barely following along to what would have to serve as her own version of a bedtime story. As she lay in their rack, her last thought before falling asleep was, *I wonder what tomorrow will show us.*

As Ronin trudged to his quarters, he also pondered what the morrow would bring. He simply was too tired to think of anything else that had to be done today, so he stepped out of his uniform, tossed it into the laundry, and had a quick shower. His desktop commlink system indicated there was a video message from his children, so he prepared a glass of herbal tea to sip while he sat at his desk to watch the video from Sarah and Edward on his screen. He was smiling when the video concluded, and decided to send a quick video reply before crawling into his rack and falling into a deep sleep.

"Hi kids! As you can see from the message header, I'm not aboard the Ike any longer. I'm captain of a brand-new ship, the Cerberus, but I wasn't allowed to tell you that until we departed, so there's the big piece of news I've been holding back. She's a huge, fast and powerful ship, but this is the surprise. We were sent out on an exploration mission to find some legends. I have to go now, but I love you and do what your grand-parents tell you. Ronin out."

Message and tea finished, Ronin fell into his rack and immediately went into a deep sleep.

The next day at 1200 hours, Ronin strode on to the bridge and walked over to Delacroix's station. "Delacroix, anything new since the morning report?"

Delacroix shook his head and said, "No, Captain. No change in aspect on the bogeys. We've detected two moons orbiting Planet Nine, and AI supposition continues to support Science Department's prelim-inary determination of the hot spot being artificial in origin," reported Delacroix.

Ronin nodded. "All right. I think it's time to move on. Let's get the Bulldogs into the game here," he said, walking over to the command chair.

"Sunderland, this is the Captain," said Ronin into a commlink chan-nel that he opened by using the console node built into his chair arm.

"Sunderland here, what can I do for ye, Captain?" immediately responded the CAG (Commander Air Group), in his heavy Scottish burr.

"Scouting mission for your Bulldogs, Lieutenant. Mount up three crews. One for a reconnaissance of Planet Nine, and the others for an intercept of several bogeys we've been tracking. Sneak and peek initially, jump to safety at the first sign of trouble, then inspect closer if nothing seems dangerous," said Ronin.

"Aye, it'll be a pleasure Captain. We'll prep for preflight, and launch the birds in ten minutes," replied Sunderland.

Sunderland opened a commlink channel to the pilot ready room using the node on his collar. The ready room was occupied with bored

Marine pilots who had been following along with the sensor scans, hoping for something interesting to happen.

"Now hear this. Bulldog crews one through three, mission briefing in my office in two minutes. Launch Master, preflight their birds. Sunderland out."

After he closed the line, Sunderland noted to himself he essentially said a spacecraft named after a dog was called a bird. "Sometimes the weird around here is hard to wrap me head around," he muttered to himself, shaking his head slightly as he prepared his thoughts.

Two minutes later, three pilot officers and their rear-seaters gathered in Sunderland's office.

"Listen up. The Captain has a reconnaissance mission for you. Our tactical situation is this," he said, throwing an image from his desk computer to the wall screen in his office.

"We've jumped around this radiation hot spot and found a dark planet with a pair of moons. Couldn't see it until we cleared the hot spot because the radiation is so intense most of our sensors are fouled except for optical, and those couldn't detect the planet from there. It is now designated Planet Nine, as we finally could see it when we got closer. We're also tracking several objects on constant bearings, increasing range trajectories for the better part of a day. By now they would've seen us if they were looking.

"Your missions are this. Bulldog 1, jump to Planet Nine and survey. Bulldogs 2 and 3, jump to these objects and investigate them. Keep your jump engines spooled up and jump out at the first sign of trouble. If the situation is quiet, we can proceed further. Questions?" asked Sunderland as he completed their mission briefing.

"Why are we tracking these particular objects and not the rest of the junk that's normally flying around?" asked Bulldog 1 Pilot Officer Erin Johnson, the petite, dark-skinned pilot from Alabama.

"That's a solid question," said Sunderland. "Sensors and visuals report very little is out here. We don't know why, but both of those two objects stand out because their courses intersect at the hot spot, and at current speeds that we've observed from optical telescopes, it would have taken both of them 753 years to get where they are from that inter-section point."

Startled, the Bulldog pilots looked at each other before Johnson spoke up again. "Um, sir? Are those objects all traveling at the same speed?"

Sunderland nodded. "That's affirmative, Johnson. Like buckshot, they are traveling at the same speed in a diverging pattern originating from roughly the same point in space, all beginning at the hot spot."

"Just like debris from a really big explosion," mumbled Bulldog 1's rear-seater, Hal Patterson, who was from Texas.

Questions answered, Sunderland looked at his pilots and rear-seaters one more time. "All right. Make it happen out there. Good hunting and don't do nothing stupid," he said as his people stood to head over to the launch bay, where the engine whine of the Bulldogs could be heard from the preflight. After he watched them board their rides and his screen showed green lights across the board for the Bulldogs, Sunderland com-mlinked the bridge using the node on his collar again.

"Captain, Sunderland here. Bulldogs 1 through 3 are go for launch on your order."

Ronin, expecting the report, simply responded, "Launch Bulldogs."

BULLDOG 1

"Bulldog 1, you are go for launch," said the Launch Master into Pilot Officer Johnson's ears as she pressed the launch acceleration button on her console to send their ride hurtling down the launch tube into the beyond. Seconds later, they were free of Cerberus' gravity field.

"We have good launch. Systems still report optimal," reported rear-seater Patterson from his electronic suite and tactical station behind Johnson.

"Thanks. Jump in three. Two. One," responded Johnson as they jumped the Bulldog away from Cerberus.

There was a small jump flare between Planet Nine and the orbit of its largest as Bulldog 1 appeared. "Jump 1 complete," announced Johnson.

"Beginning scans," responded Patterson. "Prepare for a long wait for our signals to return with data," he said.

BULLDOG 2

"Bulldog 2, you are go for launch." said the Launch Master into Pilot Helmut Meyer's helmet as he pressed the launch acceleration button on his console to send their ride hurtling down the launch tube.

"We have good launch. Systems still report optimal," reported rear-seater Sophie Schmidt from her electronic suite and tactical station behind Meyer. Both Meyer and Schmidt spoke slightly accented American because they were Germans.

"Jump in three. Two. One," responded Meyer as Bulldog 2 quickly jumped away. There was a small jump flare as Bulldog 2 reappeared near their target, now dubbed Object 1.

"Jump 1 complete," announced Meyer.

"Object 1 on sensors, distance to target, 100 miles," said Schmidt after a few moments. "Object is tumbling slowly, but we can match if needed," she noted after another glance at her screen.

"Matching target speed now," said Meyer as he brought the ship into a stationary position relative to the target.

Several minutes passed as the Germans took additional readings while they held on station 100 miles from the object, which was still too far away to see.

"Radiation readings match ambient levels," announced Schmidt. "Scopes are otherwise clear of objects," she added.

"Roger that. I'm going to close with the target. Call out any change in aspect," responded Meyer.

Bulldog 2 slowly began to accelerate, and closed the 100 miles separating them in a few minutes. Soon the object became visible, and then it quickly grew in size until it filled their forward windows from a mile away. Stunned, Schmidt and Meyer easily recognized the object as the remnant of a spacecraft. It was over 1000 meters in length, with a width of 500 feet width that was comparable to that of Cerberus.

"No life signs. No energy readings, hull temperature matches the outside temperature," said Schmidt, having a hard time tearing her eyes away from the forward windows long enough to read her screens.

"I'm going to get us closer," said Meyer. "I want to take a look at why one side of it is darkened," he continued, as he pushed the Bulldog even closer and matched the slow tumble of the ship.

"Carbon scoring readings," said Schmidt. "The entire side of the ship must have been facing something really hot to do that," she stated.

"Look, towards the rear," interrupted Meyer. "That look like melted metal to you?" he asked.

"Affirmative," agreed Schmidt.

"Time to swing us round the other side," Meyer said. Bulldog 2 began to traverse the hull, scanning the entire time.

Sophie saw it first. "Helmut, there's writing over to port!" she exclaimed.

Meyer's eyes focused on the area indicated by Schmidt, and he slowly flew the Bulldog to hover over the writing. They were speechless for a few moments.

"Helmut, why is it we can actually read that writing?" asked Schmidt in a barely audible voice, quaking with shock.

"What the hell have we found?" asked Meyer, in an equally alarmed voice.

BULLDOG 3

"Bulldog 3, you are go for launch." said the Launch Master into Pilot Antonio Russo's helmet as he pressed the launch acceleration button on his console to send their ride hurtling down the launch tube.

"We have good launch. Systems still report optimal," reported rear-seater Michael Jonsey in a southern-accented, spectacularly deep bass voice from his electronic suite and tactical station behind Russo.

"Jump in three. Two. One," responded Russo as Bulldog 3 quickly jumped away. There was a small jump flare as Bulldog 3 reappeared near their target, dubbed Object 2.

"Jump 1 complete," announced Russo.

"Object 2 on sensors, distance to target, 100 miles," said Jonsey after a few moments. "Object is tumbling. We can match it," he noted.

"Matching target speed now," said Russo, as he brought Bulldog 3 into a stationary position relative to the target.

"Running long distance scan now," said Jonsey.

"Low levels of radiation, a bit higher than surrounding space," Russo said, "Time for a closer look. I'll bring us in slowly."

Bulldog 3 accelerated and closed the distance rather leisurely. "Distance to target, thirty, now twenty, now ten miles…we're reading a power spike. Weapons lock!" yelled Jonsey, interrupting himself when an alarm sounded and Russo reflexively triggered an emergency jump back to the rendezvous point with Cerberus.

"Cerberus, this is Bulldog 3, be advised we experienced weapons lock on approach to Object 2," said Jonsey, once the link to Cerberus opened and their sensor data transmitted. "Request further orders."

Ronin heard the message while he sat in the command chair of the bridge. He thumbed open his chair's console commlink and asked, "Bulldog 3, this is Cerberus Actual. Say again. Weapons lock?"

"That's affirmative, Cerberus. We confirm weapons lock. Our sensor data shows a weak power spike accompanied by sensor lock and a targeting pulse," responded Jonsey.

"Captain, we didn't get close enough to get a visual on the target before we jumped, so we still don't know what it is other than it's hostile," added Russo.

"Wait one," responded Ronin, which meant the same thing as 'wait a minute'.

"Captain, I recommend we jump Bulldog 3 closer to the target, say thirty miles or so, and have them launch some drones on an intercept. We can aim a pair of them on a kinetic glide path to intercept Object 2, and use a third as a powered decoy," said Lieutenant LeCroy, speaking from the Tactical station.

"You thinking the drones can come in under the targeting horizon of whatever is out there before activating and trying to disable the defenses?" asked Ronin.

"Affirmative, Captain, that's exactly what I'm thinking," replied LeCroy.

"Transmit that plan to Bulldog 3 and tell them to keep us appraised," ordered Ronin.

Minutes later Bulldog 3 appeared 30 miles away from Object 2. "Jump 3, completed. Kinetic drones launching…they're flying straight and true," said Jonsey after a minute of activity. "Jump us to the launch point for the powered drone," he said to Russo.

Seconds later, Bulldog 3 appeared 30 miles away from Object 2, but this time back on the same approach vector as they initially occupied. "Jump 4, completed. Drone launch successful. Time on target, 30 seconds," noted Jonsey as Bulldog 3 jumped again to another point 30 miles from the target.

"Jump 5, completed," noted Russo this time.

"Drone convergence, 15 seconds," said Jonsey. "Ten. Five…" he counted down, when suddenly there was a bright flash through their forward window.

"Decoy drone destroyed. Appeared to be another power spike and an energy discharge," said Jonsey, reading his sensor screens. "Kinetic flight has made contact with the Object, drones activating. Telemetry data suggests they have identified two targets that appear to be gun turrets. Guns are tracking, but they can't lower their target horizon. Turrets destroyed!" said Jonsey triumphantly. "Sending the drones to scan the remaining exterior."

BULLDOG 1

Pilot Officer Erin Johnson sighed as she stood up to stretch. "Hal, I've tied the jump system to my audio commands so I can move about the cabin," she announced.

"Roger that," replied rear-seater Patterson in a bored tone as he looked over the copious data flowing in from their sensor scans. "Our drones are approaching the larger satellite to Planet Nine. We should be receiving their data before long," he said.

"While it was exciting to discover an unknown, dark planet in distant orbit around the Sol system, it appears to be just a gas giant," said Johnson. "I wonder if we can name it?" she asked rhetorically.

"From what I heard, Lieutenant Delacroix's labeling it Planet Nine seems to have prevailed already," remarked Patterson with a small snort. "I think you're outta luck on the naming rights," he concluded with a smile as he continued to stare at his data screens.

"Hey, a girl can dream, can't she?" said Johnson with a grin. "Besides, there's not much doing here so far," she laughed.

Two hours later, Patterson's scan alarm tripped. "Looks like the drones over the satellite have found something," he said excitedly. "They're reporting spotting straight lines and rectangular shapes. I'll detail one to fly over the location and take a closer look," he continued.

"Straight lines and rectangles aren't natural," Johnson noted with interest. "Hopefully we find something interesting before we finish our survey and jump back to the rendezvous."

CERBERUS RENDEZVOUS POINT

Ronin paced the small floor space of his ready room as he awaiting the returning Bulldog survey teams. *Man, I feel like a kid on holiday*, he said to himself. *Too much energy*. His thoughts were interrupted by an incoming message chime.

"Captain, this is Commander Mueller. The Bulldogs have returned and are landing in the hanger bay."

Ronin walked over to his desk and pushed the commlink screen button. "Thank you, Commander. Have the AI assimilate their data transmittals and let's meet in the main conference room at 2100 hours."

Several hours later, Ronin gathered in the main conference room with Commander Mueller, her husband, Karl, and lieutenants LeCroy, Delacroix, and Anzio. "All right. Our Bulldog crews collected a wealth of data, and Mr. Mueller will take lead to walk us through Science's conclusions," began Ronin as he yielded the meeting to Karl Mueller.

Karl cleared his throat as he stood up and walked over to the wall display. He was a tall man, with sandy brown hair and piercing blue eyes. "Thank you, Captain. As you all are aware, the data from the past few hours is remarkable. The highest-level summary is this: We have discovered remnants of at least two unknown spacecraft, one of which appeared to be hostile, and an installation of unknown origin on the largest satellite to Planet Nine," Karl began in dramatic fashion. "While those discoveries are shocking enough, it appears one of the discoveries is mostly likely human in origin and dates from before The Fall."

The assembled officers chanced looks at one another in disbelief, accompanied by some murmurs that this isn't possible. "Oh, let me assure you it's happening," said Ronin as Karl changed the wall screen to show the writing found by Bulldog 1.

"This is Object 1, and that is a word written in American," said Karl as they looked at the high-resolution image. "USS Constitution," he read aloud.

The surprise was evident on all their faces. "About as iconic an old American naval name as ever there was," commented Ronin. "Before The Fall, the old United States was governed by a revolutionary structuring document called the Constitution. The initials USS, which stood for United States Ship," preceded the names of ships.

History lesson concluded, LeCroy looked at his captain in disbelief. "Sir, are you saying pre-Fall deep spaceflight was actually real?" he asked.

Ronin looked at his officers. "It's time to fill you in now that some evidence is staring us in the face. Cerberus' true mission wasn't merely to investigate some distant coordinates before the AC arrived. Cerberus is investigating old legends. These coordinates are the possible location of the mythical jump gates which the old legends say led to the pre-Fall Colonies." Seeing the officers shocked into silence by his announcement, Ronin realized he couldn't have dropped more of a bombshell announcement on them had he revealed the second coming of Jesus Christ.

"Captain…are you being serious here?" asked Delacroix in his slightly French-accented American.

"Yes, that really is Cerberus' true mission," replied Ronin. "I know it's difficult to believe a technologically advanced spacecraft was sent on a possible archaeological mission, but Fleet Intelligence had come across data from several different sources which strongly suggested a mission out here was warranted," said Ronin. "Based on evidence we have found, I say our mission was justified."

"Sir, what do we do now?" asked Anzio. "Are we bringing this information back to Earth?"

Ronin looked at Anzio, then the rest of them. "We will, but we're not finished yet. I'm ordering a Bulldog with Bravo team as a Marine boarding party to Object 1, and another with Echo team as the boarding party to Object 2. I also plan to send several Bulldogs with shore parties to Planet Nine's satellite. Send Bravo team to Object 1, and Echo team to Object 2. I'm also ordering a Bulldog back to the other side of the hot spot to pick up the data being collected by the drone screen we left on the other side because we need to monitor our friends as they arrive in the area. If they've maintained their last known course and speed, we'll have a few weeks before they even arrive at the hot spot. We'll use that time to find what we can find," Ronin said.

"Questions?" he asked. "No questions? All right, let's get after it."

BULLDOG 1

After detailed examination of scans collected by several Bulldog surveys and drone flyby's over the course of a week and preparation of a boarding plan, Bulldog 1 appeared a mile away from Object 1 with a small jump flare. "Jump 1 complete," said Pilot Officer Erin Johnson, as she immediately began to match the course, speed and tumble of the target.

"Threat board is clear," announced rear-seater Patterson in his Texas accent. "Cleared for approach," he continued. The Bulldog approached what had been identified as a possible airlock, before landing on the hull directly over that target with the Bulldog's landing skids straddling it. "Engage magnetic landing lock. We have good lock. Docking collar extending. Collar seal is good. Corporal Mackey, you're a go," said Patterson.

Marine Cpl. Brett Mackey (Bravo 1), who had been listening over the commlink along with the rest of the Marine boarding party, simply nodded to Bravo 7, who immediately began attempting to open the airlock upon Mackey's signal.

"No joy on opening using the visible handle. It's stuck solid," reported Pvt. Ty Jeffries (Bravo 7) in an unsurprised tone of voice. "Switching to the arc cutter."

Inside his suit, Mackey was grinning like a madman, his gleaming white teeth standing out in contrast to his dark skin. Mackey had always loved the idea of boarding other vessels and he had always been entranced by pre-Fall relics. He was thinking that combining both on a deep space mission was more fun than a guy like him should be allowed.

Due to their excitement, the thirty minutes it took to cut through the hull seemed to take forever. At last, a large hole was created and the corresponding metal disc was floating down into the passage beyond. "We have an entry, moving in now," said Bravo 5 (Terry Allison) in his Alabama accent as Jeffries moved aside with his tools while Allison and the Marines piled up behind him moved into the dark tunnel.

"No gravity, no atmosphere, no power readings at all," reported Allison, as the team clicked on their powerful helmet lights to illuminate the passage to reveal a partially closed hatchway approximately 50 feet away.

Bravo team gathered at the hatch, taking up covering positions for Bravo 6 (Steve Cupper) as he widened the hatchway with the breaching jaws. Allison moved in with his weapon ready and searched the room covered by his teammates back in the hatchway. Moments later, Allison reported over the team's commlink, "It's a storeroom, with dry goods and stuff."

"How do you know that?" Bravo 4 (Carlos Guthrey) asked. "There a store or something in there?"

"Because of the sign that says 'Storeroom 3' and some boxes labeled 'Flour' and 'Beans'?" Allison said, barely containing his glee at the chance to verbally beat down Guthrey.

Guffaws of laughter broke out over the commlink. "Can it, you savages. Everybody knows Marines can't read without pictures," said Mackey, not doing a good job of hiding the smile behind his growled command.

Allison tried the hatch on the opposite end of the room. It opened easily and the team advanced to the next hatch. "It's a passageway. Too long to see either end. Going left where we saw less visible damage on the outside of the hull," Allison said.

The Marines of Bravo team leapfrogged each other as they advanced down the passageway towards the fore of the hull, passing black signs with white lettering stating the purpose of each compartment they passed in old American. They passed something called a commissary, restrooms, conference rooms, and so on until they came to a cross passage creating a T with their current passageway.

"Take the T," ordered Mackey as he approached Allison to shine lights down each direction. "If their ships were designed like ours, all the important stuff will be towards the center of the ship for greater protection," he said.

"Affirmative," responded Allison, as he rounded the corner and moved deeper into the hull. The next sign read "Astrophysics Lab." Making note of it, the team moved on, passing an armory and a logistics compartment before arriving at a tube way with ladders going down further into the hull. Following the plan to reach the center if possible, Allison took the tube way down while their exosuits kept track of their exact routes on their tactical information displays.

After passing down several levels, the exosuit AI broke into the team commlink, announcing in its calm female voice, "Bravo 1, suit sensors indicate consistent deck spacing down your current route. Twenty more levels and Bravo team will reach the vertical center."

Clicking a nonverbal acknowledgment, Mackey nodded for Allison to continue as indicated. It wouldn't have been difficult to figure out which level was the important one as the exit was marked by a sign saying "Command Level." Allison had no trouble pushing the hatchway open and looking inside.

"Bravo 1, Bravo 5. Be advised, the first command level compartment is a crypt. Multiple corpses."

BULLDOG 2

Bulldog 2 slowly approached Object 2 with Echo Team under the command of Corporal Toshi Kanagawa onboard. Pilot Helmut Meyer kept their jump engines spun up as a precaution even though no further signs of hostility were observed by drone surveys in the past week. "Jump 1 complete," said Meyer, as he immediately began to match the course, speed and tumble of the target.

"Threat board is clear," announced rear-seater Sophie Schmidt. "Cleared for approach," she continued.

As in the mission for Object 1, Bulldog 2 approached what had been identified as a possible airlock and landed on the hull directly over the possible airlock with the Bulldog's landing skids straddling it. "Engage magnetic landing lock. We have good lock. Docking collar extending. Collar seal is good. Corporal Kanagawa, you're a go," said Schmidt.

The Marines of Echo Team quickly discovered this hatchway was too damaged to manually open. "As expected. We'll do it the old school way and cut our way in," ordered Echo 1, Kanagawa, who was from Japan.

"Knock, knock," muttered Echo 3, Pvt. Rhee Lee, who was from Korea, as he applied the arc cutter to the hull. The thin hull metal cut quickly, and the team entered the compartment.

"Remind me not to use the same interior decorator," said Echo 2, Cpl. Adrian Longman from Australia. There were the visible remains of a corpse floating near one wall. "Looks like our host lost is head, poor sod," Longman, calling everyone's attention to the smashed-in skull of the corpse.

Echo 4, also known as Pvt. Han Pak, moved to the only exit of the compartment and illuminated the passageway beyond. Like Lee, Pak was from Korea. "The way is clear. Two corpses, no enemy contacts." Pak reported. Lee and Pak stopped at each hatchway and scanned the signs with their suit cameras.

"Echo 1, language analysis of the images you provided confirms the signs are written in Mandarin," said the voice of their team AI over their helmet commlink channel. "Prediction is you are approaching the remains of the aft section of the ship as the signs state various engineering functions," the AI concluded.

Kanagawa held up his hand and halted the team while he asked the AI the question on his mind. "Does our analysis hold true that this surviving portion of the ship is missing the fore and aft sections?"

"Correct," confirmed the AI. "Whatever destroyed this ship left this smaller interior portion intact."

"Halt," commanded the AI over the common commlink. "This sign translates as Primary Engineering," AI added.

Pak tried to open the closed hatchway, but it was not budging. "Echo 5, use the breaching jaws."

Pvt. David Danfries (Echo 5) from Britain brought up the jaws and made ready to force the hatch open. Within seconds, the powerful breaching jaws forced open the thin hatch metal, crumpling part of it with ease. Long dead corpses, or parts of them, were the only occupants of the compartment. "Echo 1, Echo 5, Sensors read a power source in here. It's weak, but definitely active," said Danfries, peeking through the now open hatchway. "Echo 4, take Echo 6 in. Remaining Echo Team, secure the area."

After the team set up a defensive perimeter, privates Pak and Gonzales entered Engineering. "Weapons lock! Take…" began Pak, before the two of them were rendered unconscious.

Echo 2 had been keeping an eye through the hatchway and saw the anti-intruder turret zap Echo 4 and 6. "Man down! Anti-personnel turret, 2 o'clock," yelled Longman.

"Take it out!" responded Kanagawa as he pressed up against the outer wall of the hatchway. "Launch the drone," he further ordered.

Longman detached the small, stealthy drone from his utility belt and set it to target the turret. As it flew into the compartment, the turret began wildly swinging about. The defensive system detected the drone, but couldn't get a lock on it before it landed on the turret's weapon pod and drilled down into the pod.

"Weapon neutralized, remain where you are until further notice," announced the AI, as it redirected the drone to perform a similar procedure on a second turret. "Compartment secure, it is safe to enter," called the AI.

Their corpsman, Echo 7 (Pvt. Nancy Dos) immediately went to Echo 4 and 6, while the remainder of the team continued their defensive posture. "Echo 1, Echo 7. Both Echo 4 and 6 are injured and unconscious. Looks like there wasn't enough power to burn them through," reported

Nancy Dos, the Canadian medic for the team, as she stabilized their life signs.

"All right, let's secure the remainder of this relic and bring the science types over here to find what they can after we get our injured back to the sickbay on Cerberus," ordered Kanagawa.

BULLDOG 3

With a small jump flare, Bulldog 3 appeared on the far side of the hot spot and immediately began searching for the drone screen. "Jump 2 complete," announced Pilot Officer Antonio Russo.

"Receiving challenge, sending encrypted response," said rear-seater Michael Jonsey. "Drones confirm our command codes. Receiving telemetry. They've ID'd the class of the incoming spacecraft. AC Type 22 destroyer. Crewed by 1750. Speed has increased since we last saw her," noted Jonsey.

Both of them were silent for a few minutes. "At that speed and distance, they won't be able to avoid the hot spot, will they?" asked Russo.

Jonsey and Russo looked at each other, then ran the numbers on his nav system. "Unless they've got better maneuvering than we've seen on other ships, they're going to pass right through. Are they even aware it's there?" Jonsey responded.

More minutes passed. "We're done here," Jonsey announced. "Time to get back to Cerberus."

"Roger that," Russo said, and Bulldog 3 jumped away.

BULLDOGS 4 AND 5

With matching jump flares, Bulldogs 4 and 5 appeared in orbit around the unnamed satellite to Planet Nine. "Jump1 complete," announced Bulldog 4 Pilot Officer Reggie Parsons in a soft Arkansas accent.

"Gamma team reports ready," responded rear-seater Terry Gellin, himself a Kentuckian. "Receiving drone telemetry and running new scans," Gelling noted in a slightly distracted tone as he coordinated the processes.

"All clear. No change since the last sweeps," Gellin reported a few minutes later.

"We're heading down to the site. Follow us," Parsons announced on the open commlink with Bulldog 5 as he changed course.

"Roger that," responded Bulldog 5's pilot officer, Gary Chanson from New Boise.

Both Bulldogs quickly flew down to the airless surface. "Primary entry point dead ahead," Gellin announced as they descended to what both Cerberus' AI and science staff had identified as the most likely ship landing dock. "Looks even more like a landing facility the closer we get," Gellin murmured as they got closer.

"Yes, it does," Chanson agreed from Bulldog 5, unaware he had the commlink channel open.

Minutes later, both craft settled in on matching squares on the expansive tarmac. "We're down, Gamma 1 time to earn your pay," said Gellin.

"Gamma 1 confirms. Gamma team, move out and establish a perimeter," ordered Gamma 1, Cpl. Brett Blackwater from Wales.

Gamma team swiftly moved out of the Bulldog, assuming kneeling postures with weapons drawn as they established a semicircular perimeter between the ships and the buildings 30 yards away.

"Negative contact, Gamma 1," reported Pvt. Jefferson Langley from Wisconsin Rapids, Wisconsin.

"Roger that, Gamma 2," Blackwater responded. "Breaching team to the entrance on the larger building to the right," he ordered. Gammas 3 through 5 swiftly posted themselves next to what Blackwater thought looked just like an airlock from Cerberus. Blackwater moved to get a better look at it.

Gamma 5, Pvt. David Addington from the hinterlands of the Canadian Yukon, set himself as he was covered by the team, and used the breaching jaws on the airlock door. "Knock, knock," Addington said, when the door suddenly opened with great force. "Berger, job opportunity," he announced, ducking away from the opening in case someone on the other side didn't appreciate his efforts.

"Affirmative. Drone away," responded the team's electronic warfare specialist, Private Victor Berger, in French-accented American. "Clear!" Berger reported seconds later.

"No contacts. Berger, get that inner hatch open," commanded Blackwater, who immediately ordered most of the team inside the room.

Berger swiftly repeated his breaching duties, and the team swarmed into the dark passageway beyond.

BULLDOG 1 – COMMAND LEVEL

Cpl. Brett Mackey followed Pvt. Terry Allison into the spacious command level compartment.

"Bravo 1, they look pretty dead," noted Allison.

"Roger that, Bravo 5," acknowledged Mackey. "Bravo 6 and 7, job opportunity. Move these corpses out of our way," he ordered.

"Bravo 1, Bravo 2. We've ID'd the computer core," announced Pvt. Ed Wilson.

"Already? They have a big picture on it so you grunts could find it or something?" asked Mackey.

"That's a rog, Bravo 1. And it's literally labeled Computer Core. It's written in American on the outside of the section panel," noted Wilson, who was from Brookings, South Dakota.

"Bravo 4, can we turn the thing on to copy its files, or do we want to figure out how to physically take the thing with us instead?" asked Mackey.

"Captain wants us to try to turn it on here, Bravo 1. The Science team is afraid of a possible hostile reaction if there's an AI and they don't want Cerberus too close if that happens," responded Guthrey.

"OK. We're expendable, understood. Bravo 4, let's get that process figured out," Mackey decided.

"Bravo 5, break out that portable generator and I'll open this thing up," Guthrey said, grabbing the utility took from his waistband. "Never thought I would end up using a standard screwdriver in an ancient, flying ghost ship, and find that it worked!" Guthrey interrupted his commentary as the access panel quickly popped off. He looked at Bravo 1, who was now standing near him.

"Should we be unnerved that our tools fit this relic?" muttered Mackey as he watched.

Well, I guess this has to be a power feed, thought Guthrey ironically as he explored the innards. He noticed a cable labeled "Power," which he swiftly cut into, as there wasn't a coupling to tap into. When he was ready, Guthrey motioned for Allison to start bringing up the power output of the generator. When power output hit 50 percent, the workstation suddenly lit up and came to life. Guthrey motioned again, this time for Allison to hold power at 50 percent.

The team gathered round the workstation and watched its view screen display the system boot process for a few moments. They were rewarded when the system navigation screen appeared. For a moment Guthrey studied the options, by now only slightly surprised to see them listed in American since the origin of the ship was obvious.

"Bravo 4, anything look promising?" inquired Mackey.

"Well, Logs, Records, and AI," responded Guthrey. "But only AI is clickable."

Mackey wasn't terribly pleased with that option, but gave Guthrey the go ahead anyway.

"Here goes nothing," muttered Guthrey to himself, clicking AI.

Seconds later, the entire team heard through their helmets, "Please state command authorization," through their commlinks.

"Uh, Bravo 1, we aren't supposed to hear the ancient alien machine talking to us on our own encrypted commlinks, are we?" asked Ed, managing to sound both highly concerned and dumbfounded at the same time.

"That's a negative, Bravo team," responded Mackey.

"Who are you?" asked the disembodied female voice through all of their exosuits commlink nodes.

After Bravo team all traded glances at each other, Mackey replied to the voice. "Corporal Brett Mackey, Bravo team leader, assigned to the Cerberus. And who might you be?"

"I am the artificial intelligence for USS *Constitution*," the voice responded. "Corporal, you and your vessel do not appear in my data-banks for Western Coalition forces. Please state your origin."

Even no one could see it through his helmet, Mackey's eyebrows rose in surprise before he replied. "Dothan, Alabama." No one else spoke.

"Corporal, my sensors are offline and this limits my analysis. Your accent when speaking English does not quite match my records of that location's accent. Can you explain?"

Mackey thought about his response for a moment before deciding the truth was the only smart play here. "We're a Marine boarding party. We located a ruined hull hurtling through this region of space with the markings USS *Constitution* visible on the outside. There are corpses throughout the vessel, and we brought along a power generator to aid our exploration efforts. We used it to bring you back to life. And why did you say I have an unusual accent when speaking English? I speak American."

This answer gave the AI pause.

"My last data fragments recorded a massive shockwave impacting the ship during battle. Coalition forces detonated fusion bombs to prevent eastern access to the jump gate. Do you have an estimate of when our recovery teams will arrive?"

Both stunned and saddened, Mackey decided to just tell the intelligence the harsh truth. "Recovery team? I'm sorry, AI. There will be no recovery team. Are you aware of how much time has passed since the battle?"

"No. I am presuming somewhat longer than five days. My systems were entirely powered down due to the extent of damage to the ship. Fleet doctrine is to locate and recover ship AIs within five days of combat to prevent capture by enemy forces," responded the AI. "However, you were unable to provide command authorization, suggesting you were diverted from another mission for the recovery as command authorization is not transmitted over fleet channels for security reasons."

"You have no idea how diverted we were, AI. At your current velocity and course, and factoring in the rate of radioactive decay, your battle took place 753 years ago." said Mackey. "I'd like to introduce you and our team's AI, but our AI goes to auto lockdown when an unknown AI infiltrates our systems."

BULLDOG 2 - AFT ENGINEERING

As Echo team explored the aft engineering, they didn't take long to find where the Engineering ended. It was once an "L" shaped compartment, but now they saw after rounding the inner angle of the "L" that the other end of the "L" wasn't there. Literally, it had been sheared off by the forces that destroyed the ship centuries ago.

"Echo 1, Echo 5. There ain't much to see here," reported Danfries. "The other end of the compartment is gone. Completely blown away and exposed to space," he added.

Just then, the AI broke into the commlink. "Corporal Kanagawa, my infiltration of the system has revealed a nearly spent nuclear power source here in the surviving section of Engineering. That source powered the anti-intruder system that injured privates Gonzales and Pak. I have severed the connections between the power source and the remainder of this vessel."

"Thank you, AI. Have you located any records or logs in this wreck?" asked Kanagawa.

"Affirmative. Some navigational data survived. Most logs and records were destroyed along with the rest of this ship. I have downloaded what little information remained for retrieval."

Surprised, Kanagawa called Cerberus. "Cerberus Actual, this is Bravo 1. Ship is secure."

Ronin responded moments later. "Roger that. Science team is on the way. Cerberus Actual, Out."

BULLDOGS 4 AND 5

As Gamma team swiftly moved into the passageway, Pvt. Victor Berger left signal repeaters at intersections and spacing intervals. The building was three stories tall, and about a hundred yards long on each of its four sides. There appeared to be two main passages, interspersed with laterals every ten yards on the ground floor that they traversed.

"Personnel. Galley. Power Plant. Spaceflight control. Gym. So far, this place seems pretty mundane," commented Cpl. Jefferson Langley.

"Oh yeah, what are those signs telling you, private?" challenged Blackwater.

"Uh, that it's an office building?" responded Langley.

"No, you numbskull. The signs are written in American! That means this was probably a Coalition base and not an Asiatic Collective outpost," rumbled Blackwater.

"Come on Gamma 1, everybody knows we can't read," wisecracked GySgt. Juan Sanchez.

"They should've drawn pictures in crayon if they wanted guys like us to know what was in there," added Pvt. Aldo Pena, the team's corpsman.

"Cretins like you would've thought they were dirty pictures even *if* they were in crayon," Sanchez quipped as the team located the center of the floor plan where both main passageways intersected around a bank of lifts.

"Gamma 5, open a set of the lift doors and let's see where they lead," ordered Blackwater.

"Gamma 1, this place has everything," quickly responded Addington, getting the doors on the far left lift open. "A third-floor penthouse and at least ten sub-levels below ground," he added.

"OK. Gamma team, break into pairs and let's get the rest of this building searched before we go spelunking," Blackwater ordered.

Within thirty minutes, the team reformed back at the lift bank in the center of the first floor. "The building houses administrative and cargo facilities. I'm betting the fun stuff is down below. There's no stairway, which isn't terribly surprising from a security perspective. Easier to control access if there is just a bank of lifts to guard," Blackwater said. "There's an access hatch in the floor of the lift, so let's go through there and rappel down the shaft," he added.

"Uh, Gamma 1, we're going down into the dark scary hole? That's where aliens eat your face off," said Langley, peering down into the dark shaft.

"You watch too many cheap movies, Gamma 2," commented Blackwater dryly. "None of them would find your head palatable."

After the laughter died down, Sanchez ribbed Blackwater. "Gamma 1…uh, 'palatable'? What, you get attacked by a dictionary or something? We're just grunts. We don't know fancy jargon like that."

With that, Gamma team descended down into the dark hole.

CHAPTER 10

DISCOVERY

The next week crawled by for Ronin, but it passed swiftly for the various boarding and shore parties, who found a decidedly mixed bag of success. While they explored, Ronin was getting into the rhythm of his ship.

Gotta get some exercise, he thought as he crawled out of his bunk in his quarters. He brushed his teeth to get the nasty out, and stumbled down to the gym.

As he walked along, he saw Lieutenant Delacroix in the open rec room near the gym, sitting at a table populated by a mixed group of three navy ensigns, and a Marine lieutenant. Curious, Ronin sidled over to see what card game was ongoing.

"Captain, join us?" asked Delacroix when he spotted Ronin. "We're just playing a friendly game of five card stud."

Ronin smiled and shook his head. "No, thanks. I don't need to lose my pay to a gang of pirates. Especially to you, Delacroix."

The Marine laughed.

"Yes-sir, the good Lieutenant's prowess at the table is legendary," Ronin remarked, to the amusement of the others seated with Delacroix. Ronin continued on to the gym, thankful to have escaped the card sharks swimming at that table.

As he entered the gym, his eyes were immediately drawn to a sparring match going between Charlie team's Private Kowalski and Gamma's Corporal Blackwater. Both were accomplished black belts in Tae Kwon Do, although Kowalski was also a black belt in judo as befits a close combat specialist.

"Care to join us sir?" called Kowalski.

"You don't mind sparring an old flabby guy like me?" Ronin responded.

"No sir, we could always use some fresh meat...I mean, another sparring partner. Greatest exercise ever." Blackwater backed out of the sparring ring to play scoring referee while Ronin geared up with some sparring pads.

"OK, Kowalski, I'm ready," announced Ronin as he and Kowalski faced each other in the center of the ring and bowed.

The two quickly began circling as Kowalski tried to get a read on Ronin's skill level. Ronin quickly realized his opponent didn't know he wasn't facing a rookie in the ring, so Ronin decided to play it like a rookie. He started acting nervous, and forced himself to seem unnaturally stiff, like someone who didn't know what he was doing. Ronin also began showing various openings, trying to bait Kowalski into attacking. He didn't have to wait long, as Kowalski decided to start with a showy tornado kick against his inexperienced opponent.

Gotcha! thought Ronin, as he suddenly relaxed so he could move faster as he stepped further to the side while delivering a very basic roundhouse to Kowalski's exposed midsection when it reappeared during his spinning. Ronin swiftly followed it with a sliding sidekick at the midsection to keep Kowalski's momentum going in the wrong direction while Ronin twirled into a spinning wheel kick at Kowalski's head while covering enough ground to catch up to where Kowalski had gone to.

Surprised, Kowalski recovered quickly with a spin back kick that caught Ronin in the stomach. "Ooff! Sir, nicely done. You baited me in with that whole rookie act," Kowalski said with a small laugh.

"What belt are you?" Ronin, still circling as the two threw various combinations of kicks and punches.

"Third degree black in Taekwondo," replied Kowalski.

The next hour's sparring with combinations of the three men was just the sort of hard, stress relieving workout that he craved, Ronin thought as he returned to his quarters for a quick shower.

By the tenth day, Cerberus' science teams were as giddy as kids on Christmas morning. They were uncovering all sorts of interesting stuff, and the functioning AI discovered by Bulldog 1 had been very cooperative.

Ronin, LeCroy and Cmdr. Diane Mueller met in the main conference room with the ship's science team to get the latest update. Mueller's husband, Karl, was there. "Captain, it's still difficult to believe some of the information we've located. Legends are coming true," Karl reported.

"How true?" Ronin asked.

"Data from the records onboard the Constitution and from Ninebase confirm the jump gates were indeed real, and this system's gate was destroyed in The Fall. Its location was the center of the highest density radiation in the hot spot," Karl stated bluntly.

Interesting how the ancients named the base on Planet Nine's satellite Ninebase, Ronin thought. *They must've originally counted the number of planets using the same conventions we are using today.*

"What about the colonies?" Ronin asked, hoping they weren't just going to remain legends.

"Yes sir, we've only partial data there due to deterioration, but there was enough left to confirm the existence of three coalition colonies in orbit around a star the ancients called Baidam. We initially assumed assuming it was named after the person who discovered the star, or explored the system or something like that, but data from the Constitution said it was named Baidam because it's in the shark constellation."

Ronin took a sip of his beloved coffee. "Which colonies?"

"Forrestal, Celestra, and Solara."

Ronin set his coffee down and leaned forward. "You're sure? Those names really ARE the stuff of legends." Ronin shook his head slowly as he sank back in his seat. "Seriously, we've heard those names our whole lives. They've reached the same legendary status as the legend of Atlantis in the pantheon of lost civilizations. I've never heard of a shark constellation. How do we find it?" he asked.

"There wasn't any nav data uncovered so far, just a symbol that looks like a backwards 'S' and a video fragment of some stars. We're not sure what it's supposed to mean. Confederation databanks don't have any information on where this shark constellation supposedly was," Kurt noted.

"We have another dilemma that is of a slightly more immediate concern, Captain," Mueller noted. "Bulldog 3 is still eyes on the enemy destroyer over on the far side of the hot spot. They report it's still accelerating for the hot spot, but we have time to warn them to change course before they fly though enough radiation to turn everyone onboard into a crispy corpse. What are we going to do about them?"

Ronin leaned back, and clasped his hands behind his head as he looked towards the ceiling and mulled it over before speaking. "I've thought about it and decided we will do nothing."

Looks of surprise flitted across everyone's faces at that. "Nothing? Captain, are you sure? Murder seems pretty inhumane to me," Mueller said, speaking her mind much too frankly. LeCroy, a veteran of many missions with Ronin, was shocked by Mueller's merciful attitude.

Ronin raised an eyebrow at Mueller's response, and sharply spoke his mind in response. "Commander Mueller, Cerberus is not a ship of the line! Out here, we lack the resources of a large battle formation like you're used to. For this kind of mission, Cerberus is going to be tasked to operate as a lone wolf for most of our missions. Old-fashioned notions of fairness will just get our people killed."

"But Captain, they're all going to suffer a horrible death! We can prevent that—," Mueller started, but Ronin cut her off.

With a glare and ice in his voice, Ronin spelled it out for her, "Commander, our mission orders clearly state we are not to engage with the enemy or reveal this ship unless absolutely necessary to accomplish the mission. That includes mercy calls and anything else that might happen out here. The enemy blindly flies through a kill zone, that falls under the heading of 'not our problem'. You better get used to this kind of mission environment, or you'll not succeed on this ship."

Mueller was shocked into silence. *I can't believe I have to work for this madman.*

With that, the meeting broke up and Ronin headed to his quarters to complete his progress reports. As he walked, he thought about the coming end of the enemy destroyer. *Letting their ship fry in a kill zone is just a bonus. Good thing I'm also not feeling too inclined to save them for personal reasons. Bastards never gave us any warning when they ambushed the* Frisco *and killed my wife ten years ago. I'm not going to get all broken up about that crew getting fried.*

Sitting alone at the desk in his quarters hours later, Ronin's tired eyes were unfocused and he ignored the report on his tablet as he muttered the ancient names to himself in wonderment. "Forrestal, Celestra, and Solara." *So maybe they actually did exist!*

He shook his head as he pulled up the old legend on the tablet after he signed the final report. Ronin then read aloud the skimpy legend. "Forrestal is supposed to be a planet of cold, deep oceans, snowcapped mountains and dark forests. The entire planet is rumored to be quite temperate because of the mountains near the equator. Celestra orbits Forrestal, and enjoys a similar climate."

That's it? Yeah, that's all on Celestra. Hmph. Solara was supposed to orbit somewhat closer to its star, with a hotter climate. Deserts, jungles and beaches and stuff. Great. Those are so vague we'd be lucky to recognize them even if we stumbled right into the system. Good thing we'll never be sent on that *little wild goose chase.* Ronin chuckled to himself.

At the same time, Diane also retired to her family's quarters. After putting Sonya and Sophia to bed with stories and some giggles, she curled up next to Karl on the sofa in their small living room.

Karl could read her eyes. "What's troubling you? You've been putting on a brave face since you got home."

Diane looked at him before replying quietly. "I may have made a mistake to take this duty assignment. The Captain and I disagreed about whether to save an enemy ship when it's within our power to do so." She told him about the remainder of the situation.

Karl thought about it for a few long seconds before speaking softly. "I suspect you both are just looking through the lens of your prior experiences. Your experience is with large fleet formations deep down in the inner solar system, while his is one of operating independently far away in the belt and beyond. Neither of you is wrong if this situation aligns to one of those contexts. But only one of those contexts applies to this location. We're all alone out here. The Captain might be right."

Diane rested her head on Karl's shoulder. "I was afraid you were going to say something like that. This is going to be a long tour." she said.

CHAPTER 11

WAYSIDE STATION

A month later, Cerberus jumped into space near the coordinates for Wayside Station. "Jump complete, Captain. We're on approach for Wayside docking," announced Lieutenant Perez.

"Captain, we're receiving a coded message from Admiral Rodding. It's marked "eyes only" for you and Commander Mueller," reported Lieutenant Delgado.

Ronin and Mueller looked at each other a moment before they simultaneously began moving towards Ronin's ready room.

Inside the ready room, both Ronin and Mueller sat at his desk and verified their identities through the retinal scanner on his screen. Moments later, a video message from the admiral popped up.

"Captain Ronin and Commander Mueller, welcome back. First item is your mission was a resounding success. Second item is, your mission created more questions than answers. Many more. The data you sent ahead with the Bulldog crew will keep our scientists busy for some time. Your Bulldog and its crew is returning to Cerberus as soon as you dock. Report to me at my office by 0900 station time tomorrow for further briefing and orders."

"Questions," said Mueller, glancing at Ronin. "They have no idea how many questions WE have!"

Ronin nodded with a small smile. "We've been gone for about two months. And while we brought back a large assortment of data scraps, we didn't manage to find more than a few answers. For now, let's focus on getting Cerberus docked and stocked before tomorrow's briefing."

The next morning, Ronin and Mueller were shown into the Adm. Jessup Rodding's office promptly at 9 a.m. Mueller admired the beautiful real wood doors to his office, wondering for a moment how long it had been since she had seen actual wood.

"Captain, Commander, come in!" said a chipper sounding Rodding. "I trust you managed a good night's sleep?" he joked as he motioned to the slightly dark rings under their eyes, knowing they would get the quirky humor. Nobody got much sleep the first night after docking and stocking. Too much to do.

"Oh, yes, sir. Like a vacation out there," responded Ronin with a smile and chuckle.

"Funny you should mention vacation," Rodding said. "You're going on vacation. Mandatory two weeks of R&R, and the clock won't begin to run until you've arrived in Green Bay."

Ronin was surprised, as he'd been expecting more deployment orders. Just as he opened his mouth to protest, Rodding stopped him.

"No use arguing, Captain. The Fleet Admiralty is requiring you to get your long-delayed downtime so you stay sharp. Commander Mueller will handle your ship in the interim."

Ronin and Mueller glanced at one another. "What will Cerberus be doing while the Captain is away," Mueller asked.

"Good question, Commander. You'll deploy Cerberus back to Planet Nine and deliver research teams to both the two ancient ship hull fragments and Ninebase. The teams also include archaeologists, who very nearly came to blows over who would get to investigate what. It's the discovery of a lifetime for that profession."

Mueller nodded, happy with those orders. She and Karl likewise couldn't wait to return to those relics to do some more investigating.

Rodding continued, his gravelly voice warming up as he spoke to his two officers. "Ronin, there's a shuttle leaving tomorrow at 1300 hours. Be on it, and go see your kids. There are some new videos from them in the commlink system's buffers. By departure time, we figure most of the restocking process that would require your involvement will be done."

"Yes, sir!" Ronin said smartly. There was more he wanted to ask and he figured now was the time. "Did our scientists make any new discoveries?"

Rodding was ready for the question, as it was obvious the two were dying to find out. "There's a ton of conjecture so far, and our AIs are also hard at work trying to connect all those data fragments, but here's what we know for sure. The colonies are real. That's the biggie here. Problem is, there are still no records identifying which celestial objects we're supposed to look at to know where the shark constellation is, which is disappointing.

"The power facility you found down inside Ninebase might be a type of power totally unknown to us. Something called dark matter. We don't know what that is yet, but one of the research teams will attempt to reverse engineer the power plant.

"I dunno much about all that, sounds like rocket scientist stuff. We have an AI who volunteered to work with the surviving AI on the Constitution. Hopefully that goes well, but the AI knows it will have to be isolated to protect our own systems. Oh, and the linguistics teams are in an uproar over something you stumbled across," Rodding lectured.

"Sir, would it be the name of the language?" Mueller asked

Rodding nodded with raised eyebrows. "Correct, Mueller. Those relics call our language English, while in today's world it's simply called American. We had no idea.

"The AI on Constitution provided a short primer on the evolution of that language and how it was heavily influenced by other languages and borrowed words from them. The AI even explained the ancient language had developed a host of accents over time, and that it came from Britain where a portion of the island was called England. In fact, Britain apparently colonized the Americas using wooden sailing ships, if you can believe it. Colonists from a variety of nation states brought their native languages with them. American eventually became the dominant language. As you can guess, most of those other languages became extinct during The Fall."

After the three continued discussing other matters for a while, Ronin and Mueller returned to their ship. "That part about extinct languages sounds like some old stories told in our family," Mueller mentioned as they walked the corridor leading back to Cerberus.

"Oh, yeah?" Ronin asked, prompting Mueller to elaborate.

"The family historians who have researched the family lineage as far back as they can spoke of the main native language in Germany being called Deutsch. The country name was pronounced "Deutschland" in that language. And that there were multiple dialects, generally originating from different tribes scattered around the area as eventually they joined together to form a nation state with a common language. That's about all we know though."

Ronin was impressed. "Our family history basically begins with The Fall. Before that, we have nothing that was carried forward. After you, Commander," he said, motioning for Mueller to proceed before him into the open passageway that lead into the heart of Cerberus.

Ronin managed to catch a few hours of sleep after they arrived at Cerberus. Mueller did likewise. Both of them were exhausted from the frenetic pace aboard the ship as it was made ready to depart again.

By the next day, Ronin was still exhausted by the time he needed to depart to catch the shuttle home. Mueller met him at the passageway into the Wayside docking area.

"Have a good time reconnecting with your family, Dan. Cerberus will be in good hands while you're away," Mueller announced with a salute.

Ronin returned her salute. "Thank you, Diane. I know you'll take good care of her. Remember what I said about operating as a lone ship. *Cerebus'* safety is paramount to concerns of civility. And you get to explore those old-world relics some more, which makes me a bit envious!"

Mueller forced a smile to hide her thoughts about killing the enemy, her blue eyes contrasting with her blonde hair. "The twins have been bugging me for stories about the old world for weeks. Hopefully we'll be able to come up with some more material to send them off to bed with. We'll jump back out there in a few days, and rendezvous back here with you in a few weeks." They shook hands, and Ronin left to catch his ride home.

Ronin hurried as he didn't want the shuttle to leave without him. Turns out he needn't have worried, as it had been ordered to wait for him. An old veteran like Rodding knew Ronin might be a little late in this situation.

As Ronin settled in to his seat on the shuttle, the flight crew sealed up the ship and prepared to leave. "All passengers, prepare for departure," announced the pilot as the engines began to whine louder with increased power. Ronin was quiet, his mind blurry with exhaustion, and he closed his eyes. He was sleeping before the shuttle even left the station.

Mueller stopped by her quarters for a few minutes before returning to the bridge. "I'm taking command of Cerberus for a few weeks while the Captain finally gets a break to take the edge off. He really needs a vacation." she said to Karl after the doors closed behind her.

"What are going to do with the ship? Take her out for an interstellar joy ride somewhere?" Karl joked. His smile fell when he got a look at the expression on Diane's face.

"We're going back to deep space on a mission to Ninebase and the flying hull relics." she deadpanned.

Karl's eyebrows shot up. "We are?" he asked.

"It won't be a trip without danger," Diane replied.

CHAPTER 12

GREEN BAY

Ronin slept half of the five-day trip to Earth. He kept to himself the rest of the time, partially because he outranked the other passengers and they didn't want to bother a fleet captain. After the shuttle docked at the Confederation's orbiting transfer station, he was swiftly transported to the surface on a full surface to transport. It wasn't difficult to find one headed to a major city like Green Bay, as they departed for the city every few hours.

The short trip to the surface seemed to take forever because Ronin was so excited to finally come home and see his family. Once the shuttle landed on the designated pad at the port, he quickly exited and was grateful to hear familiar cries of "Daddy!" when he entered to waiting area. His arms quickly wrapped around Sarah and Edward as they did their best to burrow into his neck area.

"You two have gotten so tall!" Ronin exclaimed as he glanced up at his father, Robert. "What have you been feeding them? They're monsters!"

Robert was already grinning, glad to see his son at last. "We feed them steroids and cows! Only way to grow 'em big and strong," he said, using the same old joke he used to tell his own father when little Ronin would visit his grandparents. "I've got some steaks ready to grill, and the beer is ice cold. How about we head home and get started?" he said to Ronin.

"Nothing in this world sounds better!" Ronin remarked, as they walked out to the car park with Edward riding on his shoulders. Once they arrived at Robert and Julia's home, Ronin and Robert settled into the comfortable patio furniture while the steaks began cooking on the grill in the early summer evening of northeastern Wisconsin.

"What word from space? You were gone for so long due to the unexpected mission extension. We were afraid we're losing the battle for space because of it," Robert said as he handed Ronin one of his favorite oatmeal stout beers from the small brewery nearby.

Ronin took a long sip of the icy, thick beer with a brown frothy top before responding. "Well, Dad, first thing you should know is I was relieved of command of the Ike."

Stunned, Robert looked at his son. "What! What happened?"

Ronin took another sip as he enjoyed tormenting his dad with that teaser. "Mark Toft assumed command when I was given a brand-new ship, the *Cerberus*. She's far more advanced than *Ike*, Dad."

Robert stood up to flip the steaks at the grill. "So, is *Cerberus* a newer class of destroyer then?"

Ronin grinned as he walked over to stand next to Robert, admiring the steaks with a hungry eye. "*Cerberus* is a whole other class of ship. A different animal entirely, Dad. She's a heavy cruiser. Weighs in at 100,000 long tons, crew of 2,500. Carries two full squadrons of Tomcat fighters onboard, and a top-secret propulsion system. Soon she'll have a few sister ships joining the fleet. Armaments are classified. The new heavy cruiser class can crush a destroyer before they knew what hit them."

Robert pulled the steaks from the grill, and the two of them walked over to the outdoor dining table where the rest of the family was setting the table. "Julia, Dan is captaining another ship now," he announced as they sat down.

"That's fantastic!" Julia replied, beaming with pride at her son.

"Dad! Is that as good of a ship as *Ike*?" asked Edward.

"Oh, yes. Brand new ship, much larger and more powerful." Ronin interrupted himself by attacking the steak, as he couldn't wait any longer for real food after eating the spacecraft food for so long.

"I also have one heck of an announcement," Ronin said, again interrupting himself with a sip of a second of those excellent oatmeal stouts. "This will be released to the public soon, so I've already been cleared to tell you. *Cerberus* was sent on an exploration mission the past few months. Remember the old legends about the space colonies, Forrestal, Celestra and Solara?"

Sarah nodded at her father, wondering why he was referring to the subjects of many a bedtime story. "We found proof that they were real, and we found the spot where the jump gate to them existed."

While he chewed the steak, Ronin chuckled internally at how he managed to stop each of them mid-bite while they stared back at him in complete shock.

"Wait, there actually *were* colonies?" his mother asked, putting her fork down on her plate.

"Yes, we found a ninth planet way out in the outer reaches of the solar system. It's a dark planet, so telescopes on Earth can't detect it. Its satellite held an intact, ancient western coalition base. There were many fragmentary records that hadn't broken down too far from the passage of time for our AI to retrieve. Some of the recovered data indicated the colonies were indeed real. We just don't know where they are beyond some clues that are classified top secret. There were also other relics we found."

Robert couldn't take it anymore. "What relics? Don't keep us in suspense here!"

Ronin smiled, reeling in his captive audience like a hooked steelhead from Lake Michigan. "The jump gate was real, once. All that's left are a few highly radioactive debris from the battle to control that gate during The Fall. It's a hot spot now, certain death for any ships passing too close. Some pretty powerful nukes had to have been used to create a death zone like that, and for it to still be a death zone after so much time has passed. We also found two ancient ship hulls hurtling away from the hot spot. One from the old Collective. It was heavily damaged. The other was less so. It was the USS *Constitution*."

Robert was floored. "THE *Constitution?!* Legend says she was the pride of the coalition fleet! What did you find aboard?"

Ronin shook his head. "I can't tell you what we found on any of those old relics, even if I knew what all of it was." *Notably,* Ronin thought, *I also can't tell you we opted to let an AC destroyer become a flying coffin by not warning them about the hot spot.*

"Enough about work. I want to find out what my family has been up to!" Ronin announced.

Edward and Sarah were all too happy to fill him in on their musical and sports interests. Julia and Robert had already brought him back up to speed on their schooling while he was out of contact the past few months.

A few evenings later, the family was relaxing around the television in the family room when the program was interrupted with breaking news: "We interrupt this evening's broadcast to bring you an important announcement from the Confederation Fleet." said the network's evening news personality Anna Champlain in her strong, alto voice.

Ronin was instantly focused on her, and not solely because he'd had a crush on her the past few years. The scene changed to the press podium at Fleet Headquarters in Green Bay. An admiral Ronin didn't recognize delivered the news briefing about Cerberus' voyage and her discoveries, while a banner at the bottom of the screen scrolled a text summary of the announcement.

Moments after the admiral finished, Champlain's image again filled the screen over the banner scroll at the bottom. "Once again, ladies and gentlemen, Confederation Fleet has confirmed the existence of pre-Fall jump gates, and the space colonies, Forrestal, Celestra and Solara.

"We're informed a new type of fleet warship was sent to investigate some coordinates at the far edge of our solar system. Admiralty describes the *Cerberus* as a heavy cruiser, and her Captain is Dan Ronin of Green Bay, Wisconsin. We will bring any new developments to you as we get them. Thank you, and goodnight. We'll return you to the regularly scheduled broadcast now," said Champlain.

"Son, I think you just became the most famous guy on the planet for the moment," Robert commented wryly, knowing how much his son detested the press.

"I don't understand why they had to identify the captain," Ronin groaned.

"Maybe it's to make you look forward to returning to the ship to escape your newfound celebrity," his dad responded as he placed his phone on mute because it had already started buzzing with multiple incoming messages.

"Yeah, I'm sure that's it," Ronin responded in a playfully sarcastic manner as he, too, muted his phone because it was now buzzing with incoming messages and requests for media interviews. "Bah. I'm on a long-awaited vacation. I'm not giving that up to help out fleet media flaks by letting them and their press releases commandeer my personal time."

CHAPTER 13

WAYSIDE STATION

Weeks later, Ronin and Mueller met outside Admiral Rodding's office. "You look positively refreshed! Must've been a good vacation," noted Mueller when she caught sight of Ronin's tanned face. After taking *Cerberus* back into the dark under her own command, Mueller had a new appreciation for what it meant to operate far away from any expectation of assistance if trouble arose because they would be dead before a call for help was even halfway home. Now she was hoping to start building a better rapport with Ronin and to learn to work together because the danger they encountered while she was in command was sobering.

"I heard it got pretty dicey when that old enemy hull woke up a bit and suddenly tried to take out the research teams and the Bulldogs," Ronin said by way of reply. It was his top worry.

"Yes-sir, it wasn't pretty. It was a sobering illustration of how fast something can go wrong when we're too far away from help if we needed it. You were clearly right about the mindset needed for deep space missions." Mueller answered. "Being in command drove that point home quickly," she added. *Especially when I realized how much my children's safety depended on me making the transition to commanding a ship with no expectation of rescue if something went wrong*, Mueller thought, but didn't say aloud.

Ronin decided that merited overlooking the lack of trust he had still been feeling toward Mueller after she disagreed with letting an enemy ship plunge to its death instead of putting Cerberus at risk by warning the enemy ship away. *Better stay professional while we work on function-*

ing as a team based on how she responded to commanding a deep space mission, he thought.

"I selfishly admit to having a good time with my family, although we had to avoid crowds and commlink nodes after the fleet's announcement." Ronin, said, now responding to Mueller's initial observation.

Mueller looked startled for a moment. "Why's that?" she asked.

"I take it you didn't hear the news? Cerberus is world famous after they announced our discoveries. I couldn't have my commlink nodes on most of the time because of all the media requests for interviews. My dad could barely go anywhere without someone asking him about his son's ship, or requesting to talk to me, or to set up an interview. We finally escaped to his cottage up in the woods along the bay shoreline to get away from people," Ronin said. "It had been tough on my kids and parents to suddenly need to go into hiding because of our missions."

"My God! I hadn't heard about any announcement. Guess they didn't get word out to the ship or to Wayside Station," Mueller commented as Admiral Rodding opened his imposing wooden office doors.

"Come on in you two. We've a lot to cover."

The three moved to the admiral's conference table and sat down. "Dan, I trust your vacation wasn't terribly imposed upon by the timing of the media announcement down on Earth? Those media weenies ignored my request to delay it until you returned."

Ronin nodded his thanks for Rodding's understanding of the situation, unsurprised that Rodding knew what had played out. "Thank you, sir. My family pretty much had to escape to my father's cottage up north to escape the furor. There were reporters camped outside the house and knocking on the doors seeking interviews. It was ridiculous," Ronin said with a shudder at the visibly distasteful memory.

"Let me offer my sincere apologies for the fleet's media circus. There was no reason not to wait until you were safely away from that. My sources have confirmed those weenies are paying a price for bungling the timing like that. Something about being assigned to a garbage scow I hear."

Ronin and Mueller both chuckled at the admiral's choice of language. Rodding was clearly a man who both understood his people, and would have their backs as best he could. His people reciprocated, and did their best for a good boss.

"Thank you, sir. It's very much appreciated. What's next for Cerberus? A public relations tour now that she's world famous?" asked Ronin.

"Well, so far there hasn't been any rumbling inside the fleet to send you on a PR tour, which I know you would loathe as much as I would, and enemy activity dictates otherwise. *Cerberus* is being temporarily detached to the Argo's latest location. While I would love to send you back out to track down the colonies, priority goes to launching your sister ships. Argo is about to complete two more Cerberus-class heavy cruisers. They're identical to *Cerberus* and include all the upgrades and modifications you've outfitted your own ship with.

"You're to join with a small group of frigates and a destroyer that have been assigned for Argo's protection. A guarded courier will bring aboard the coordinates as Argo changed locations twice while you were gone. We need those ships, and the AC has ramped up their operational tempo lately."

Ronin and Mueller both nodded. "Have there been any further developments on the whereabouts of the colonies?" Mueller asked.

Rodding nodded briefly. "Indeed, there has. Not that it helps much, but our scientists and their AI's have reached an agreement on what they believe is most likely the shark constellation. Consensus probability is 80 percent."

Mueller sat straighter at that news. "They have? What distance? How did they figure it out?" she exclaimed.

Ronin leaned forward, his curiosity almost overwhelming his self-control as Rodding responded. "The main clue was a pattern of stars forming what appeared to be the letter S. Factor in another clue that the AI discerned from ancient customs is actually related to figuring out where the constellation is.

"The islanders of the South Pacific tell of an old legend about a fisherman casting out his incompetent crew and making them fish from the northern hemisphere while he stays in the south, only allowing them to return to herald the beginning of shark mating season. The only stars fitting this S pattern are some stars in the Big Dipper. When these stars appear in the north over New Guinea, islanders know the mating season of the shark is starting."

Ronin and Mueller both stared at Rodding as he explained the simplified version of how the constellation was located. "You don't quite believe me, do you?" Rodding asked.

Ronin chuckled softly in response. "Sir, normally I would think you were putting us on, but unless you've become a poker player as skilled as Lieutenant Delacroix, I can tell you're being serious."

"A pirate like Delacroix has the card sharking skills to empty the pockets of the best players, but yes, this is totally serious. Unfortunately, we can't just send you there to nose about and see what there is too see because you won't have enough fuel to return, or even to do anything once your there. For now, they're too far away because we don't have an interstellar gas station you can pull into for a quick fill up."

CHAPTER 14

ARGO SHIPYARD

Cerberus' arrival at the outer marker that was previously placed by the Argo navigation crews was preceded by the ship's jump flare. "Jump complete, Captain Ronin. Receiving identification challenge from the outer marker now." announced Perez. "Ident accepted. Coordinates and course received," he added.

"Captain, two Confederation picket ships are approaching. They're sending a password challenge," said Delacroix from his scans station.

"*Cerberus*. Answer challenge, Taurus." squawked the lead picket ship pilot into the commlink that opened between the vessels.

Ronin responded, "Send reply, Medallion," he ordered.

"Challenge accepted. Follow us to the inner marker on course 124.212," came the reply after a moment's hesitation.

Ronin looked over at Perez, who nodded. "Acknowledged, follow you to the inner marker on course 124.212," said Perez. *Cerberus* accelerated to follow the two small picket ships in to the asteroid field.

"Seems like a rough neighborhood to park a shipyard in," commented Ronin to Mueller as she stood next to his seat as they watched the front view screen.

"My thoughts exactly! They must have found a safe spot somewhere in here," Diane replied. They fell silent as Perez did his thing to drive *Cerberus* through the floating debris. They came to a clearing between a trio of large asteroids that blocked most of the detritus from entering a protected lee in the middle space between them.

"There's our answer," she remarked. Argo had parked itself right in the middle of the safe zone, safe from prying eyes.

"Captain, Argo's not showing up on our scans even though we can literally see it. Too much debris and iron dust blocking the signals," Delacroix reported.

"Captain, we're receiving a laser commlink channel. They aren't using wireless radio. There's a lot of interference, but I've filtered out most of the static it up so it's usable," called out Lieutenant Delgado as she put the message over the bridge comm.

"*Cerberus*, this is Ike Actual. Welcome to the neighborhood," said a familiar voice.

"Captain Toft! This is *Cerberus* Actual. We like what you've done to the place. Very homey. I understand you've got some updated tactical and situation data for us?" Ronin replied.

"That's affirm, Captain Ronin. A commlink drone is on its way to you now. Security protocols have restricted us to laser commlink when we're close enough for them to punch through the interference, or using messenger drones. Now that you're here, orders are that you are the chief in charge of the task force with that fancy looking new ship of yours. Rumor mill says *Cerberus* has a few secrets and surprises, but no one over here seems to know what they are."

"You wouldn't believe me if I told you," Ronin commented dryly. "The drone is here, we'll get busy with it. *Cerberus* Actual, out."

Ronin looked at Diane as he said, "Lieutenant LeCroy, why don't you join Commander Mueller and me in the ready room? We have work to do."

The trio was soon gathered around the table in the ready room as they reviewed the tactical data. "Sensor drones have been sending tactical data by laser into a commlink net to keep messages secure. Otherwise they've been running dark to avoid detection. Argo will complete construction of our first two sister ships in roughly two to three months as construction did not start on them at the same time, with a third to follow sometime later. Get those birds in the air, and the fleet will have a lot more options," Ronin mentioned to get the conversation started.

"Sir, I'd like to send out some Bulldogs to scout the area and see if we can find some holes in our sensor coverage," LeCroy requested.

"Granted. That's an excellent idea, then we can see if the current deployment of the picket ships still fits with whatever you might or might not find," Ronin responded.

"There are plenty of sensors and weapons on the far sides of the rocks that are hiding the shipyard, but I'm guessing they weren't deployed with *Cerberus'* jump capabilities in mind," Mueller said in a distracted tone as she studied the tactical data.

"Agreed. I'm betting we can spread those further out to create a kill box on transit lanes like the one we used to get in here. Let's rethink setting up some ambushes, plus let's make an exit strategy for Argo. I don't like how it can be trapped in here if the existing routes in and out have enemy ships inbound," concluded Ronin. "I'll ask Chief Engineer Lazarus to look into whether *Cerberus* can create a hidden exit using the gravity produced by our jump drive," he added.

The team studied the tactical display a while longer, making several more adjustments and a list of things to look into before dispersing to get started.

Mueller returned to the bridge with LeCroy. "Lieutenant Sunderland, this is Commander Mueller. I've sent some tactical information to your station for a Bulldog deployment. How soon can your crews deploy?" she asked over the commlink node on her collar to Sunderland.

"Yes, ma'am. I already called my drivers to the pilot ready room. Briefing in 5, then they'll be away," Sunderland's deep Scottish brogue responded.

"Excellent. Work with Lieutenant LeCroy as needed. We need to make sure the sensor net is complete. Mueller out."

While Mueller handled the Bulldogs with LeCroy and Sunderland, Ronin migrated down to Engineering to talk to Lt. Cmdr. Elvis Lazarus about moving some rocks. As he walked into the Engineering area, he spotted Lazarus immediately.

"Lazarus, I've got a crazy idea to run past you," he began before describing his idea to make an exit for the Argo.

Lazarus looked at Ronin like he'd lost his mind. "Well, Captain, that's a new one. I don't think anyone has thought to reverse the jump drive's gravity field to push something *away* from *Cerberus*."

Ronin nodded, "Yeah, I'm thinking it might be possible to temporarily turn *Cerberus* into an interstellar equivalent of an icebreaker. If we can do that, we can improve the tactical situation out there."

Lazarus thought for a moment, rubbing his dark brown goatee absentmindedly. "I'll see if we can do that. That might have other useful applications too."

"Great! Let me know as soon as you can," responded Ronin. "I don't like the situation we're in unless we can change things to our advantage."

BULLDOGS – SCOUTING MISSION

"Jump 1 complete," announced Pilot Officer Erin Johnson to Hal Patterson, the rear-seater, as they flashed into space near the outer marker they passed on the way in.

"Scans are clear, no threats detected," Patterson responded. "Launching drone package now," Patterson added, someone what unnecessarily because Johnson could feel the slight jolting as they left the Bulldog. "Prepare to jump."

Bulldog 1 flashed away again while the drone package spread out and scanned the area. Bulldog 2 appeared above the asteroid belt.

"Jump 1 complete," said Pilot Officer Ensign Helmut Meyer.

"Launching drone package number 1," replied Pilot Officer Sophie Schmidt, from the rear seat as her words were accompanied by slight jolts from the launches.

"Prepare to execute Jump 2," Meyer quickly said, as he jumped the Bulldog again. Bulldog 3 repeated the same process below the asteroid belt.

It felt like days passed before Meyer announced, "Jump 15 complete," said Meyer.

"Final drone package away," confirmed Schmidt as they launched the last set of drones.

"Preparing for jump 16," Meyer noted.

Soon, all 3 Bulldogs made their final jumps. "Final jump complete. Schmidt, how are our babies doing?" Meyer asked after they appeared in the shadow of a larger rock.

"Receiving burst telemetry from all drones. They're on station, and going dark now," Schmidt replied.

"Time for us to do the same," muttered Meyer as he maneuvered the Bulldog into a parking spot.

"Going to be a long couple weeks until we're relieved," Schmidt commented. "Good thing we brought plenty of books."

Meyer snorted, "Books? You mean you didn't bring that ancient disco music you've been listening to so you could torture me again?"

Schmidt laughed. "Oh no! I needed to up my game and come up with something more diabolical to torment you with. You were getting too used to that stuff."

***

The scene in Bulldog 1 was little different as they lurked in the shadows of another large rock.

"Johnson, want any jerky?"

Johnson's eyes appeared to open wide with fear. "No! You didn't bring that horrid stuff, did you? The smell lingers for days!"

Patterson's grin became evil as he laughed in reply. "Don't worry. I only brought two pounds of it."

Johnson nearly tripped as she came back towards the rear of the ship. "What!!"

With a dramatic flair of terribly exaggerated triumph, Patterson reached into his go bag to fetch a snack. "Wait! That's not jerky!" he cried, looking sadly at the sack of sweet treats he had pulled from the go bag.

Now it was time for Johnson to laugh evilly. "You didn't think I knew where you hide your go bag?"

"You will die a horrible death. It'll be a tragic end for the ages," he grumbled as he pulled out two of the treats and tossed one to Johnson.

CHAPTER 15

ICEBREAKER

"**C**aptain Ronin, this is Lt. Commander Lazarus," called Elvis Lazarus as he opened a commlink using his collar node.

"Ronin here," answered Ronin.

"Captain, can you come down to Engineering? I'd like to show you what we've come up with."

Seconds later, Ronin was on his way while Commander Mueller took his place. He arrived minutes later and was met by Lazarus at the hatchway.

"Thanks for coming, Captain. If you'll follow me to the workstation?" Even though he had phrased it as a question, his tone was more of a command and statement.

"What do you have for me, Lt. Commander?"

Lazarus touched a screen button and brought up the holoimage of the ship with the estimated gravity field highlighted and shown to scale with the ship. "Captain, you were right. Remember the gravity lenses you and LeCroy toyed with for improving our sensor suite? We refined the software which operates the lenses to push out the gravity field generated by the jump drive to create a buffer in front of the ship instead of jumping away."

Ronin studied the holo thoughtfully. "How much mass can we push?" he inquired.

"Our calculations show we can push roughly 10 megatons of rock around, as long as we don't have too much velocity built up before the field comes into contact with the target," Lazarus replied as he also looked at the holoimage.

Ronin broke into a grin at that mental imagery. "It'd be a heck of a bang if we did that. Quite a way to go out," he remarked. "How long before we can get started?" he asked.

"Within the hour. We've already made the preliminary preparations under the assumption you'd green light the rest of the production when you saw what we came up with."

Ronin nodded his approval. "Excellent work, Mr. Lazarus. Get started and let the bridge know when we're ready."

When he returned to the bridge, Ronin walked over to LeCroy and motioned both Mueller and Lt. Pierre Delacroix over. "The Chief says we'll be rigged up to push rocks within the hour. Delacroix, filter your existing scan results to exclude everything over 10 megatons of mass. LeCroy, make sure Perez is working from your updated tactical map, especially for making the new escape route and designated ambush zones. Any questions?" he finished.

All heads nodded in the negative. "OK, let's get ready to make it happen," said Ronin.

The hour crawled by for Ronin. Finally, his commlink's collar node buzzed.

"Captain, this is Chief Lazarus. We're ready."

Ronin pushed the screen button. "Acknowledged. Ronin out."

He looked up at Delacroix and LeCroy. "OK. It's your show. Let's get started."

Cerberus began the long process of pushing stones. *It's like Sisyphus just got drafted from forever pushing a rock uphill into pushing rocks around in the universe's largest landscaping project,* Ronin thought as they approached the first target.

CHAPTER 16

BATTLE OF THE BELT

Space and time took on totally different meanings, depending on a person's perspective. For the Cerberus and her crew, they were exceptionally busy playing galactic landscaper. It took five weeks to arrange the strategic situation more to their liking.

Everyone knows time passes quickly when you're busy, thought Mueller as she shook off the exhaustion of another short night of sleep. She looked at Karl, who would still be sleeping for several more hours, as would their children. *Well, you wanted to become XO of the amazing new ship. Suck it up, cupcake,* she said to herself as she slowly stood up to stretch quietly for a few moments before stumbling into the washroom for a quick shower.

It was a similar story in Ronin's quarters as he swung his legs off the bed onto the floor. He stood up as he yawned and stretched. *I swear I just went to bed a few minutes ago! Must start the magic go juice machine,* his bleary mind told itself as he slowly migrated towards his precious coffee machine. Minutes later, he was showering up in a near scalding spray of water as the magic go juice machine perked away.

Once he finished, he grabbed a cup from the new pot of coffee, and sipped while he threw on his daily uniform. Ronin was happy he remembered to top off his mug this time before he went to work.

It was an entirely different story in the Bulldogs. There the enemy was boredom, causing time to drag by for the crews working their ships. Pilots and rear-seaters alternated twelve-hour shifts while their opposite half tried to rest or find something to do while they remained dark and on station for a week at a time.

As he approached the bridge, Ronin's commlink node on his collar beeped with an incoming message.

"Captain, this is Lieutenant Delacroix. The drone sensor net just reported they've spotted inbound enemy war birds. Are you on your way to the bridge?"

In lieu of acknowledging the message, Ronin simply walked onto the bridge seconds later. "Lieutenant Delacroix. Number and composition of enemy fleet?" he asked, ignoring the surprised looks of the bridge crew at his sudden appearance instead.

"Five enemy war birds, Captain. Four frigates, and a destroyer approaching the outer marker of the path we followed to here," Delacroix began saying when he was interrupted by an incoming transmission that demanded his attention.

"Captain, Bulldog 2 has detected two more enemy frigates coming through the other known pathway through the field. Looks like they're taking up blocking positions to keep Argo from escaping."

Ronin nodded. "Obviously they've located the *Argo*. Lieutenant Delgado, open a Tacnet commlink to our task force."

Moments later, Lt. Maria Delgado responded, "Tacnet channel open, Captain."

Ronin nodded his thanks at the quick response. "By now each of you in task force 58 has a clear picture of the situation. Seven enemy vessels, two of which are in a blocking formation, while the main five try to chase the prey right into them. Cerberus has a few surprises for them, so as per the plans previously sent to you by drone, sit tight and let the ambushes do their thing before we provide an update on battle damage assessment. Ronin out."

THE *IKE*

Capt. Mark Toft closed the commlink and looked at his tactical officer. "Lieutenant Savoy, sound Action Stations."

Savoy looked at Toft after the klaxon sounded, "All stations report combat-ready, Captain. Any thoughts on what kind of ambush Cerberus has planned?"

Toft shook his head. "Nope. Captain Ronin kept that under wraps for security purposes, but knowing him, it will be quite a nasty surprise."

BULLDOG 1 - ALPHA STATION

Bulldog 1 had been deployed to the pre-positioned asteroid designated Alpha Station for five days on its latest deployment to the same spot.

"Four frigates and a destroyer," remarked Patterson, staring at the formation of enemy ships displayed on his screen. "They haven't seen us and we're still dark so this is just from our passive optics. Cerberus has confirmed we're a go for the ambush. Frigates are arrayed around the destroyer in their standard protective formation."

Pilot Officer Erin Johnson listened intently while she chewed on a piece of Patterson's beef jerky. "OK, Patterson, vector six of the drones in this group with the weapons pods into the destroyer first, then send the two nearest groups this way, ASAP."

Patterson nodded to himself before counting down, "Time on target, one minute. Thirty seconds. Fifteen seconds. Optics confirms multiple impacts!"

Johnson grinned. "Yeah! How much damage?"

Patterson shook his head. "I can't tell, too much junk in the way. Needs time to clear." Patterson's board beeped for his attention. "Next drone flight arriving in five minutes. They are moving at extremely high velocity now."

The cabin of the Bulldog fell quiet for a few minutes as they watched their screens. To help ease their nerves and pass the time, both of them chewed on some of Patterson's beef jerky that he snuck past Johnson's defenses the next time they deployed. The smell slowly permeated the cabin as they ate.

"Optics show minor hull breaches on the destroyer, but there must be some internal damage as she's venting a stream of atmosphere from her port side. Looks like the drones took down a couple of weapons turrets," murmured Patterson, not looking away from his screen. "Drone impact, 30 seconds." he added just as the starboard side of the destroyer lit up with point defense fire.

"I see it," noted Johnson. "We may have to launch our weapons soon, then make ourselves scarce fast," she continued. They watched as two more drones impacted the destroyer, this time on the starboard side.

"Only two drones got through, their point defense stopped the others," Patterson confirmed. "Observation drone sending damage assessment. Several starboard maneuvering thrusters were destroyed," Patterson added.

"That'll hurt when they try to navigate their way further into the belt to get at the *Argo*. The destroyer will take a lot longer to make their course changes without those thrusters." Johnson said approvingly.

Job nearly done, the two of them fell silent again as they unconsciously mimicked their Bulldog, which was itself quietly lurking in the shadows of an asteroid. They continued to watch the fleet as it passed by their position. Patterson's workstation commlink beeped with an incoming message from Captain Ronin.

"Excellent work, Bulldog 1. After they've passed by, launch your Grasshoppers and bug out before you're spotted."

Johnson thumbed her screen button and responded, "Affirmative. Estimate five minutes until Grasshopper launch."

Johnson and Patterson silently watched their screens as the passive sensor's plot of the fleet continued crawling forward at a slower pace than before the ambush. Patterson had put a countdown timer on the corner of their displays, which was adjusting its remaining time to factor in the enemy's slowing pace as it approached the next attack zone, where a passing asteroid would temporarily block the fleet's line of sight to the Bulldog, so they could jump without the flare being spotted.

As the countdown finally reached zero, Johnson spun up the Bulldog's jump engines and put some space between them and their hiding spot. "Ready for jump," she called to Patterson.

"Grasshopper launch in ten seconds," Patterson responded. "Five. Four. Three. Two. One. Launch!"

The two Grasshoppers shot out of the weapons pod mounted between the landing skids. "Jumping," Johnson announced, as they jumped away from Alpha Station to return to *Cerberus*.

BULLDOG 2 - BETA STATION

Pilot Officer Ensign Helmut Meyer watched his screen carefully. He was startled when the quiet was suddenly broken by Pilot Officer Schmidt's quiet musing.

"Our little backwater is getting more exciting than we we're hoping for," Meyer watching the passive optics plot of the two AC frigates slowly working their way through the navigation channel to get at the *Argo*.

"Tacnet data says the main fight is near the outer marker of Alpha Station. Bulldog 1 is about to launch their Grasshoppers," Schmidt added a few moments later.

Meyer eyed the countdown time Schmidt had placed on their screens until the pair of frigates arrived at the pre-selected ambush spot that had previously been designated Wolf 99. "These guys are about to learn the hard way they've been seen," he responded as the number ticked down to thirty seconds to drone impact.

Schmidt began the countdown soon after. "Five, four, three, two, one. Impact!" All five drones that had been mounted with weapons pods impacted on the lead frigate at an extremely high velocity because they had plenty of time to accelerate due to the early sighting.

"Observation drone optics imagery coming in now. Lead frigate is holed with at least three through and throughs because the velocity was so high," Schmidt observed.

Meyer was also watching the same show play out on his screen. "Looks like the main engines were erased by one of the impacts and the warhead detonation. That ship isn't going to come back from the dead," he said.

Schmidt laughed in response. "Those drones were practically turned into kinetic weapons because they'd built up so much velocity!" she said excitedly.

Still maintaining their dark and silent status, they watched as the remaining frigate launched a screen of drones to give itself a larger sensor net as it accelerated away under full power. "Unsurprisingly, they're not even bothering to check for survivors before dashing into the navigation channel at reckless speeds," Schmidt commented as they followed the plot on her screen as they waited for the frigate and its drones to pass by their deeply shadowed hiding spot.

"The Collective doesn't have citizens like the Confederation does, they have subjects. The Collective just doesn't care about its powerless subjects or their lives. It just cares about the State, and its ruling class," Meyer responded.

Schmidt nodded without taking her eyes from the screen plot while she replied. "Yeah, that's the natural end point of all socialist, communist, or collectivist systems by whatever name. They all end up the same way because human nature inevitably results in some folks saying or doing whatever they need to do in order to become more powerful."

Meyer also didn't take his eyes from the screen plot in front of him. "The irony of it is, those collectivist or socialist systems which purport to make everyone equal are far more susceptible to certain people taking power for themselves and making themselves the rulers over the little people. At least the Confederacy tries to avoid that by spreading power between equal branches and having a democratic vote. It's not perfect but realistically, people themselves aren't perfect either so it's the best system ever devised." he said.

Schmidt's countdown timer that she put onto both of their screens adjusted itself to thirty seconds while they watched the frigate shrink into the distance.

"Spinning up the engines," Meyer announced as the Bulldog separated itself from its asteroid. "Ready for jump," he called to Sophie a few seconds later.

"Grasshopper launch in ten seconds," Schmidt responded. "Five. Four. Three. Two. One. Launch!" The two Grasshoppers shot out of the weapons pod mounted between Bulldog 2's landing skids.

"Jumping," Meyer announced as soon as the Grasshoppers flashed into hyperspace. Bulldog 2 then jumped away from Beta Station and the ambush at Wolf 99 to return to Cerberus.

CΞRBΞRUS – ΛT YΛNKΞΞ STΛTION

The space occupied by Cerberus had been designated Yankee Station. As Captain Ronin cut the link with Bulldog 1, Lt. Matt LeCroy looked over from his tactical station.

"Captain, Tacnet shows Bulldog 2 launched their Grasshoppers and jumped back to Cerberus for a reload, and Bulldog 4 is conducting the battle damage assessment of Bulldog 2's engagement via passive scans only."

Ronin nodded. "Acknowledged. Thank you, LeCroy."

While LeCroy was busy with the overall tactical situation, Mueller was closely monitoring both the rearming of Bulldog 1 and the second ambush point of the incoming fleet. "Bulldog 1 reports ready to launch in five minutes," she noted to LeCroy and Ronin. Mueller then added, "Captain, Bulldog 4 reports the two-frigate task force has been destroyed. Survivors are unlikely due to the extent of the damage. The two Grasshoppers turned the second frigate into spare parts."

Mueller looked up from the screen plot she was following, then she glanced at Ronin with her eyebrows raised. Ronin met her eyes, his eyebrows likewise shooting up. Mueller switched screens to pull up an image of the last frigate that was taken by Bulldog 4.

"Captain Ronin, I think the Grasshoppers packed more punch than we anticipated," she said as LeCroy leaned over to look at the screen that showed a debris field with some larger hull pieces slowly spinning away. LeCroy whistled softly to himself as he examined the images.

Ronin walked over to where they were standing. "Wow!" he exclaimed, then he, too, whistled softly. "Turns out the hulls weren't designed to withstand explosions from the inside, huh?"

LeCroy and Mueller chuckled, while they continued to watch the screen. The commlink beeped at LeCroy's workstation to signal an incoming message from Bulldog 3, and he turned to answer it.

"LeCroy here. Sitrep?"

Both Ronin and Mueller listened to the situation report intensely.

"This is Bulldog 3. Damage assessment as follows. Bulldog 1 drones caused minor damage to the destroyer, but notable for starboard thruster damage that decreased maneuvering effectiveness by an estimated 50 percent. Some port side turrets were destroyed. Grasshoppers destroyed two frigates. Two frigates are undamaged and are in an escort formation with the damaged destroyer. Estimated arrival at Wolf 184, the second marker, in two hours."

LeCroy sent and acknowledgment of the report, while Ronin and Mueller glanced at each other.

"I have my doubts if the remaining enemy formation will even make it to the fifth marker, where we planned to let the Tomcat squadrons out to play," Mueller concluded.

"Agreed. The destroyer will be even more of a sitting duck than we hoped when it has to negotiate the sharp turn at the second marker. When Bulldog 2 returns for its re-arming, deploy them with Bulldogs 1 and 3 to the second marker vicinity as planned. Bulldog 4 will stay in a passive observation role for now to keep shadowing the enemy." ordered Ronin.

Ronin returned to his command chair while LeCroy and Mueller continued coordinating the various efforts. He observed Mueller's body language for a moment. *She still is reluctant to hit a vulnerable enemy,* Ronin thought.

Ronin opened a line to the *Argo*. "Captain Smith, this is Cerberus Actual. Have you finished your departure preparations?" Capt. Reggy Smith wasted no time in replying, his harried voice rising from Ronin's chair arm commlink.

"That's affirmative, Cerberus," said Smith. "We're ready to shove off with our escort vessels as soon as you give the word."

Ronin was pleased with their progress. "The word is given, Captain. We'll join you as soon as we can. Cerberus Actual, out."

The interesting thing about combat, Ronin mused as he waited for the next two hours to pass, is that it always has a hurry-up-and-wait aspect to it, no matter what century it is. Even with the dawn of the era of jump ship combat that drastically compressed the relative distances involved in combat actions, suddenly the flow of action ebbed for a few hours while they waited for the enemy to stumble into the next ambush. His thoughts were interrupted when Mueller walked over to stand next to him.

"Bulldogs 1, 2 and 3, have redeployed to the second marker. They jumped to their predetermined hides behind the asteroids we moved into position with Cerberus so the enemy formation couldn't see the jump flares."

Ronin nodded at the expected report, and glanced at his screen. "Now we wait," he remarked.

Ninety minutes crawled by with very little conversation on the bridge as they waited for round two to begin. Cerberus continued to actively scan the area around Yankee Station in a search for new threats.

BULLDOG 1 - AT FOXTROT STATION

Johnson and Patterson appeared behind the pre-positioned asteroid designated Foxtrot Station. "Jump 1 complete," she said, restarting the jump count because of their rearming return trip to Cerberus. The two of them quickly shut the Bulldog down, relying on the drone optics that had been likewise been pre-positioned.

"The clock is at ninety minutes," Patterson noted as they went dark. Foxtrot station appeared tranquil once again.

BULLDOG 2 - AT KILO STATION

At the same time Bulldog 1 appeared, Bulldog 2 appeared behind their own pre-positioned asteroid, which had been designated Kilo Station.

"Jump 1 complete. Prepared to go dark," Meyer announced.

"Go dark in five. Four. Three. Two. One. Shutdown," Schmidt counted down.

Unknown to them, Bulldog 2 had set a speed record in going dark.

BULLDOG 3 - AT OSCAR STATION

Tony Russo and Michael Jonsey likewise appeared behind their own asteroid hide, that was designated Oscar Station during the mission planning.

"Jump 1 complete. Ready to go dark," Russo stated in a somewhat absentminded fashion as his attention was mostly occupied by his instruments.

Seconds later, Jonsey counted down. "Dark in five. Four. Three. Two. One. Shutdown."

Russo glanced back at Jonsey for a moment before asking, "How's the drone telemetry?"

Jonsey pressed a few buttons as he refined their data link. "Five by five, Russo. Optics synced with our systems, and the countdown clock is at ninety minutes and falling. Visual clarity is so high, we even have eyes on each of the drones out in their screen."

Russo smiled. "The Captain has us set up beautifully out here. All that scrambling around the past few weeks might have been worth it."

Jonsey nodded, murmuring "umm-hmm" softly as he watched the screen plot and chewed his mint gum.

CHAPTER 17

YANKEE STATION

Some two hours later, Ronin and Mueller watched the Tacnet plot on the main view screen. Three remaining AC ships slowly approached the second marker, an ambush point that had been designated Wolf 184 during the mission planning.

"I know they've been slowed down by the loss of their starboard maneuvering thrusters, but they're even slower than we anticipated," Mueller whispered.

LeCroy overheard her as he approached them. "The destroyer's name translated into American is The Dragon, but despite her name, our sensor readings from before the attack suggests The Dragon's maintenance is in poor condition. The engines are way out of tune, and that has reduced thruster efficiency by 23 percent. In fact, the sensor readings of entire enemy fleet revealed them all to be in similar condition. One of the destroyed frigates even suffered a reactor mishap not long ago because the hull was still fairly radioactive. That crew was destined for an early grave."

Glancing at LeCroy, Ronin nodded in agreement. "That tells me the perennially weak economy of the Collective can't keep their ships maintained properly anymore, and it is likely a sign their economy is collapsing. No one has any incentive to work or provide superior craftsmanship in a socialist or collectivist economy, so they always lag far behind in nearly all areas."

Mueller muttered in response, "Hopefully they don't get desperate and do something stupid as their economy collapses."

Ronin turned to look at her as he nodded again. "Exactly what the Admiralty is afraid of. But all we can do is take care of the business we have in front of us today. Let's worry about tomorrow when it's time to start worrying."

A beeping on his station console drew LeCroy's attention.

"Captain, the Bulldogs are spinning up their jump drives. Targets are nearly stationary as they negotiate the turn. Missile launch in 45 seconds," LeCroy reported.

"OK, time to hammer down," Ronin responded. "Lieutenant Perez, execute Jump 1."

Lt. Antonio Perez acknowledged the order, and jumped Cerberus to another pre-positioned asteroid designated Whiskey Station, which was its attack position behind near Wolf 184.

"They had to wonder what that big flash was," LeCroy commented, although spotting the larger jump flare coming from behind the rock couldn't be helped. Cerberus was too big to completely hide in this area, so it had to wait until the trap sprung to jump in and participate in the combat.

"Too late for them to do anything about it," Ronin replied as Mueller started issuing the orders to reconfigure the jump drive gravity lensing to turn the ship into a rock pusher.

Seconds passed before Mueller reported, "Reconfiguration complete, Captain. Commencing with the Potato Masher. Lieutenant Perez, proceed."

Mueller's commanding attitude and lack of noticeable hesitation in ordering the Potato Masher to proceed surprised Ronin for a moment. *Maybe she's coming 'round*, he told himself.

Perez quickly pressed screen buttons on his console as he verbally replied, "Aye, aye, Commander." Cerberus quickly turned to face the rock, before pushing its nose close to it as the ship slowly accelerated to make contact with its gravity field from the jump drives. Once the field had a steady grip on the asteroid, Perez began increasing power with the sub light fusion drive. The rock resisted the pressure for a few moments, then began to accelerate. Slowly for the first few seconds, rapidly picking up momentum as Cerberus' fusion drive flared when it reached max power. The verbal reports came in quickly.

"Captain, the Grasshoppers have destroyed the two frigates. One Grasshopper also damaged the destroyer. Looks like The Dragon's engines were heavily damaged from the impact. Her thrust levels have dropped to about 10 percent," said LeCroy as he read the report from Tacnet.

Delacroix added, "Captain, The Dragon is nearly stationary. Bull-dogs have jumped back behind their asteroids again."

Suddenly the acceleration gravities eased off as Perez reported, "Rock is released! Ready to jump away, Captain."

Ronin nodded briefly. "Mr. Perez, jump us back to Yankee Station." Perez acknowledged by jumping the ship away.

Cerberus reappeared at the Yankee Station staging area, followed by Perez saying, "Jump 2 complete."

Ronin looked over at LeCroy. "Report, Mr. LeCroy."

LeCroy didn't respond for a few seconds as the data link to Tacnet was reestablished. "Taking a reading now. The Dragon is attempting to avoid the incoming asteroid. Engine output just ceased, her engines couldn't handle the demand. She's adrift. Aim is good. Estimated time to impact, ten minutes."

Ronin responded quickly. "Recall Bulldogs 1 and 2 immediately. Keep 4 in an observation role as they've got the special optics pod. Keep 3 at Oscar Station in reserve for now."

LeCroy immediately sent a message. "Bulldogs 1 and 2, priority recall order. Bulldogs 1 and 2, this is a priority recall order. Execute immediately. Bulldog 4, continue observations."

The Bulldogs confirmed receipt of the orders.

BULLDOG 1 - YANKEE STATION

Bulldog 1 smoothly arrived in the Cerberus hangar bay, then taxied to its designated parking spot. As Johnson powered down the systems, Patterson noted, "Two minutes until impact, Johnson."

As she finished her task, Johnson called over her shoulder to Patterson, "I kind of wish we could've lingered to see the show, but it's good to be home anyway."

Patterson laughed before he said, "Me too! Let's hit the showers. We're pretty ripe smelling after days in our suits."

As they exited and stepped down onto the Cerberus deck, deck chief Adam Taylor couldn't resist taking a swipe at them. "Ripe? You two are ready to be pickled. Get off my deck before someone dies from the fumes," Taylor said with a slightly evil grin.

Patterson and Johnson laughed as they walked away. They turned to watch Bulldog 2 taxiing to the adjacent parking spot.

Meyer and Schmidt soon exited and joined the waiting crew of Bulldog 1. Patterson had to start with the razzing as the four walked to the flight crew quarters. "Schmidt, when did you ditch Meyer and replace him with a wolf man?"

Meyer laughed loudly, as he touched his now impressively thick blonde beard as he flashed a huge grin. "You just wish you were man enough to sprout this mane, girly man."

Now it was Patterson's turn to laugh, this time along with the rest of them. "C'mon wolf man. Let's hit the showers before you confuse the tears in our eyes with happiness to see you!"

Up on the bridge, Ronin noted the arrival of Bulldogs 1 and 2, before LeCroy interrupted his thoughts. "Thirty seconds till impact, Captain. Tacnet plotting says it'll be a glancing blow due to The Dragon's accrued momentum before her engines flamed out."

The bridge fell silent at that, while Ronin eyed his screen plot and countdown timer.

"Bulldog 4 reports the asteroid hit The Dragon, Captain." LeCroy reported. "Damage assessment is she's a total loss despite being a partial hit. Speed at impact was .1 lights." LeCroy continued looking at the Tacnet report by the observation Bulldog for a few moments before adding, "Clarification. The Dragon was totally destroyed. Kinetic energy of the impact equaled about a 100-megaton nuclear warhead. Bulldogs 3 and 4 are jumping away to avoid the shockwave."

"Recall the Bulldogs and let's get out in front of the *Argo* to scout for more threats," Ronin ordered. LeCroy quickly ordered Bulldogs 3 and 4 back to the ship, while Perez plotted their next jump, this time to the new escape channel that Cerberus created a few weeks ago. Minutes later, the Bulldogs were parked in the hangar and Perez was ready.

"Execute jump, Perez," Ronin commanded. Cerberus jumped.

CHAPTER 18

NOVEMBER STATION

Cerberus appeared at the staging area previously designated November Station. This was the final waypoint before the *Argo* would leave the confines of the belt. Cerberus had placed a host of monitoring sensors and early Tacnet warning devices around the exit to let them know if the Collective was waiting for them.

"Jump 3 complete, Captain," announced Lieutenant Perez.

Lieutenant LeCroy read Tacnet for a moment to confirm what the telemetry sent via the repeaters had reported. "No ships have been here since Cerberus last left the area, Captain," noted LeCroy when Ronin looked over to his station with the question written on his face.

Lieutenant Delacroix finished his more thorough scans. "Confirmed, Captain. No exhaust residue from passing Collective ships found by the sensors. Task force is showing up on our sensors. Arrival in ten hours," he said.

Ronin nodded acknowledgment. "Let's keep our Bulldog crews home for now and they can grab some rest while our sensor net does the heavy lifting." Mueller passed Ronin's order along to the pilot ready room.

"Captain, incoming message from Captain Toft," announced Lieutenant Delgado from the bridge's main commlink station.

"Send it through to my console," Ronin ordered. He answered the soft beep.

"Cerberus Actual, this is Ike Actual. Tacnet reports all enemy ships destroyed. Is that for real?"

Ronin smiled slightly, the corner of his mouth turning up in a half smirk. "That's affirm, Mark." The commlink was silent for a few moments before Captain Toft spoke again.

"Dan, I don't understand. How could you have wiped them out in just a few hours? That's not possible!" This time Ronin's smile spread wider as Mueller also glanced over with a smirk on her face.

"Remember when I said you wouldn't believe what Cerberus could do if I told you? We're the new sheriffs in town."

"You're enjoying not telling me, aren't you?" Toft said in a half-teasing voice.

"Oooh, I'm taking so much pleasure in not telling you. That much enjoyment should probably be illegal! Cerberus Actual, out." Ronin closed the line before speaking to the bridge crew:

"We have a slow period coming on. Call in your replacements, and go get some rest. We're not out of the woods yet."

Over on the Ike, Toft shook his head slightly as he glanced up at his new XO, Christine Hansen. A capable veteran of both fleet politics and multiple engagements, Johnson had been on the Ike for three years before Toft chose her as the new XO.

"What do you suppose Captain Ronin meant by that?" she asked Toft.

"I don't know. Captain Ronin isn't usually so cryptic, unless there's a security reason for it. The way he's phrasing his response tells me there is a big security reason for it. Cerberus must be really fast to cover so much ground that quickly."

Hansen nodded, commenting, "Heavily gunned too. I've never heard of anything that could wipe out a fleet coming in from two widely separated directions in a matter of hours."

Now it was Toft's turn to nod. "Yeah. It would have taken us days just to cover the distance, and we would still have been too late to stop the second group from reaching *Argo*. And how did they manage to do it without being damaged at all?"

While Toft and Hansen were trying to noodle out how Cerberus seemed to pull off the impossible, Ronin had changed clothes and was walking into the gym when he spotted his sparring partners, Kowalski and Blackwater.

"Ready to work up a sweat and trade a few lumps, Captain?" Blackwater said with a predatory smile while Kowalski was still putting on his sparring pads.

"You betcha! Been sitting still for hours. Got a need to work off some stress here," Ronin replied as he started putting on his own pads.

Blackwater and Kowalski knew exactly what Ronin meant. Ronin just wished he were down in the pilot ready room to partake in quaffing one of Sunderland's home-brewed celebration beers that he figured would be served at the debriefing.

Mueller noticed the time as she walked to her family's quarters, which prompted her to walk quicker. They should all still be awake and she wanted to get some time in before everyone got some sleep. She was only two steps inside the hatchway when Sophia and Sonya attacked with hugs and excited cries of "Mommy!"

As she soaked in the love, Mueller sighed and said, "I really needed this!"

After the hugs, Karl held out a plain brown bottle that had a note attached. "Lieutenant Sunderland said I should give this to you. He said you'd know what it is?" Karl said in a tone that was both statement and question.

"Honey, get the beer mugs!" Diane said excitedly when she saw what Karl was holding.

Delacroix decided to relax the way he loved best. That meant a trip to the impromptu poker table that was temporarily set up in Marine Country, which is the section of Cerberus occupied by the Marines. In their briefing room, the Marines often had the ship's poker tournament going on.

Interestingly, while there was a personal note on file from the captain of *Achéron* on Delacroix's last tour to beware Delacroix's poker skills unless you'd like to become bankrupt, only Ronin seemed aware of the cautionary warning in the file. Ronin had promised Delacroix that he would tell no one about Delacroix's talent, but not to be surprised if Ronin would have a need to draw upon Delacroix's poker skills someday.

Down in the pilot ready room, the freshly showered crews of Bulldogs 1 through 4 gathered for their debriefing. Lieutenant Sunderland walked in, followed by his wife, Amie, who was carrying an unmarked box. The expression on his face was stern.

"All right, you animals, grab your seats. First off, somehow you all managed to survive, which is itself an outright miracle."

The pilots snuck worried glances at one another, wondering why Sunderland seemed to be in such a foul mood after their victory.

"Secondly, I'm shocked you didn't trash your birds. Another minor miracle. And thirdly, the Captain has requested, and I agree I might add, that you have earned one of my celebration beers!"

As Sunderland said this, he couldn't keep the fake stern expression on his face any longer and the pilots broke into whoops and cries of excitement. Sunderland's craft brew making skills had long been perfected and had become legendary in the Confederate fleet.

After his sparring, a very sweaty Ronin stumbled into his quarters for a shower and some sleep. Although he didn't notice it due to his haste to get into the shower to clean up, after he changed into fresh clothes he noticed a large, plain brown bottle with a note attached to it that said "Captain's celebration beer" on it.

After pouring a mug of the cold oatmeal stout, Ronin took a sip and sighed contentedly at the smooth, creamy malt taste. Sunderland really should have been a brew master running his own brewpub because the man knew how to brew beer styles matching exactly what everybody seemed to like.

CHAPTER 19

BIRTHING PAINS

eeling refreshed, the prime bridge crew had returned to their posts on Cerberus, which remained at November Station. Commander Mueller stood next to Captain Ronin in his command chair as they reviewed the after-action reports.

"So far we haven't had to engage the Tomcat fighters," Ronin noted.

"Haven't been close enough to need the sub light fighters," Mueller responded with a grin repeating something Ronin had mentioned earlier. He chuckled at hearing his own remark thrown back at him.

"The scout team we sent back to Wolf 184 and Wolf 99 reported there isn't enough remaining of those ships to bother with. They never knew what hit 'em, so they won't know to adopt new tactics yet," Ronin responded, with no small amount of satisfaction.

"Captain, the *Argo* reports ship launch is imminent," Lt. Maria Delgado broke in.

The main view screen was changed to show the optics of the now very close *Argo* Shipyard. A minute or two later, the left side of the shipyard's rigging (as seen from the perspective of the optical image on the Cerberus view screen) appeared to be giving birth to another ship.

"Ladies and gentlemen, I give you the Ceres, the second Cerberus-class heavy cruiser," announced Ronin, before opening a commlink at his console. "Cerberus Actual to Ceres Actual, welcome to the world!"

Seconds later the reply came back. "Cerberus Actual, this is Ceres Actual, it's good to hear from you, Captain Ronin! Like old times, but with new stuff!"

Smiling broadly, Ronin responded. "Captain Michelle Rodgers, as I live and breathe. Looking forward to taking your new toy out for a spin?"

On the bridge of the Ceres, Captain Rodgers was grinning broadly as her XO, Tom Chastain, looked on with a bemused expression.

"Captain Ronin, Captain Hu Nagun of the *Kitty Hawk* and I were best friends in the academy at Green Bay," Rodgers explained in her East Texas accent.

Tom's eyebrows rose in acknowledgment as he nodded slightly before the corner of his mouth quirked up into a slight smile at the banter between the ship captains.

"That's affirm, Captain Ronin. After what Cerberus did in the Battle of the Belt, we're dying to see what she's got under the hood." Rodger's bright teeth contrasted sharply with her dark skin, as she didn't bother to try to conceal her excitement at finally launching Ceres into space.

Ronin's upcoming reply was interrupted by another ship wide announcement. "Second ship launch imminent."

The bridge crews of *Ceres* and *Cerberus* gave their full attention to their respective view screens as the *Argo* superstructure opened to reveal the birth of another dark gray Cerberus-class vessel. Before Ronin or Rodgers could issue a greeting, their commlink nodes chimed with an incoming conference call.

"I hear they let anybody into this party!" said the German-accented voice of Capt. Alfred Jurgenson, the new captain of the Cygnus.

"Welcome to the show, Captain!" replied Ronin. Rodgers greeted Alfred a few seconds later.

"Now that you're underway, our orders remain unchanged to conduct your shakedowns while we escort the shipyard to its new location. How soon do you anticipate beginning?" Ronin asked.

He wasn't surprised to learn that it was immediately.

CHAPTER 20

WAYSIDE STATION

Three months later, Cerberus arrived at Wayside Station. Its latest location was directly opposite that of the Earth as they orbited around opposite sides of Sol. Ronin and Muller were quickly ushered into the office of Adm. Jessup Rodding. They were only mildly surprised to see one of the chairs in the room occupied by the mysterious Colonel Hobson.

"Dan, Diane, good to see you! The past few months have been quite successful for Cerberus," Rodding said in a tone indicating he was mostly in a good mood as he shook hands with them.

"Yes, sir, it went better than we ever hoped," Ronin said. Rodding poured dark caramel-colored bourbon into four glasses and handed one to each of them.

"First, a toast. I understand Cerberus is the best flying brewpub in the galaxy because of Lieutenant Sunderland's brewing expertise, but I guarantee even he can't match this Kentucky bourbon. Salute!" Rodding said.

Feeling the burn as the expensive liquid went down, Ronin nodded in appreciation as he looked down at the bourbon remaining in his glass. Rodding wasn't given to many indulgences, but his taste in fine bourbon was top grade.

"Ah. That's good stuff. Been saving it for your return," Rodding noted to Ronin. "Captain, I have a little surprise for you. You children and parents are here on Wayside, so you'll get some quality family time in before your next deployment."

Ronin looked at the Admiral in surprise. "They are? Why are they here?"

Rodding looked grave for a moment before he responded. "Two reasons. The first reason is you have become so famous on Earth, we feared for their safety and privacy. The media wouldn't leave them alone, and we didn't want agents of the Collective to potentially have any access to them. The second reason will be explained by Colonel Hobson," Rodding said, nodding in the Colonel's direction.

"Captain, as you noted in your log entry after the Battle of the Belt, your suspicions about the economic collapse of the Collective matches our own observations. We're afraid the AC is gearing up to start a new war on Earth before its time runs out. It needs resources, and the Confederacy is the only place the Collective can look to for them. That strike force you wiped out in the Battle of the Belt was a last-ditch attempt to keep the Confederacy from having unfettered access to the solar system and beyond."

Mueller spoke first. "Sirs, is the Collective's fleet still a threat?"

Rodding nodded. "Yes, there are enough remaining frigates and destroyers to cause problems, but we're much more concerned about the situation down on Earth. Now that the fourth Cerberus-class ship is about to launch, we have achieved battle space supremacy and we intend to ramp up the pressure on the Collective with the entire Cerberus-class of ships. Your sister ships are being dispatched on raids to clean up known outposts and the Collective's space stations, locations which were learned from reading the enemy's communications thanks to our AI's cracking the encryption between *Shanwei* and the command and control shuttle you captured."

Ronin nodded. Cutting off the Collective's lifelines to the resources of space would inflict a major hurt on their ability to contest the Confederacy for economic or military victories. It was also the obvious strategic goal, even if the Collective had no idea how the Confederacy was going to achieve that end using the new jump drive ships. Ronin supposed it would come as a terrible shock to the Collective when they finally realized what the Cerberus-class ships could do. He was just glad they brought his family to join him. For the first time in his life, space was safer than remaining on Earth.

"Cerberus will join this rapid reaction force to achieve the objective of cutting the Collective off from space borne resources, Hobson added. "Your raids will generally be against targets in near Earth proximity, with the goal of making the Collective overextend its resources to guard everything because they no longer will be able to predict where we will strike next.

"Also, don't be surprised if Cerberus is called upon later for satellite destruction or orbital bombardment of planetary targets," Hobson concluded.

Ronin's eyebrows rose at the phrase "orbital bombardment." The old legends spoke of some orbital bombardment precipitating The Fall, and it had not happened since.

"Sir, would the Confederacy really abandon the Treat of Midway by launching nukes from orbit?" Ronin asked with a great deal of concern.

Hobson realized he hadn't adequately clarified what such bombardment would involve. He took a sip of the bourbon and responded, "No, we would not initiate a nuclear strike unless responding in kind, or to some other unforeseeable emergency situation. Your rail guns will have targeting information fed to them from Tacnet. We've created some special slugs for you. Their kinetic velocity will be high enough to cause a heck of a blast, but there won't be any toxic or explosive material contained in the slugs. They're just super hardened titanium alloy shells over two-ton solid cores, so they won't burn up entering the atmosphere. Speed will do all the damage that's needed for small targets. They're part of your resupply while Cerberus is here for the week."

Satisfied, Ronin sipped the wonderful bourbon. It was going to be an interesting week.

"Got another interesting item for you," Hobson said.

Ronin and Mueller both looked at him.

"Our AI had some success in descrambling some of the data you brought back from Ninebase. It turns out dark matter was an old, pre-Fall energy source research project. They had pretty much perfected the theory and power generation on a small scale. Their scientists had set up shop at Ninebase to scale it up in a safe, distant place, but they didn't get the chance to finish before the war brought it to a halt. They died where they worked when their air and food ran out."

It was an interesting history lesson, but Ronin didn't see the relevance until Hobson added, "Ceres will soon be on her way to reestablish Ninebase and startup the project. We think we can finish what they started and hopefully upgrade the range of Cerberus' jump drives."

Now that *was interesting,* Ronin thought as he and Mueller shared a glance.

"Maybe we'll have some time to do some exploring a little further from home someday," Mueller noted in a somewhat hopeful tone.

After Mueller and Ronin left Rodding's office, Mueller turned to Ronin out in the hallway. "Never have I been so glad to have my family with me on the same ship," she said to him with a worried face.

"Me too. Now it's my turn again, too. I'll have to take over one of the family-size quarters to accommodate having my kids with me."

Mueller patted Ronin on the shoulder. "I'll take care of having you moved to larger quarters. Go see your family."

As Mueller left to return to Cerberus, Ronin asked the station's AI where his family was staying. The AI informed him. "Your family are currently in the station's guest accommodations, which are quite far from your current location. Do you require directions?"

Dan responded he would need directions as that section was unfamiliar to him. As he followed the AI-provided route to a maglev tube station, Ronin again marveled at the sheer size of Wayside Station. It seemed endless.

A week later, the ship's AI woke up Ronin. For a moment, he was slightly disoriented because he was still unused with the new family quarters. The family had moved in the prior afternoon. As he rubbed the sleep from his eyes, his son, Edward, came in, looking as equally sleepy.

"Dad, it time to get up already?" he groaned as he half fell into Ronin's waiting arms for a good morning hug.

Ronin grinned, "You're as slow to wake as me," he said as he squeezed the boy. "Go get ready for work, hey?" he half told, half asked his son. As Edward stumbled out of Ronin's room to go shower up and get dressed for the day, Ronin's commlink node next to the bed chimed with an incoming call.

"Captain, we're ready to depart," said Lieutenant Anzio. Ronin had rotated Anzio into the third watch while they were in port to start getting her some command experience. "We're resupplied, and the new ordinance is stowed," she added.

Ronin replied, trying not to sound like he just woke up. "Understood, Lieutenant. Take the ship out and I'll be along in about a half hour or so."

Ronin quickly stood, stretched, and hit the showers. *Throw some grub to the little wolves out there, and it'll be just another day at the office,* he thought as he quickly dressed.

As he walked out into his family's common area that was the center of their quarters, Edward and Sarah were eagerly awaiting his arrival. They were very excited at their first full day on Cerberus, and were looking forward to meeting their new schoolmates in the ship's small classroom.

"Dad, does the ship have good food?" Sarah asked, causing Ronin to laugh.

"You'll get used to it kiddo," he said knowingly as the three left to go to the galley for breakfast.

CHAPTER 21

WOLF 14, BATTLE OF THE DARK SIDE

months later, Cerberus appeared near the dark side of Earth's moon, taking a cloud of enemy Type 112 fighters by surprise.

"Launch Tomcats," ordered Captain Ronin as soon as the jump was complete. The war birds rapidly shot out of the ship's launch tubes, in minutes all eighty of them having formed up into two squadrons.

While they were doing so, Lt. Matt LeCroy loudly said, "Incoming ordinance!" as if they all somehow weren't expecting such a hot reception. "They're throwing everything at us, Captain" he added after another moment of reading Tacnet.

"Lieutenant Perez, execute jump," ordered Mueller as soon as the squadron launches were completed. With a flash, Cerberus vanished about a minute before the ordinance arrived.

"Your calculations were perfect, Lieutenant LeCroy," noted Mueller after the jump. "They missed us by a minute."

LeCroy nodded, without taking his eyes of the Tacnet plotting. "Thank you, ma'am. Drone telemetry now reaching us. The Collective's heavy guns can't hit the Tomcats. They're too small, fast and maneuverable. Type 112 enemy fighters are about to engage with our squadrons."

Inside his Tomcat, Sunderland and his rear-seater Chris Tagget were plenty busy. "I count 125 Type 112s," Chris said.

"Roger that. Let's draw them off and keep them busy." Sunderland responded to Chris. Sunderland activated the all-fighter commlink.

"Taurus and Leo squadrons, remember the game plan. Draw them away from the base defense network, then engage," Sunderland added.

A chorus of confirmations acknowledged the order as the fighters began their cat and mouse game to lead the Type 112s out of position.

On the Cerberus bridge, LeCroy followed the clearing of the airspace over the target. Minutes later he reported, "Captain, the squadrons have drawn them off."

Ronin nodded his understanding. "Launch Bulldogs," he responded.

Down in the hangar bay, the four Bulldogs that were waiting heard the order over their open commlink before the deck chief followed by announcing the green light launch status of each ship. "Bulldogs 1 through 4, your boards are green. Launch in sequence," Ronin said.

Each Bulldog quickly left the safety of Cerberus. As they prepared to jump, Pilot Officer Erin Johnson opened a commlink to Corporal Mackey, who was riding in the back with his Bravo team. "We're ready to jump, Corporal," she noted.

"Roger that. Haul the mail, and we'll deliver the pain, Pilot Officer," acknowledged Mackey, who had been following the battle on Tacnet.

Johnson rolled her eyes to herself. *Do Marines recruit for both corniness and cockiness? That was painful.* "Jump in five. Four. Three. Two. One. Jump," she announced over the open commlink channel to all the Bulldogs.

As the other three Bulldogs were synced to Johnson's, the Marine assault group arrived simultaneously roughly two hundred feet over their landing zone. "Jump complete. Nobody's home. Landing now," Johnson announced over the commlink channel.

The Bulldogs settled on the surface, and the Marines spilled out in less than a minute. As soon as they were clear, the Bulldogs lifted off and jumped away.

"Bravo team, Bravo one. Move out," ordered Mackey as the team quickly went into the nearest access building. As the new designated breacher, Pvt. Carlos Guthrey positioned himself outside the airlock as the rest of the team lined up behind him along the wall.

"Execute breech," ordered Cpl. Brett Blackwater.

Since stealth wasn't necessary, this particular breaching didn't involve the breaching jaws. Much to Guthrey's pleasure, it involved placing explosives and blasting their way through.

Bravo team felt the concussion as the airlock blew inwards, making Blackwater thankful they couldn't hear sound in space.

"Clear!" yelled Guthrey over the commlink channel as the next in line quickly scooted through with weapons drawn. The team quickly located the closed hatchway leading to the tunnels to the underground base.

"It's unlocked, Bravo One," reported Bravo 5, Pvt. Terry Allison. "Sounds like an invitation to pay them a visit," he noted.

"Yeah, that's what your mama said last time, too," Guthrey quipped.

"You only wish!" replied Allison, to the guffaws of the rest of the team.

"Alright you animals, get your heads in the game. Move out!" Blackwater replied.

CΞRBΞRUS – DΞLTΛ STΛTION

"Captain, the Bulldogs have returned. They report successful insertion of the Marine teams," reported LeCroy from his Tactical station.

"Good. Alert the deck chief they're back and have them made ready to resupply the Marines as soon as possible."

LeCroy nodded quickly. "Chief Taylor, Bulldogs are incoming. Confirm ready to receive?"

"Aye, we're ready for them! Taylor out," replied a harried-sounding Chief Taylor seconds later.

Ronin opened a commlink from his console node to Capt. Hu Nagun. "Cerberus Actual to *Kitty Hawk* Actual. Boots are on the ground. What's your status?"

The open commlink communicated the sounds of combat from *Kitty Hawk's* bridge for a second before Nagun's voice filled the comm. "We took a few hits from their guns when we got a little too close because we had to help your squadrons as bait for the 112s to draw them off. Damage wasn't to mission critical areas of the ship, and light casualties. Your

Tomcats are still heavily engaged keeping the Type 112s off us. We're staying just below the sight horizon so the base's guns can't target the ship."

Ronin couldn't ask for more than that. "Roger that. Keep us informed if the situation changes. Cerberus Actual, out." He looked over at LeCroy. "How are Taurus and Leo squadrons doing?"

CERBERUS TOMCAT SQUADRONS - WOLF 14

The sunless sky on the moon's dark side was filled with bright missile streaks and engine flares. If he wasn't so busy jinking and trying to stay alive, Sunderland would have thought it quite pretty.

"Sunderland, we've lost another bird in Taurus squadron," reported Chris.

"How many are gone?" came the reply. "Fourteen destroyed in Taurus, three more disabled. Twelve gone from Leo, four disabled. Thirty-eight Type 112s destroyed. Unknown number disabled."

The view outside the Tomcat suddenly spun wildly as Sunderland rolled it and nosed down towards the moon to get a better attack angle on a couple of 112s who themselves were trying to gang up on someone from Leo squadron.

"I sure hope those Marines find what they're looking for fast," muttered Sunderland after he closed the channel.

BRAVO AND ECHO TEAMS - STAGING AREA

"Echo 3, Shift your fire to the right and take out that turret!" Blackwater yelled over the combined commlink used by Bravo and Echo teams.

Echo team's heavy weapons specialist, Pvt. Rhee Lee, immediately shifted his fire. For the moment, he was in a reasonably protected position shooting through the narrow line of sight created from behind a pair of metal shipping containers. Bravo team already lost three Marines in the trap sprung by the Collective's troopers who were waiting in the other end of the large underground staging area. There were only three ways out of the staging area. The way they came in, and the two passages on the far side, which were currently defended by troopers not terribly inclined to give them up. Once the trap was sprung, Echo and Bravo quickly blew away the defensive auto-turrets, but the troopers were much more difficult to dislodge.

"How far do you think it is to the far end?" Blackwater asked his opposite number, Echo 1.

Cpl. Toshi Kanagawa risked a quick glance over the top of his cover position. "About 75 yards, give or take," he replied. Just then, the catwalk along the upper right side of the chamber blew up in a spectacularly pyrotechnic display after Bravo 6 launched a rocket grenade at it to stop the troopers who were advancing along it. Kanagawa's question that followed his reply was drowned out by two more explosions and gunfire.

"Echo 1, say again?" Blackwater yelled.

"I said, we can provide covering fire for our rocket grenades. See if we can take out their positions inside those passages? They're pretty far."

Blackwater thought about it for a moment as he watched Bravo 6 try to get under cover despite the light gravity, which gave him an idea. "We can throw grenades there!"

Kanagawa shook his head in disbelief. "What! Nobody can throw that far!"

Blackwater smiled evilly. "You mean, nobody can throw that far, on Earth."

Kanagawa froze for a moment as he processed that. "Oh, YEAH! I didn't factor in the low gravity!"

Blackwater responded quickly, "Echo and Bravo teams, on my count, use hand grenades synced to my signal. Echo team, take the left tunnel, Bravo take the right. Make sure you adjust your aim for the low gravity."

While the rocket grenades relied mostly on their kinetic energy to cause damage by punching holes in target, the powerful hand grenades relied solely on explosive power for more of an area damage effect. Moments later, both teams had the pins pulled on their grenades as they crouched behind their cover and waiting for the signal.

"Three, two, one. Now!" Blackwater called, as they all did their best to throw the grenades without exposing themselves to the incoming fire. Most of the grenades were thrown accurately enough, and as they arrived in the target area, Blackwater eye-clicked the Detonate All button option that was shining on the inside of his visor as he braced himself.

The thunderous simultaneous explosions of fourteen grenades shook the entire staging area, with several pieces of shrapnel ricocheting off the walls behind them and from the cover they were hiding behind.

"Bravo 4, send up the Butterfly! Where are the rest of them?" Guthrey screen-clicked the Launch button to send the tiny Butterfly drone that was attached to his back up into the air for a look. Its sensors wasted no time in marking the remaining enemy targets. "Acquisition. Sending targeting info to your screens," Guthrey reported.

Blackwater and Kanagawa saw there were fourteen remaining troopers. Three of them appeared wounded.

"Echo 2, job opportunity." said Kanagawa. "Link your Stinger rounds to the targeting data from the Butterfly."

Cpl. Adrian Longman was quite pleased to comply. He quickly selected Airburst mode as he wanted to inflict a lot of pain. The guided rounds would burst into deadly slivers of metal just before hitting the designated target. He was ready within seconds. "Firing now," he said as he fired the large, guided rounds to the target hiding behind a loading vehicle as the targeting data indicated this trooper had the clearest view of fire.

The magnetically propelled, hypervelocity round was far too fast for the eyes to follow, but its downrange effects could not be missed as the round passed over the loading vehicle and burst into shrapnel that was automatically directed towards the designated target.

"Target one, down." Longman noted dryly in his Aussie accent. He methodically fired at the next most dangerous target. "Target two, down." Longman repeated this process until all the targets were down and half his ammunition expended.

"Echo team, secure the far end of the room. Bravo team, search for survivors," ordered Blackwater as he was in overall command of the combined assault team.

Kanagawa did a weapons and ammo check after the room was secured. "We're running pretty low on ammo," he said to Blackwater, who nodded at the expected report.

"I've already called in Bulldog 4 for resupply." Blackwater then opened a commlink to Private Cupper. "Bravo 6, take Echo 5 and 6 with you to ferry the resupplies Bulldog 4 is bringing to our landing zone."

The assigned three acknowledged and they quickly returned to the landing pad because they were getting dangerously low on ammunition.

C≡RB≡RUS TOMCAT SQUADRONS – WOLF 14

"*Kitty Hawk* Actual, this is Cerberus CAG. Can you shoot these guys off our tails if we swing them past your position?"

Sunderland was jinking his Tomcat wildly trying to shake the four Type 112s pursuing Sunderland and his wingman. They were too good.

"Cerberus CAG, this is *Kitty Hawk* Actual. We can do you one better. Sending you the coordinates for a hot spot. Go through there in two minutes. If you're coming through fifteen seconds later, you're a dead man."

Sunderland didn't know what to make of that. From what he knew of Captain Nagun, he was all business during a fight so if he said don't be late, you best not be late.

"Affirm. We'll be there! CAG out."

Sunderland switched to the commlink with his wingman. "Bouncer, you hear that? Two minutes fifteen seconds. The clock on your screen is counting down."

Bouncer wasted no time in responding. "Affirmative. Right behind you."

As he closed the commlink, Nagun turned to his tactical officer. "OK, Petty, time to see if you're right. Execute hot spot."

The *Kitty Hawk* synced computers with Sunderland's and his wingmen, then suddenly launched several missiles and a cloud of rail gun rounds at the designated spot. Due to the distance from the ship, they would arrive at the designated spot when the synced timers reached zero.

"I hope we can keep these guys occupied for two more minutes without getting blown outta the sky," Sunderland muttered to himself as he threw his Tomcat into a wild spin to barely avoid a line of lead tracer ordinance spewed by one of his pursuers. The tracer rounds passed by so close they lit up the Tomcat's cockpit, and Sunderland was sure there would be scorch marks along the side of his fuselage.

"That's way, way too close for comfort, CAG!" said Chris from the rear seat.

Sunderland snorted in reply before he was able to think of anything witty. "Just trying to keep them entertained!"

It was the longest two minutes of Sunderland's life. His Tomcat took a few rounds through the fuselage, but the ship integrity wasn't too compromised. As the two Tomcats' flew through the soon-to-be-hot-spot, Sunderland felt the hairs on his neck rise with that feeling you get when you just managed to avoid a speeding car.

The Type 112s never stood a chance, as two of them were obliterated by the kinetic ordinance that was timed to impact the fighters. The following two realized the trap too late, and attempted to bob and weave the rounds. They were too busy to see the missiles, which ended them from behind.

As his pursuers were suddenly erased from his long list of concerns, Sunderland looked at his Tacnet plot. "Scopes have cleared up quite a lot. Only thirty bandits remaining, and they're bugging out," Chris noted. "What's our status?" Sunderland asked.

Moments later, Chris responded, "Taurus down to ten effectives, Leo only has nine. There's a handful of disabled Tomcat's that might be repairable. Search and Rescue birds are collecting our survivors. Six are alive so far."

CERBERUS – DELTA STATION

Ronin was shocked at the carnage in the Cerberus Tomcat squadrons. Seventy-five percent of Taurus squadron wiped out, slightly more for Leo. He knew this would be a tough assignment when the orders came down to hit the newly discovered moon base, hard, but that did nothing to make him feel better about the exorbitant cost in pilots and crews. "This had better be worth it," he grumbled to Mueller when she approached. She nodded, not saying anything. What was there to say?

"Cerberus Actual, Gamma 1. We've taken out the base's surface-to-ship defenses. Do you copy?" Ronin thumbed his reply button. "Gamma 1, Cerberus Actual copies. *Kitty Hawk* is sending reinforcement unit to your position. ETA five minutes."

Blackwater quickly acknowledged the update.

BRAVO AND ECHO TEAMS – STAGING AREA

The 6s (Bravo and Echo) and Echo 5 finished unloading the resupply from Bulldog 4. As Pilot Officer Reggie Parsons lifted off, he was just about to jump the Bulldog back to Delta Station when a weapons lock alarm suddenly sounded.

A second later, the Bulldog exploded from the missile impact. "There's someone still alive in that turret next to the landing pad!" As they were in an airless environment up in the landing area, all the Marine teams heard the unidentified call at the same time over the commlink channel.

"Gamma 3, Gamma 1. Do you have eyes on the target?" called Blackwater over the commlink. The target had already been designated by Bravo 5 over the Tacnet.

"Roger that. We're setting up rocket grenades now."

Suddenly a loud voice broke into the commlink, "Belay that! Take cover. Incoming!"

There was barely enough time for the warning and command to register before two unseen kinetic bombs impacted directly on the turret. Despite being 500 yards away from where the resupply was unloaded by the three Marines, the force of the impact knocked them off their feet in the low gravity.

Captain Nagun had fitted out his ship's Bulldogs with a kinetic weapons package in case some extra boom was needed to help get the reinforcement Marine units safely to the surface. "Target eliminated," announced the pilot of the lead Bulldog, as they settled down and quickly discharged four units of Marines.

With all the extra hands, the resupplies were quickly delivered to the underground staging area where Echo and Bravo teams held station.

Corporal Mackey spoke to the four teams now under his company command. "Echo and Bravo, gear up. Two minutes till we move out."

Blackwater didn't bother to ask about casualties. Despite their armored exosuits, his Tacnet feed reported three dead on Bravo team, two for Echo, and one wounded but operational. Zeta and Theta teams obviously had none as they'd just arrived.

The teams quickly made ready for the push further down into the base. Zeta team's electronic warfare specialist, Private Gregory Paulson had hacked into the base network.

"Bravo 1, Zeta 3. Intel from the base net coming over your screen now." Paulson announced over the commlink.

Blackwater watched the screen display on the inside of his helmet that Private Paulson sent. The path to their objective was clearly marked, giving him the route from the choke point they now held. He opened a separate command channel to the 1s of the three other teams in the company.

"Ones. There's only the single route down. Easily defensible because there's another choke point, here." As Blackwater emphasized the word "here," their screens lit up with the point he had designated.

"I don't like this target profile," muttered Theta 1 muttered.

"Yeah. They know we're here now. It'd be a shooting gallery," agreed Zeta 1.

Blackwater's AI had been listening in, of course, and startled the team leaders by suddenly speaking. "Corporal Mackey, analysis of the base blueprints that were obtained by Private Paulson suggests there may be an unconventional, alternate route to consider."

Blackwater's first thought was something back on the surface or something, so he asked the AI to continue.

"The base has a large air duct system. I suggest your team gain access through this wall, then follow the route indicated on your screen maps." As the AI said this, a red arrow blinked on all the 1's individual screens to identify the wall that needed breaching, followed by a map with the alternate route superimposed over it.

Theta 1 thought about it before commenting first. "Runs right through the main air plant, but we can get through that."

Echo 1 quickly added a highlight to the map. "Right here we can pop back into the main passageway behind the choke point, and it's on the inside of the security perimeter for their safe zone. We can hit them from behind and grab the objective."

Pleased, Blackwater, who was company leader by virtue of the earliest swearing-in date of among the 1s that were on the mission, decided. "I like it. Simple. Easy to remember. Avoids a near certain kill box of a choke point. AI, you're not getting paid enough."

For some reason, Blackwater's AI had developed a somewhat quirky personality in its time with Blackwater, which isn't unusual. Marine AI's had been designed to develop their own personalities to better mesh with the team leaders. The AI's quirky personality startled the other three team leaders when it suddenly responded in a very seductive female voice, "Oh, I couldn't agree more, darling!"

"Darling?" smirked Echo 1.

"You call me that again, I'll kill you so hard you're whole family will die along with you." threatened Blackwater. The other 1s burst into laughter at the exchange. Their own AIs often did something similar to them, so they knew this kind of stuff happens.

"Echo 5, job opportunity," called Kanagawa.

"You got something for me boss-man?" responded Pvt. David Danfries as the rest of Echo team perked up now that the leaders had obviously decided how to continue their incursion.

"Blueprints for the base are telling us we want to be in the air duct on the other side of that wall to avoid a kill box downrange. Make it happen." Kanagawa ordered. The team's helmet screens likewise showed a blinking spot on the wall where they needed to make a hole.

"My pleasure, Echo 1." Danfries responded as he grabbed his gear and some boomsticks before bouncing over to the wall. He inspected the wall for a few moments and compared his thoughts to the blueprints. "Echo 5, can you make a hole?" asked Echo 4, Pak.

Danfries smirked inside his helmet even though no one could see it. "One boomstick should do it," he responded before spending the next few minutes rigging up his breaching explosive. The rest of the Marines migrated over behind cover in anticipation of the blast. *Knock, knock,* thought Danfries as he finished the rigging.

"Fire in the hole! Fire in the hole!"

The blast was way more boom than either Zeta or Theta teams had fully expected, because while Danfries had said one boomstick ought to do it, he used two under the time honored Marine boomstick formula of "P" for Plenty. Why use just one, when two is twice as satisfying? Since Bravo and Echo teams were plenty familiar with Danfries faithful observance of the P for Plenty formula, they weren't *completely* taken by surprise by the powerful explosion that shook the staging area and filled it with smoke and debris. They just hadn't figured Danfries was crazy enough to use two full sticks.

After the dust settled, Echo 4 sent a Butterfly drone into the gaping hole into the wall. "Clear left. Clear right. Sending the drone down the ventilation shaft now."

Pak and the rest of the company watched the feed on the inside of their suit screens as they held their positions. In minutes, the speedy little drone arrived at the giant air circulation plant.

"Clear to the air plant, Bravo 1!" reported Pak.

Blackwater nodded inside his suit helmet, so no one actually saw it. Old habits die hard.

Mackey wasted no time. "Echo team, take point. Then Zeta and Theta. Bravo team is vanguard. Go! Go! Go!"

No one argued with Bravo team moving to the rear as the team had sustained the most casualties. There wasn't truly a safe spot when fighting your way into an enemy base anyway. Twenty minutes later, Echo team reached the air circulation plant and designated entry point.

"Echo 5, can you breach or no?" Kanagawa asked.

After Pak drilled a hole in a small spot and flew a Butterfly through to the hall way to confirm it was empty, Danfries was joined by Gonzales as they began tearing apart a side panel to remove a piece of machinery so they could crawl through the space into a large air vent into the hall. With the extra power of their exosuits, and the help of a military grade cutter, they were ready in merely five minutes. Following their progress, Pak reported "Still clear, Echo 1."

That was all Kanagawa needed. "Echo team, set up a defensive perimeter while the following teams join us."

Echo team scrambled to make it happen. Soon the company was in the hallway, as Echo team led the way to the objective. Taking point, Echo 2 signaled for the company to halt as he stealthily approached a T-intersection. "Echo 4, have your Butterfly peek around that corner."

The drone had no sooner rounded the corner than an energy beam fried it and burnt out its electronics.

"Found it," Longman remarked with a grin as he and Pak watched the video and Tacnet feed.

"Auto turrets, and gunner hiding behind that portable barrier on the right." Pak noted.

"Grenades on three?" Longman asked Pak with a note of excitement in his voice. "Oh, I LIKE grenades!" Pak enthusiastically responded.

They pulled their pins, and Longman counted down. "Three. Two. One. Throw!"

Their grenades flew the twenty yards to the defensive position held by the enemy. Despite the speed and the fact there were two of them to choose from, the auto turret still managed to ricochet a few rounds off Longman's armored arm as it threw the grenade around the corner. "Argh!" he responded in surprise, unintentionally managing to sound like an old pirate from the legends and accidentally meriting a new nickname at the same time.

"Echo 2, are you injured? Your suit isn't showing damage on Tacnet." asked the Echo team corpsman, Nancy Dos.

"No, I'm fine. The rounds ricocheted without damage. Just took me by surprise because it was so fast." Longman said.

"Oh, then you're telling us you're now a pirate with that 'argh' business?" noted Pak dryly with a teasing tone.

Longman suddenly stopped, only too late becoming aware he was getting stuck with a new nickname. "I REALLY hate you guys!" he said with a sheepish sound, and causing the Echo team commlink to fill with all sorts of laughter at his expense.

The next Butterfly launched by Pak showed the powerful grenades had done the job. Both the gunner and the auto turret's were down. "Clear!" he called, prompting the rest of the team to pour down the passage to a closed, armored hatch.

"Armored. Who armors a hatch deep inside some base?" asked Longman when he reached it before the rest of the team.

"Echo 5. Job opportunity. And don't blow up our objective with too much Plenty in your formula this time."

Danfries shooed his team back to safety around the corner at the 'T' again while he rigged up some plastique and shaped charges. Once he inserted the remote detonators, he too scrambled back to rejoin his team, while the other teams kept watch.

Knock, knock, Danfries said to himself, triggering the charges. He had set them in a cascading circular pattern on the wall about two feet beyond the outline of the hatchway. "That was very civilized and totally unsatisfactory," he muttered as he looked at his handiwork. They had blown a hole into the wall and he easily pushed the armored hatchway down. No massive explosion. What a letdown.

Echo team and Zeta team quickly secured the three rooms behind the armored former hatchway. "Bravo 1, we have the objective. No resistance. He decided not to swallow the cyanide pills they gave him and put his country first, so we bound him up. Ready for egress."

As they were bringing the bound prisoner out, there was a Tacnet warning accompanied by distant gunfire and two explosions. "Contact! Bravo 1 to all teams. Enemy troopers massing beyond our entry point! Hustle up and get the objective out here. Theta team, join us in the vanguard and reinforce our position while Echo and Zeta escort our guest."

Theta team was moving back to Bravo's vanguard positions at high speed. Echo and Zeta were right on their heels. The entire company needed to become scarce before the Collective troopers recovered enough to get themselves organized and counterattack in force instead of the piecemeal resistance encountered so far.

CƎRBƎRUS – DƎLTⱯ STATION

"Captain, Tacnet shows the assault teams have captured the objective and are engaged in a fighting withdrawal from the facility," LeCroy reported to Ronin.

"Status of the enemy fighters?" Mueller asked.

"Still bugged out. They lost way too many to mount a return unless some new squadrons show up," LeCroy noted.

"Alert Lieutenant Taketa to expect incoming casualties from the ground assault teams," Ronin ordered. Taketa acknowledged the order, and reported in that he and his medical team had patched up a handful of injured pilots who had been returned to the ship by the search and rescue teams.

MⱯRINƎ COMPⱯNY – STAGING ARƎⱯ

The fighting withdrawal by Bravo and Theta teams had taken a terrible toll on the Collective's troopers. More than a hundred of those troopers lay strewn and broken for the entire distance back from where contact had been made.

As Bravo and Theta prepared to follow Echo and Zeta and reenter the staging area they had taken earlier, the 2s of Bravo and Theta quickly planted magnetic mines while the rest of the teams occupied the troopers with heavy fire. Zeta 2 also laid mines at the actual passageway into the staging area, which they skipped by venturing into the air system.

"Bulldogs, this is Bravo 1, ready for evac. Over," Blackwater called after they were ready and on their way to the surface landing zone. The enemy troopers were hanging back and not trying to rush straight into their guns or mines for the moment.

The answer came quickly. "Bravo 1. Sixty seconds, mark."

Blackwater relayed the message. "All teams, sixty seconds! Echo 1, get the objective onto Bulldog 1 with your team. Bravo team on Bulldog 2 with Gamma team, which is holding the landing zone and waiting for us. Theta and Zeta, your ride is the last Bulldog."

Blackwater's orders were quickly acknowledged by each team's leaders as they organized themselves to speed the loading process.

C⊑RB⊑RUS – D⊑LTA STATION

"Captain, Bulldogs 1 and 2 have returned. I've notified the medical bay of their arrival." LeCroy reported when Tacnet updated their position.

Ronin looked over at Lieutenant Delgado. "Lieutenant, open a commlink to *Kitty Hawk*."

A moment later, Delgado responded, "Commlink open, Captain."

Ronin cleared his throat before speaking. "*Kitty Hawk* Actual, Cerberus Actual. Our birds have returned to the nest. Interrogate status."

From his ship's position just over the horizon from the base, Capt. Hu Nagun responded. "Cerberus, this is Kitty Hawk Actual. Our birds are aboard. Tomcats are still controlling the skies. Kitty Hawk standing by."

An ancient general once observed a military truism that no plan survives initial contact with the enemy. Which meant Ronin was surprised because this seemed to be the first time that everything seemed to follow the plan as originally approved. "Execute Operation Goodbye."

Nagun acknowledged the order.

Leaving it to Kitty Hawk to collect its own squadrons of Tomcats as well as Cerberus' Tomcats, Ronin ordered Cerberus to jump away with its prize.

KITTY HAWK – WOLF 14

Nagun looked at his tactical officer. "Execute Operation Goodbye. Helm, get us in position to bring the pain."

Seconds later, the helmsman confirmed the coordinates that had been pre-selected during the operational planning before the battle. "Coordinates laid in, Captain."

Nagun nodded, then replied, "Take us in."

Kitty Hawk reached its bombardment position a few hours later. "Rail gun crews report ready to open fire, Captain," reported the tactical officer.

"Fire!" Nagun ordered. He was in no mood to delay, and it was time to get away before it was too late. The main view screen was showing a split screen of optics taken from several observational drones that had been positioned so they could watch the show and assess damage. Nagun allowed the rail gun volleys to continue for one minute. He wanted to erase the still dangerous base to avenge all the Tomcat crews and Marines that had been sacrificed to grab their high value objective.

"Evasive action," added Nagun, somewhat unnecessarily.

While there wasn't any ordinance on the way to wipe out the Kitty Hawk that they could see, there was little need to take the risk when the drones would take care of watching the show.

Several hours later, the high-speed kinetic rail gun ordinance had crossed the huge distance between where it originated on the Kitty Hawk, and the lunar base. Each of the one-ton slugs impacted with the equivalent power of a one-megaton nuclear weapon. Still sitting on the bridge, Nagun watched the base disappear forever under the wrath of thirty rail gun impacts. There would be debris floating over the site for centuries before the weak lunar gravity could pull it back down again.

"Heck of a calling card, Captain," murmured the XO, Steve Fisher, to Nagun as the two watched the show on the view screen while standing next to each other. "Hopefully the Collective will be too discouraged to try to build any more secret lunar bases in the future. Think they'll invite us to any more house parties?" he added.

Nagun had a slight smile turning up the corner of his mouth as he softly snorted with a slight "humph" sound. "I reckon they're too civilized to invite barbarians like us in the future. We're boorish house guests. Always leave behind a huge mess."

Nagun watched for a few more minutes. "Fisher, take over and get us underway for Wayside Station. Have the section heads copy their reports to my attention. I want to take a look at our damage and repair progress before I head to my ready room. After that I have work up a post-battle assessment for the big brains at the Admiralty."

Minutes later, Kitty Hawk finally departed while the debris cloud on the dark side of the moon continued to expand.

CHAPTER 22

WAYSIDE STATION

Cerberus wasted no time docking with Wayside Station and delivering its high value passenger. Even thought it was a relatively short mission from Ronin's perspective, they needed to take on more Marine ordinance as well as replace the Marines they had lost. While that was occurring under the critical eyes of the Cerberus load masters, Ronin and Mueller were reporting as ordered to Admiral Rodding's office.

They were quickly shown in to his office. They sat at the conference table while Rodding poured glasses of his preferred bourbon from his crystal decanter for all of them. "Time for some Old Prohibition bourbon to celebrate, and to commemorate our dead," Rodding said somberly as he handed the glasses to them. "To those who are no longer with us," he toasted, holding his glass up for Ronin and Mueller to clink theirs against before they took sips.

"Sir, I've been wondering what your brand of bourbon was," Ronin remarked as he looked approvingly at the glass and its dark, smooth contents. "Strange name, though."

Rodding's left eyebrow cocked upward in surprise. "You mean why is it called Prohibition?" he replied. Seeing nods of confusion on their faces, it was time to impart a little knowledge.

"Prohibition is a little-known era in American history from well before The Fall. It was still a young country at the time, and there was some sort of morals based political movement that managed to ban the production and consumption of alcoholic beverages. Like all such movements, it was a complete failure. It gave birth to violent organized crime syndicates loosely referred to as The Mob, which were created to cater to the country's continued alcohol indulgences. The failure was of such magnitude, the law was repealed a few years later, but the problems it created continued on for many years."

Impressed by Rodding's historical alacrity, Ronin said, "I had no idea! Our schooling didn't make mention of the period for some reason."

Rodding nodded. "I'm not surprised. I had a few history classes in college, but so many records were lost in The Fall that not much is known about Prohibition beyond those broad brush strokes I painted for you."

Rodding took another sip of Old Prohibition. "New orders for you. Cerberus is to stay in the vicinity of Wayside Station for the moment and make yourselves available to us if called upon. Due to the rapidly crumbling situation on Earth, we're going to sweat the high value package you retrieved from the moon base during what's being dubbed The Battle of the Dark Side. If he provides us good intel, Cerberus might be ordered in to action on short notice to take advantage of it."

Mueller's curiosity finally got the best of her. "Admiral, who was the high value target that we snatched from the base?"

"Now that it's been decided that Cerberus is likely the ship that will be used to act on any intel he provides, you're cleared to be in the know. It's Igor Kuznetsov. He's the head of the State Security apparatus for the entire Collective. Igor came from the part of Asia that was once called Russia before The Fall. Up north near the Arctic Circle where the radiation and virus never reached. He's valuable enough that Kitty Hawk was ordered to obliterate the base and any trace of our presence at the end of the operation."

As Rodding finished, he took another sip to wet his whistle.

"Any word on dark matter, Sir? It's been months."

Rodding shook his head. "Nothing, so far. The big brains that went to Ninebase are a secretive bunch. They'll have something to say when they have something to say. Until then, radio silence."

After they finished up with Rodding, Ronin and Mueller stopped for a bite to eat at one of the station's restaurants.

"What do you think about what the admiral said regarding the current state of the Collective?" Mueller asked Ronin before she took a bite of her club sandwich.

Before replying, Ronin took a spoonful of the wonderful chicken and vegetable soup. He had delighted in the discovery that the establishment served steaming bowls of Booyah – the chef also hailed from the Green Bay area and specialized in its local cuisine. Booyah, as was traditional in Green Bay, was just a soup made with whole chickens (without the feathers), and stringed vegetables. The most 'sacred' part of the meal's preparation required cooking it overnight in a large vat under the careful watch of a chef who drank beer throughout the cooking process. Dan thought with amusement as he ate, *It's always debatable whether more beer is consumed during the eating of the Booyah, or the making of it.*

"The Admiralty and fleet intelligence believe the economic collapse of the Collective will drive them to open warfare down on the planet very soon to try to cull the troublemakers in their population by using the damage from our retaliation to help keep them under control. Just like how the old legends say The Fall began."

That was not the hopeful sounding answer Mueller wanted to hear. "I just hope we can stop it from happening again," she said quietly. "Things are so desperate, we can't take any chances and go easy on them anymore."

Ronin nodded slowly, with a resigned look on his face.

CHAPTER 23

WOLF 78

Three months later, the Cerberus crew was exhausted by the frenetic pace of operations. They were still on call for Wayside's needs, but that meant they had been on duty without any relief and thrown into one combat action after another. "We've been extremely lucky to sustain as little damage as we have so far, Dan," noted Mueller as the two of them sat in his ready room and discussed the next, upcoming operation.

"Three kinetic strikes repaired. One hundred and twelve crew dead, and some fifty-plus Marines gone. Another 200 injured and rotated for replacements. Hard to quantify that as lucky, but somehow it is. We should have been erased by any of those strikes, instead of them passing through non-critical areas," Ronin replied. "The crew is tired," he added.

Mueller leaned back in her seat and stretched for a moment. The two of them had noticeably dark circles under their eyes. She yawned as she tried to speak through it.

"Seems like we've been operating nearer to Earth orbit each time we've been sent out to cause trouble."

Ronin nodded. "I haven't told you this, but I spoke with my counterparts on the Ceres and Cygnus. Captain Rogers mentioned the Ceres has been operating much like we have with the exception of the Battle of the Dark Side. For them, it's been all hit-and-runs. Cause some hurt, blow up something, and disappear before they can be targeted. What stands out is she also noted they've also been getting closer and closer to Earth with their missions. Same as Cerberus."

Mueller looked up at him. "What about Cygnus?"

"Cygnus has been guarding the *Argo*, wherever it's currently hiding, and launching strikes further out in the system. It has hit some more distant targets and cleared the known bases on the outskirts of the system. Two more Cerberus-class ships are nearly ready."

Ronin finished, taking a sip of his very dark, strong coffee and trying to stay alert.

"These all seem like signs the Collective is collapsing, and the area of the system under its control rapidly shrinking."

Ronin nodded. "My thoughts exactly. Like a rope tightening around the victim."

Their discussion was interrupted by a soft beeping indicating an incoming message.

"Captain, priority message from Admiral Rodding."

Ronin glanced over to Mueller as he leaned forward to accept the message.

"Here we go again," he said before opening the video channel. "Cerberus Actual, go ahead, Admiral."

Rodding wasted no time on communication protocols. "Captain Ronin, we've become aware of a small, three ship detachment of the Collective's vessels streaking away from Earth orbit at unusually high speeds. The ships seem to be using fusion booster rockets for some reason, so they're arriving in the belt far sooner than would be normal for a trip from Earth. The detachment is one larger ship that we believed was a cargo vessel, and two of their newer frigates, which have never been used in combat before. Intercept and destroy the frigates, and figure out what the story with the cargo ship is."

Mueller and Ronin looked at each other, then Ronin replied. "Admiral, what are we to do with the cargo vessel? Destroy it?"

Rodding shook his head. "You have carte blanche discretionary authority regarding the cargo vessel. Other than being high value cargo, as told to us by the package you retrieved from the Dark Side, we don't have insight as to exactly what it's hauling. Nor do we know why it was boosted to the belt so quickly other than the obvious observation that it's cargo was deemed precious enough to go to such precautionary extremes."

Ronin's eyebrows rose a few millimeters. "If it's that valuable enough for the Collective to protect, it's valuable enough for us to try to keep them from keeping it. We'll look into it, Admiral."

Rodding forced a tired smile. "I know you will. The pace of operations is wearing on us all, so try to avoid unnecessary risks. Good luck, and good hunting. Rodding out."

Ronin pulled up the Tacnet data forwarded with Rodding's message. As he and Mueller began studying it, he noticed the enemy formation's predicted flight path took it into an area of the Belt which spacers had informally dubbed The Cloud. It was so named because long ago, several large asteroids had met catastrophic ends and broken up into massive dust clouds sprinkled with plenty of decent sized rocks. "They're running for The Cloud. Good place to get lost quickly and not be found if you don't want to be found." he remarked.

Mueller nodded as she looked at the Tacnet plot. "You thinking what I'm thinking, Dan? Jump out there ahead of them and prepare a hot reception for them in The Cloud?"

Ronin smiled coldly. "My thoughts exactly. That cargo ship can't be maneuverable at all, especially with the boosted speed. That means a high probability of entry into The Cloud at the predicted entry point at a predictable time. Perfect setup for an ambush."

Mueller smiled coldly in response. "We know when and where, so now we just need to map out the how."

Ronin expanded an area of the plot that was inside The Cloud, and he thought for a few moments as he considered the setup. "They'll be flying blind, and will have burned much of their available fuel to reduce speeds for safe transit inside The Cloud. We know this particular point right here is a natural choke point from past experience. Only one possible route through. Let's designate this ambush point, Wolf 78, and spring the trap here."

As he spoke, the area marked by him began flashing in red. He labeled the point "Wolf" to reflect the traditional pre-designation of an attack coordinate in space. The two of them looked it over for a while, then Mueller opened a commlink using her collar node to Cerberus' tactical officer, LeCroy, who was off duty and working up a sweat down in the gym.

"LeCroy, sorry to bother you during your workout, but can you come up to the Captain's ready room right away?"

The sounds of an active gymnasium provided an acoustic background to his reply. "Yes, ma'am. Be prepared for the smell though." Both Ronin and Mueller laughed at his reply.

* * *

A few days later, Cerberus jumped into The Cloud. "Jump one complete, Captain," announced Perez from the helm.

"Scanners are fouled, as expected," Delacroix noted right after.

"Lieutenant Sunderland, launch your Bulldogs," Ronin ordered over the commlink he opened from his console. Sunderland acknowledged, then switched over to the commlink for the Bulldog crews.

"All right, you savages, you heard the Captain. Time to go to work."

The waiting Bulldogs quickly launched, and jumped away. After they left, Cerberus began launching drones, then micro jumping elsewhere to seed even more drones. This process would repeat itself for some time.

***

Days later, Perez was finally able to report after they finished drone seeding. "Jump twenty-two, complete, Captain."

LeCroy swiftly began reading the telemetry from the drones. "All drones online and functioning correctly, sending the go dark order now."

Mueller and Ronin glanced at each other as she stood next to his command chair. "Now we wait," she remarked.

"Optics from the observation drones outside The Cloud confirms the enemy formation is still approaching the predicted entry point on the same vector. Time of arrival in two days." reported LeCroy.

Not quite two days later, Ronin fell out of bed early and caught up on intelligence reports while his children still slept. He always had difficulty sleeping the night before an operation. Today was no different. As he sat in the common area and read, one report in particular caught his attention:

> Sources inside the Collective have reported food riot driven acts of rebellion occurring throughout the Collective. Government control over St. Petersburg and Liuzhou ended violently when they were seized by the rioters. In an act of vengeance for their brutal suppression of the people, the former officials and their families were captured and publicly tortured to death.

Things are worsening rapidly. What happens when their government lashes out? Ronin wondered as he sipped his coffee. His answer was located several paragraphs later, where the report noted the Collective's government troopers slaughtered tens of thousands in a failed takeover of a medium-sized city in Siberia.

Hours later, Ronin stepped on to the bridge. "Report," he said to LeCroy as we walked out of the hatchway.

"Enemy detachment is right where we want them. They're entering The Cloud outskirts now. They have scouts forward of their position, but nothing we can't handle."

Ronin already knew all that as he had been following the progress while he was catching up on the overnight intelligence reports. He walked over and sat in the command chair that was just vacated by Mueller as she had been standing watch during his downtime.

"Step into my parlor, said the spider to the fly," he murmured to her as they glanced at each other with a knowing look.

The corner of her mouth curved upwards in a cold smile. "Nobody here to bother you big, tough brutes. Come on in. Everything is nice and safe."

LeCroy put the Tacnet plot on the forward view screen while they tracked the ships. Hours later, LeCroy broke the quiet on the bridge.

"They've reached the first turn and are starting down the next lane. Estimated arrival at Wolf 78 in three hours," Ronin said, nodding. The hours were going to crawl by.

BULLDOG 1

Johnson watched the progress of the enemy detachment for hours as it approached Wolf 78. If time could stand still, she was sure it could only happen while waiting to spring an ambush.

"Patience was never your virtue," wryly noted Patterson as he heard Johnson shifting in her seat. Again.

Soon he heard Johnson snacking on chocolate. "You got chocolate?" he asked hopefully. Anticipation always made him get the hungries, same as happened to Johnson.

She half turned and tossed one his way. "Good boy!" Johnson said.

Patterson managed to bark out an "Arf!" before chomping away as he continued watching the Tacnet plot that was being lasered on a tight beam to their Bulldog from passive drone optics only. Finally, the count-down grew short. "Thirty seconds to Wolf 78," he said.

Patterson began counting down aloud. "Ten seconds. Five. They've reached the target area, and they're slowing to make the turn."

The turn was unexpectedly sharper than the Collective's navigation charts showed, courtesy of Cerberus' pushing rocks around to make it that way in the days before the detachment arrived.

Johnson nodded. "Time for the dramatic unveiling," she remarked.

Patterson had been just waiting to push the button for hours. "With pleasure," he responded.

KURSK

On board the bridge of the People's Ship that was named the Kursk, Capt. Ivor Remus and his navigator were engaged in a heated discussion.

"Comrade-Captain, the navigation charts do not align with the route we have taken! There's no guarantee we can make it to the safe zone," said Michail Kamisky, the navigator.

"You saw for yourself, the way was blocked," Remus replied, somewhat annoyed. "You wish to drive us through a cluster of asteroids instead?" Neither Captain Remus or Kamisky noticed Dimitri Volodovsky, the ship's political officer, approaching them.

"Comrades. Is just a small field? Comrade-Captain will return us to prior course soon. Yes?"

Kamisky and Remus had worked together for years, so there was a level of trust between them. They both trusted their instincts to avoid political officers like the plague, which was the unspoken message that passed between them with but a brief glance in each other's direction.

"Comrade Volodovsky, I will endeavor to return us to the proscribed course as soon as is warranted based on what our scanners show is the safest route through The Cloud."

Wang, the ship's liaison officer from southeastern Asia, overheard the conversation, and decided the safer place for him was in his office. There were no government political officers lurking about down there.

BULLDOG 1

"They're about to have a very unpleasant surprise," muttered Patterson, as he pressed the button at last. Bulldogs 1 through 3 were flying in a close (for spaceflight purposes) formation in the path of the oncoming enemy detachment.

"Optics confirming. Two Collective frigates, and one vessel of unknown type not matching previously observed long range transports," he noted as the synced Bulldogs activated their reconfigured jump drives to project an image of Cerberus in front of the detachment. Twenty seconds passed in silence, which was finally broken by Patterson.

"Bulldogs 2 and 3 confirming image projection. Let's hope this works."

KURSK

The discussion between Remus, Kamisky, and Volodovsky was interrupted by the tactical officer as he quickly read the alert that chimed at his station.

"Comrade-Captain, Confederation heavy-cruiser detected! It's the Cerberus!"

Remus quickly stepped over to the tactical station. "Combat stations!" he ordered loudly. He quickly glanced at the plot, before issuing a series of commands. "Reverse course! Launch missiles. Activate point defense batteries."

Liu, the tactical officer, quickly pressed the proper buttons to make all that happen. A shower of missile launches issued from the small fleet detachment while they maneuvered to reverse course in the narrow channel that Cerberus had left open in The Cloud.

CERBERUS

Lieutenant Perez nearly shouted, "Detachment attempting to reverse course, approaching relative motion dead stop point."

Ronin understood his excitement, because the hunt was afoot. "All right, Perez. Jump us behind them when LeCroy confirms his readiness."

Perez glanced over at LeCroy, who nodded in his direction immediately.

"Jump in five. Four. Three. Two. One. Jumping!" Perez counted down as the ship jumped to approximately one hundred miles behind the three ships. "Jump thirty-three complete!"

Ronin nodded sharply, then ordered "Anytime, LeCroy."

LeCroy wasted no time. "Ordinance away. Recommend jump now, Perez."

Cerberus quickly jumped away again. "Start the five-minute timer, LeCroy. That should be sufficient for the ordinance to cause the desired amount of chaos," noted Mueller.

Ronin put a small five-minute timer on the main view screen. *This better work*, Ronin thought to himself. *Best not telegraph my uncertainties or it'll affect the crew.*

KURSK

Remus and Liu stared at the plot on the tactical scanner. "Forty seconds until impact, Comrade-Captain," Liu noted, without taking his eyes from the plot.

Remus was staring so intently, he didn't notice the beads of sweat that began trickling down the side of his face. As they stared, Liu's attention was suddenly drawn to a new threat warning.

"Comrade-Captain! Cerberus-class vessel has appeared aft! Distance, 100 miles."

Remus was shocked. "There's TWO Cerberus-class vessels? Why didn't our drones or scans detect this new ship earlier? Evasive maneuvers!"

Even as he roared these questions and command to Kamisky, both Remus and Liu realized the situation was hopeless. Trapped nearly motionless in an asteroid tunnel between two exceptionally powerful Confederation warships, one of which appeared out of nowhere a mere 100 miles aft. They were sitting ducks.

"I have no explanation why we failed to detect either vessel, Comrade-Captain! It's like they just appeared out of nowhere."

While he said this, Liu opened fire with the Kursk's point defense weapons and anti-missile fire. Liu wiped the sweat from his eyes as he quickly glanced at the incoming ordinance timer. It was counting down far too quickly. "Two minutes until impact. Our weapons fire is… three minutes from the fore Cerberus-class vessel and sixty… it's gone! The aft Cerberus-class vessel has disappeared from our scanners!"

"What? Impossible!" Remus knew better than to demand Liu recalibrate his scanners while they were exchanging naval gunfire with a pair of vastly more powerful Cerberus-class war birds. Even if they seemed to appear and disappear like ghosts.

"Where could they have gone?" As Remus said this, another beeping indicated the situation changed yet again.

Liu nearly shouted as he said, "The fore Cerberus-class vessel has vanished from our scopes!"

"Did we damage them?" Remus asked hopefully, although it was too early for their ordinance to have arrived at the ghostly target.

"Negative impact. Sixty seconds to last known target location," Liu responded. "Scans indicate the bulk of the enemy ordinance is directed at our escort frigates."

Upon hearing that, Remus relaxed slightly. At least they were unlikely to die immediately.

"Thirty seconds to impact," Liu called out.

The seconds counted down, before Liu unhelpfully announced, "Impact!" as the Kursk was slammed hard. He would never learn why the fore vessel didn't fire at them like the aft vessel did.

CERBERUS

All ordinance should have reached their targets by now, Captain," LeCroy announced.

"Split up our Bulldogs and have them jump in for a damage assessment run." Ronin ordered.

"Bulldogs 1 through 3, return for a damage assessment. Disperse accordingly. If there's any sign of trouble, jump away immediately," LeCroy ordered over the commlink from his workstation.

BULLDOG 1

"You heard 'em. Jump in five, four, three two, one. Jump!" counted Johnson. "Jump thirty-seven, complete," she added.

Without comment, Patterson immediately began scanning the area with both active scans and passive optics, while he waited for the observation drones to report in. As he did this, Johnson reminded Patterson of something he was pretty aware of.

"Jump engines are still spun up. Any signs of trouble, and we jump away, Patterson." He only managed to reply "Mmmmm," while he quietly munched on his beef jerky.

Johnson reached behind her with a slight snap of her fingers to get Patterson's attention, which was barely enough to get him to absentmindedly place a few sticks of jerky into her hand while his eyes remained glued to his screens. The cabin of their Bulldog smelled of candy and jerky.

"Got a read on the situation," Patterson suddenly said, causing Johnson to jump at the break in the silence.

"Both frigates took it on the chin. AI estimates they're wrecks with 90 to 95 percent confidence, and their hulls are in uncontrolled spins. It also positively identified the larger vessel; a converted cargo ship formerly named the *Kursk*. What it's been converted into is unknown."

"Patterson, forward that to Cerberus. I'm going to jump us in closer and to clear this area because we've been actively scanning from this location."

Patterson nodded, and pressed the buttons to make it happen before Bulldog 1 jumps again. "Ready," he announced, giving Johnson the go ahead to jump away.

CΞRBΞRUS

"Captain, good call on trying to disable the Kursk," Mueller noted as she and Ronin sat in the main conference room with LeCroy discussing the battle damage reports from the Bulldogs and their drones. "Our pilots and boarding parties want to have a go at the Kursk instead of waiting for her systems to completely fail or for them to initiate a self-destruct, even though the command crew had to have died when the bridge was erased by a hit. Kanagawa and the Brett's still think it's unlikely the ship's conversion would have included significant anti-intruder measures, and the risk is acceptable. I'm inclined to agree. Thoughts?" Mueller asked.

Ronin replied, "I agree."

They both looked at LeCroy, who wasted no time in responding to the question being asked merely by looking at him. "Me too. Let's get in there and see what there is to see."

Ronin nodded slightly, then opened a commlink through his collar node to the CAG. "Sunderland, I'm ordering the Marine boarding parties to execute immediately. Get your Bulldogs in position to haul the mail."

Down in the pilot area, Sunderland acknowledged and opened another link to the Bulldogs. "Bulldogs 2, 3 and 5, prepare for boarding maneuver. Marine boarding teams are headed your way."

Meanwhile, Ronin had already opened another commlink and advised the Marine team leaders they were green lighted.

"Captain, can I ask? The Brett's?" Mueller quietly inquired after the orders were given. "What are, the Bretts?"

Ronin gave a small laugh at her confusion. "The first names of both corporals in charge of Bravo and Gamma teams is Brett. Thus, the Brett's."

Mueller and LeCroy both laughed. "I hadn't heard of anyone calling them that yet. I like it though. Fitting," Mueller replied.

"Using the Bulldog's jump drives to project the image of a Cerberus-class ship was pretty effective. Even OUR sensors were reporting the sudden appearance of our mirror image. Spooked the Collective's vessels into an emergency course change that left them sitting ducks for a while," LeCroy noted excitedly. He liked having new abilities to play with for his tactical planning.

KURSK

"Is not repairable, da?" asked the Kursk's chief medical officer, Irina Stanislav, hoping her guess was completely wrong.

"Da," responded the very young third-class engineer who had been trying to repair the ship's life support systems, Petor Gregor. He was the only living engineer left on the Kursk after the attack destroyed Engineering. The fact that his youth saved him was not lost on Gregor. Because as the newest engineer, he had been sent away from the now missing Engineering section to try to fix a glitchy food replicator and was still working on it when the sudden attack from nowhere left the Kursk a dying husk of a ship.

Since the attack, Gregor had been in a desperate race against time to fix the ruined air system, and had enlisted Stanislav in the effort due to her medical expertise to help figure out the parameters of acceptable air quality. The two of them were greasy and sweaty from the fruitless effort. "Is, what? About two hours of breathable air remaining," Gregor noted.

Stanislav nodded slowly, not having the heart to tell Petor that the air was already pretty fouled due to the smoke from the fires inside the ship, so their time was even shorter. They both knew everyone aboard would die unless their poltergeist-like attackers chose to reappear and rescue them. No sense in belaboring the obvious.

Stanislav pushed aside a limp blonde strand of hair from her face. "I guess this is the end, then." Gregor simply nodded, too tired to do anything else. He had noticed the air quality was rapidly deteriorating as they rested from their efforts.

"Cannot seem to catch my breath," he noted as his eyes closed. He was so sleepy and tired. Why not just stay here next to such a beautiful doctor? As he thought this, he glanced over to where Stanislav had already passed out. Not long now, he thought before he, too, succumbed to sleep.

Minutes later, Bulldog 5 jumped into the space near the Kursk. "Jump one seven, complete," announced pilot Gary Chanson, from Idaho.

"Space is clear, insertion point is identified on your plot," said the rear-seater Akira Nakamura, from Okinawa. "Gamma 1, two minutes until we make contact with the insertion point on the Kursk hull," Nakamura added over the commlink.

"Roger that," responded Blackwater in his thick Welsh accent, before switching over to his team's commlink channel. "All right, lads, time to earn your pay. Two minutes!"

The line was silent for a moment, before Gamma 3 made a remark in their native French to Gamma 4 about boarding an active enemy vessel was perhaps not the healthiest of plans.

"Stow that froggie croaking," Blackwater ordered to the great surprise of Pvt. Louis Caron and Pvt. Victor Berger. Neither of them had yet figured out Gamma 1 was fluent in French. They grinned as they looked at each other. Who knew?

"Gamma 1, YOU speak French? What was her name, anyway?" asked Gamma 4 (Victor Berger) in a teasing tone, causing a chorus of similar responses and catcalls from the rest of the team.

"I really hate you guys and hope you die horribly!" responded Blackwater in an exasperated sounding tone. His only response was another round of whoops and wolf whistles from the team. They would make sure to drag this story out of their 1 whether he wanted to tell it or not.

Bulldog 5 quickly settled on the insertion point their AI had indicated was likely unguarded. "Gamma 5, do your thing," ordered Blackwater. Private Addington quickly began using his various tools to cut through the thin hull of the cargo vessel. Much easier to breach than the armored hull of a warship.

Within minutes, Addington called out, "Gamma 1, we have entry."

Blackwater wasted no time. "Gamma 4, get your bugs in there and tell us what the story is." Victor was already waiting. He launched a Butterfly drone.

"Empty, Gamma 1. Air's fouled," said Berger in his French accent.

"All right. Keep your suits buttoned up. Let's go," said Blackwater as he jumped down into the dark hole. As the team entered the insertion point, Gamma 6 buttoned up the entry behind them to keep the ship's atmosphere from spilling out if the Bulldog had to depart suddenly.

BULLDOG 2

"Jump two zero, complete." announced Meyer.

"Scans are clear, insertion point on your plot now," Schmidt confirmed after a few moments. "Echo 1, sixty seconds to insertion point," Schmidt added over the commlink.

"Sixty seconds, make ready!" Kanagawa informed Echo team over the team's commlink. "Contact, Echo team, go!" Meyer announced as he landed the Bulldog.

"Meyer, Bulldog 5 has sent their boarding party into the Kursk," Schmidt noted as she kept an eye on the Tacnet plot. "No resistance, and the air is fouled."

Kanagawa was also listening in on the command channel and heard Sophie's report. He passed the information to the rest of Echo team. "Stay buttoned up," Kanagawa ordered his men.

"There's an airlock!" Meyer announced excitedly. "I'll drop the party there." Kanagawa responded quickly. "Excellent work, Meyer. We should be able to gain entry much faster while the ship still has some power to operate the airlocks and hatches."

Minutes later, Echo 5 had the airlock cycling so the team could enter the Kursk. As it opened, he gestured in to Kanagawa. "Age before beauty, Echo 1."

Kanagawa couldn't resist throwing out a quip in response. "Then you'll never enter, Echo 5!" That retort brought a chorus of hoots and jokes from the team.

"OUCH!" and "Burn!" and the like. The team entered the ship and cycled the airlock before Danfries could get roasted any further.

KURSK

The Marine boarders quickly made their way into the ship.

"Gamma 4, there's a net node. Hook in and give a sitrep." ordered Blackwater when he saw the connection port.

Berger was only too happy to follow through. He quickly stepped up to the ship wide network node and used his bag of toys to rig up a connection. His AI took no time at all to assert itself.

"I've gained entry into the ship's neural network," said the AI over the circuit to Blackwater and Berger.

"The Kursk's system security was minimal. Last system upgrade was over twenty year's ago," noted the AI. Berger and Blackwater glanced at one another, each thinking the AI sounded a bit smug about that.

Kanagawa looked around as he listened to the AI's progress report. "This ship is old, and doesn't look like it was kept in top of the line status even before we made a mess of it," he replied.

"I have control over the ship's command systems," the AI suddenly stated. "There isn't much left to control. Bridge, auxiliary bridge and engineering are destroyed, along with most of the crews for those sections. Atmosphere quality has stabilized, but that's mostly because it's bad enough not to be able to support more fire. Please stay inside your exosuits." added the AI.

"AI, where are the defensive systems in the Kursk?" asked Berger. *Safety first,* he thought.

"All Kursk defensive systems are offline, and no Collective environmental suits were activated due to the suddenness of our attack," responded the AI.

That startled Kanagawa. "You mean there isn't any armed resistance?" he asked.

"That is correct, Corporal."

Kanagawa and Berger looked at each other. "I guess we have a look around and figure out what the story behind the Kursk is then," Kanagawa remarked.

The AI unexpectedly responded, because neither Kanagawa nor Berger had closed the line to it. "The ship's orders were in the main computer and I have accessed them. Kursk was transporting refugees from the families of high-ranking party officials within the Collective. Most of the refugees come from the Collective's main population centers, which are located in both Southeast Asia and near Europe."

"How many refugees are we talking here?" asked Berger.

"Three thousand, one hundred three boarded the Kursk. Two thousand, two hundred eight remain, although their health is deteriorating rapidly due to onboard conditions."

Berger and Kanagawa looked at each other, stunned. "I thought it was transporting weapons, or supplies or something!" said Berger.

Kanagawa nodded, visible even in his exosuit. "We need to contact Cerberus ASAP, or there won't be anybody left to rescue soon."

C≡RB≡RUS

"That's right, Captain, 2,208 survivors for the moment. All Marine boarding teams have spread throughout the Kursk and confirmed there is no resistance, nor is there anyone still conscious due to the poor atmosphere conditions," Kanagawa said through the commlink. "AI has taken control of the ship's systems that still function. They're political families from the highest levels of the Collective."

"Provide what assistance you can to keep them alive until our medical and transport teams arrive. Transfer them to Cerberus as soon as conditions permit," Ronin ordered. He looked at Mueller with raised eyebrows that matched her own expression.

"Lieutenant LeCroy, follow me and Commander Mueller please." He activated a commlink from his collar node. "Lieutenant Commander Elvis Lazarus, meet me in the main conference room right away, please."

he said over the commlink as he stood and walked towards the exit to the bridge on his way to the main conference room.

Minutes later, the foursome was deep in discussions. "Yes, Captain. We can keep everyone alive long enough for us to drop them off somewhere. Provided we don't take too long in transit, and feed everyone aboard half rations to stretch the onboard food stocks. It won't smell too fresh in here with that many bodies," Lazarus reported after running some numbers.

"Thank you, Lazarus. Go make your preparations, and we'll get underway as soon as is practicable." Mueller said.

Lazarus nearly ran from the conference room. He would be very busy for the next few hours.

Mueller sat back in her seat, and she and Ronin just looked at one another for a moment.

"Well. Here we are. Refugees of the political class. Do we need any clearer signs that the Collective is rapidly collapsing? I read classified reports this morning about armed revolts springing up in their cities, and now they're leaving while they still can," Ronin concluded.

LeCroy nodded, thinking. "Aye, Captain. The end is coming. Hopefully they don't try to take down the West like what they did to start The Fall. What do we do with the refugees?" he asked.

"Refugees? Might be that the Admiralty prefers to make them pawns in their political machinations instead. I don't know. What I do know, however, is that we save as many as we can, and get the heck out of Dodge while we can and make contact with the fleet for further instructions. This was anticipated to be a hit-and-run raid, not a rescue mission. If it were supposed to be a rescue mission, Cerberus would've been kitted out much differently, especially in terms of food and medical supplies."

The look on Mueller's face showed her agreement. "Yes. As we are now, we won't be able to sustain that many people for long at all. The clock is running as soon as they're aboard," she noted.

Ronin reached his decision. "LeCroy, work with the Marines to keep Cerberus secure from these refugees. I don't want any harm coming to our ship or to them from their presence."

LeCroy nodded without further reply.

"Mueller, take command of Cerberus while they're brought aboard. In the interim, I'm going to conference with the Admiralty and figure out where to take them. I'll join you on the bridge as soon as I've got something."

While Mueller and LeCroy left to return to the bridge, Ronin slipped into his ready room. Ronin composed his thoughts while he made a cup of coffee, and then sat at his desk to open a commlink to Admiral Rodding.

He answered it seconds after the link was secure. "Rodding, go ahead." At this distance, the delay was about two minutes, but Dan needed options now so he just had to endure the lag time.

"Admiral, this is Captain Ronin. We have a bit of a situation here."

"What's the situation, Captain?" Rodding's face showed both surprise and interest at Ronin's blunt announcement. He was also concerned at the unusual communication from Ronin while Cerberus was still away on a raid.

"Admiral, we've found the secret cargo of the Kursk was actually 2,208 survivors from the ruling families of the Collective's government. There were more, but not everyone survived the disabling attacks on the ship prior to the arrival of our boarding parties. I took the liberty of assuming you would want Cerberus to deliver them somewhere instead of leaving them here as the ship was dying rapidly."

Rodding's eyebrows rose sharply. "Survivors! From the ruling families? That totally doesn't fit the mission our AI profiled for the detachment. We were expecting weapons and the like." Rodding slowly stroked his chin while he thought for a moment. "Dan, how long can you host all those extra bodies?"

"Four days, no more," Ronin responded crisply. "We can stretch the food supplies and recycle all the water, but breathable air is the primary limiting factor. Our life support systems were never designed for that kind of capacity and can't recycle enough air in sufficient quantities."

Rodding pressed a button and shared his screen with Ronin so they could both see a map. "Four days," he muttered. "Ronin, what do you know of Oasis?"

Ronin shook his head. "Nothing, sir. First I've heard the name."

A spot on the shared map screen began blinking in response to a command from Rodding. "Oasis is a small base on Triton, in retrograde orbit around Neptune. We can send Cygnus there with adequate food supplies and a large detachment of Marine guards. There is sufficient water for hydrogen, and nitrogen, to help generate the necessarily atmosphere for life support. It'll be a bit tight from an elbow room perspective, but it's a good spot for temporary lodging purposes."

Ronin thought about it for a moment. "We can get our guests squared away aboard Cerberus, then jump them out to Oasis after Cygnus has arrived there. Where do you want Cerberus after that, Admiral?"

"Leave one of your Bulldogs to search for intel in the remains at The Cloud before you leave for Triton. After you depart Triton, jump to Wayside Station. Fleet intelligence is itching to review the computer records you've recovered. There's a lot going on back Earth side, and the situation is dangerously volatile. The intel weenies are nearly certain a high value escape mission like you found is bound to have inside information about the Collective and its security apparatus."

The shared screen vanished and was replaced by Rodding's face. "Keep us apprised of your situation, Dan. Things are happening quickly now. Expect something to come up with no notice."

After Ronin signed off, he returned to his quarters for a bit. Edward was in the kitchenette making a sandwich. "Dad! I'm making a bite to eat for a quick dinner. Sarah is on her way here too. All the kids were ordered back to quarters for some reason. Want a sandwich?"

Ronin smiled and gave him a hug. "I would love one! Just famished here." As they sat down to eat their meal, Ronin decided Edward needed a cautionary word from him. "We've picked up a large number of refugees from the Collective, which is why all the civilians have been returned to their quarters unless they're needed elsewhere. It's a dangerous situation, so I need you to promise to stay here with Sarah until we deliver them to safety. They could be violent, some are hurt, and there's no telling how unpredictable they'll be, which is why you need to stay away. They find out you're my son, and one of the desperate or militant refugees might try to take you hostage or kill you. Understand?"

Edward was no dummy, and understood immediately. "Yes, Papa. I'll stay put right here until we can offload them somewhere else."

Ronin smiled approvingly. "Smart lad. The entire crew has to remain super alert while they're here as the refugees are not our friends or allies."

Hours later, Ronin left the bridge and quickly arrived in the Cerberus' main hanger where the refugees had been situated for accommodations. He was accompanied by a security detail consisting of Bravo 2, Ed Wilson from Brookings, South Dakota, and Bravo 5, Pvt. Terry Allison. Both of them were in their exosuits and kitted up for close quarters combat to discourage troublemakers, or end them if they couldn't be discouraged.

"Captain, we've processed all the refugees and identified who is who. There are a few surviving naval officers, including a chief medical officer named Irina Stanislav, and a young third-class engineer by the name of Petor Gregor. Nothing much of note there. What is of interest is a person with an identity discrepancy that caused the *Cerberus* AI some excitement," Wilson reported to Ronin as they walked to the hangar.

"How so?" Ronin inquired, which prompted the AI to speak directly.

"Captain, this identity appears recent in origin. The Kursk's records included the Collective's identification database, which was protected by heavy security encryption, but one that wasn't difficult for me to breach. This person does not appear in that database, which suggests a manufactured identity. He was accompanied by two other persons who rarely leave his immediate vicinity, according to our observations. Those other two also have manufactured identities."

"So why the focus on this guy instead of the other two?" Ronin asked. "What's different?"

The AI provided the key bit of information. "The database encryption is keyed to respond solely to this person's DNA, but not the other two, which leads us to believe he is somewhat more important."

Just then, the hatch to the hanger opened to admit Ronin, Wilson and Allison. What they saw was organized chaos, with a medical triage area off to one corner, and a soup line in another. Immediately after the impact of taking in the scene hit Ronin, the next wave of sensory impression hit. The smell of unwashed bodies, blood, food, smoky clothing,

and a somewhat sour smell floating above it all that Ronin couldn't identify. Nor did he want to. *Yikes! It's going to be a long four days,* he thought
to himself as they stepped into the hanger bay.

Ronin spotted Taketa where he expected to find him. Running the
impromptu medical triage area, and quickly made his way over to him.
"Lieutenant, is there anything else that we can get to you down here?"
he asked.

His surprised chief medical officer turned to look at Ronin. "Captain, hi! Wasn't looking for you. I think we've got it under control for
now that all hands are on deck. I'll message you if something comes up."

Ronin nodded as Taketa quickly turned to the next patient needing
his care. Next Ronin walked over to Corporal Mackey. "Mackey, report."
he ordered.

"Captain, security perimeter established. We have the refugees cor-
ralled into the hanger, which will obviously impact flight ops. Sunderland
said he can work around the delays so long as we don't have a combat situation or something equally dicey that requires a faster tempo of operations. Has Bravo 2 brought you up to speed on our special guests?"

Ronin nodded without taking his eyes off the crowd in an effort to
appear nonchalant. Mackey caught on immediately.

"Yes. Keep him under close scrutiny for now, but don't tip him off.
Cull him from the herd before we reach our destination, and his two
friends, but do it quietly. Put them someplace secure," replied Ronin.

Mackey nodded, also not taking his eyes off the crowd in the same
way Ronin hadn't. "Roger that, Captain. We'll make it happen."

The Cerberus AI also confirmed that it, too, would keep the three
special guests under constant scrutiny.

As Ronin looked around, a mother with two children stopped as she
was passing by.

"Why you attack us? Women and children? You are barbarians!" she
wailed in heavily accented American, spitting for emphasis at Ronin's
feet as she was shooed away by another Bravo team Marine.

"I'm sorry, Captain. We'll keep that from happening again," Mackey
said apologetically.

Ronin looked at him, unmoved. "They knew there were families aboard the Frisco when they attacked it years ago and killed my wife, Corporal Mackey. Then they lied and said it was a military ship when it was clearly a scientific vessel. I don't have any sympathy for collateral damage to the Collective or its ruling families anymore."

Mackey was stunned, as he hadn't heard how the Captain's wife died before. "Oh, I'm sorry, sir. Didn't mean to pry open old wounds."

Ronin half smiled with a hint of sadness, and without any humor. "Nothing to be sorry for, Mackey. It's not a secret, but after this long, it just is a fact of life for me now. I'd better return to the bridge. We'll be getting underway shortly."

CHAPTER 24

OASIS

Cerberus appeared with a jump flare in an orbit of Triton, which itself was orbiting Neptune. "Interesting moon, Dan," murmured Mueller as she stood next to him watching the forward view screen. It's the only moon in Sol system with a retrograde orbit opposite to its planet's rotation."

Ronin half-smiled back at her and replied, "I was always kind of fascinated with Triton for that reason. No one knows why it's in a retrograde orbit."

LeCroy interrupted their reverie by announcing, "Receiving hostile challenge from the local defense network. Sending coded reply." Seconds passed, then he added, "Response accepted. Receiving navigation instructions and forwarding them to Lieutenant Perez."

Down at the helm, Perez nodded, and responded, "Course received and laid in, Captain. Taking us in."

Ronin opened a commlink from his console node to Corporal Mackey, who was still holding post down in the hangar. "Bravo 1, we'll be commencing the transfer operations soon. Execute Plan Takedown immediately."

The reply was immediate. "Acknowledged, Captain. Will report back when completed."

For today's festivities, Mackey had all the ship's Marines in their exosuits and kitted up for close quarters combat. He wanted no back talk from any of the refugees, preferring that they meekly obey commands given by the scary Marines carrying lots of big guns and wearing scary looking combat suits.

"Bravo 1, targets are twenty-five meters to your ten o'clock. Echo 1 is shadowing them." said the *Cerberus* AI over Bravo team's open commlink.

"Stay sharp, Bravo team. Echo 1 is dressed as a civvie for this op," Mackey reminded the team as they swiftly closed in. Their special guests didn't click on to what was happening until they found themselves surrounded by Bravo team.

"Why you do this? What is happening?" shouted a scared looking man who was clearly the ranking member of the three.

Bravo 7, Ty Jeffries, didn't even bother responding. He just grabbed the diminutive man with the inexorable power of his exosuit, spun him around and pushed him face down on the deck while Bravo 6, Steve Cupper, cuffed his hands behind his back before attaching leg irons for good measure. The rest of Bravo team delivered similar treatment to the other two special guests.

As soon as the three were stood up, Mackey ordered, "Let's go." Bravo team stormed out of the hanger with their three prisoners. Unnoticed by the refugees, Kanagawa melted away from the scene as his shadowing skills were no longer needed. The Marines quickly passed him through their cordon so he could get his exosuit on and resume his life as Echo 1.

CHAPTER 25

WAYSIDE STATION

Two weeks later, *Cerberus* appeared alongside Cygnus at Wayside Station with a matching pair of jump flares. The commlinks on both ships immediately indicated an incoming priority message from Admiral Rodding.

Capt. Alfred Jurgenson answered first as he was already in his ready room. "Cygnus Actual, go ahead, Admiral," he stated.

Captain Ronin echoed him moments later, as the three-way video call was established. "*Cerberus* Actual, go ahead."

"Captains, we need you both to dock with Wayside, immediately, and prepare to receive extra ordinance for your rail guns and to make way under a Class One deployment," Rodding said bluntly without preamble.

Surprise registered on the faces of both Ronin and Jurgenson. "What's going on, Admiral?" asked Jurgenson before Ronin could ask the same thing.

"The special guests that Dan brought back from the trip to Oasis are what's going on. Turns out the guy being protected by the other two is the Minister of State Security for the entire Collective. Vladimir has kindly defected and provided us with his access codes in exchange for becoming a new citizen of the Confederation. The Collective is collapsing rapidly and is planning on initiating an Earth-side attack to start a full-scale war before it weakens too much to stop the Confederacy. It also is intending to try to distract its population and keep it from revolting further, and hopes we will solve their overpopulation problem with a counterstrike before we disappear. In fact, they're preparing to launch more ships to evacuate their ruling families like they did with the Kursk."

Both Jurgenson and Ronin were stunned. "The Treaty of Midway has forbidden all forms of combat on Earth for centuries," countered Ronin. "How are they planning on attacking?"

"Vladimir claims it's a biological attack using a wide area dispersal mechanism. As far as the Admiralty is concerned, it's The Fall all over again. Ronin, we need to jump one of your Bullfrogs down to the planet surface with an advance insertion team before Cygnus, Ceres, and Cerberus are called in for other duties. Orders and intel have been cut and will be sent to your desk forthwith."

Ronin nodded and replied, "Yes, sir. We'll get on it immediately."

Rodding looked right at Ronin for a moment. "This is Class One Mission here, Dan. Make it happen."

After the call ended, Ronin opened the order packet that had arrived. After scanning it for a few minutes, he opened a link to the 1s in charge of the three Marine teams on *Cerberus.*

"Corporals, meet me in my ready room, immediately. Whatever you're doing, drop it. We've received an order for immediate execution."

Minutes later, Marine team leaders Brett Mackey, Brett Blackwater and Toshi Kanagawa and the other 1s were gathered in Ronin's ready room. "First thing, gentlemen: Fleet finally approved your promotions to Gunnery Sergeants. Congratulations, when you leave here, upgrade your chevrons to reflect your new ranks. Your 2s are advanced in ranks to Corporal, so tell them to upgrade their respective chevrons as well. Thanks to the special guest we captured before the delivery to Oasis, we have a Class One mission."

The newly made gunnery sergeants glanced at each other at hearing of a Class One mission. None of them had ever imagined actually participating in a mission with a priority so high – it superseded all other orders and missions. Ronin thought of the classification as a "hair on fire" type of classification. When your hair is on fire, literally nothing takes a higher priority for you right then.

Ronin took a sip of his coffee before speaking again. "This is a specialized insertion op to jump via Bulldog deep behind enemy lines, right into the heart of the Collective. The insertion team will deliver a specially designed viral payload, upload it into the Collective's defense grid, and exfil. This ad hoc team, which I'll call Force Omega, needs to go heavy on both stealth and electronic warfare specialties."

Kanagawa nodded, thinking out loud, "Heavy firepower won't be terribly useful if the team is trapped in the middle of enemy territory, but Echo 6 might be a key element for inclusion in Force Omega. He's a trained assassin and camouflage specialist," Kanagawa said.

Ronin smiled. "My thoughts exactly. Force Omega by necessity must be small, and possessing key skills for the situation. Review the intel provided by our new citizen and devise a mission fitting the key parameter of stealth. We don't want to telegraph that we were ever there."

Sergeant Blackwater decided to ask a question, as he was bothered by the thought of executing a potentially lethal mission in the middle of hostile territory. "Captain? Isn't a mission like this prohibited by the Treaty of Midway? It's a potential hostile action on Earth," Blackwater asked.

Ronin and the others looked at Blackwater. "Sergeant, Fleet Intelligence has learned the Collective is planning to launch a biological first strike against the Confederacy on Earth in the near future, before its economic collapse leaves it too weakened to carry on against us. Even contemplating such an attack is a major breach of the treaty, and the Collective has already been moving its assets into place in preparation to launch the attack. We don't have much time to prevent another Fall so we can save our civilization and families."

Blackwater nodded. That was all he needed to know. "Yes, sir," Blackwater said. "We'll begin our mission planning as best we can in the available time before we jump off. Will he have a redundancy just in case the expert can't complete the mission?"

Ronin shook his head. "No. Not enough time, so all we can do is hope this goes off well. None of us likes a rushed mission and we have to execute 24 hours from now."

Kanagawa and the other 1s nodded, with Kanagawa speaking for them all, "Proper Planning and Preparation Prevents Poor Performance." They all knew this ancient adage by heart.

Hours later, they regrouped in the main conference room of *Cerberus* along with the 2s and electronic warfare specialists from the Marine teams.

Gunny Mackey was ready to begin the briefing over the mission plan. "All right, settle down. Time to talk through the tentative mission plan and hope we don't get killed from inadequate planning and poor preparation.

"Force Omega will jump in a Bulldog from its max range to this forested area outside the city of Nizhny Novgorod. The air defense grid around Nizhny Novgorod is a dense web of detection, radar, and missile launchers. Certain death for anything unfortunate enough to fly into. The forest is unguarded, and represents the area closest to the city where a Bulldog can safely jump to without tripping a nightmare of alarms and hostility. Rebel partisans have a cell there standing by to provide transport and assistance."

"Code words for the rebels?" asked Gunny Blackwater.

"Code phrase is, 'the night is dark and I am far from home.' According to our intel packet, say anything else and the rebels will end you without further ado, so you will be drilled in how to say it in Old Russian, which is the prevailing language there. The Force Omega team will be led by the Pirate, Echo 2. It will be composed of the three electronic warfare specialists from all Cerberus Marine teams, plus two from the Cygnus Marine teams, and Echo 6," responded Mackey, with a nod to the five electronic warfare specialists seated together at the briefing.

Mackey advanced the screens to show a picture from Nizhny Novgorod. "These are from defense satellite imagery we had in our records. The Collective's defense ministry is located here, which is called the Kremlin. As you can see, it is a hilltop fortress with over a mile of ancient walls dating back to the 1500s from centuries before The Fall. While a Kremlin in Old Russian means a citadel within a Russian town, the name of this Kremlin is meant to call to mind an ancient, secret police structure by the same name from before The Fall. It was located in Moscow, in the old Soviet Union, before it was nuked."

Ronin watched closely as Mackey continued on with the briefing for the next two hours. The plan to infiltrate was close to crazy, and high risk.

Mackey and the other 1s were very experienced Marines, and always followed the Simple is Better rule for mission planning. The simpler it is, the higher the chances of success because there were fewer things to go wrong. When the briefing finished, Force Omega left with the 1s to walk through the plan until they got the movements down.

CHAPTER 26

THE KREMLIN

As they boarded Bulldog 7, Jason Priest and Dale Dannon, the two borrowed electronic warfare specialists from the Cygnus Marine teams, noted the number of the spacecraft — seven. In a ship's compliment of six Bulldogs.

"The tradition for Bulldogs is the replacement crew for one killed in action is they take the next higher number as counted from the top crew number, right?" whispered Priest to Dannon, who were respectively designated Omega Five and Six for this mission.

"Yes, Bulldog 7 replaced 4, who were KIA at the Battle of the Dark Side," answered the Pirate, who overheard Jason's whisper.

"Now settle in," ordered Corporal Longman.

On the bridge of the *Cerberus*, Ronin looked over at LeCroy, who was monitoring readiness at his Tactical station.

"Bulldog crews report ready, Captain," LeCroy said after a few moments.

Ronin then nodded towards the helmsman. "Jump the ship, Perez."

Cerberus jumped from its staging area position to the dark side of an asteroid in the belt above and behind the Earth.

"Jump complete, Captain," reported Perez from the helm.

Commander Mueller was now standing next to LeCroy, waiting for a look from Ronin. She got it. "Launch Bulldog 7, LeCroy." Mueller said.

Down in the launch bay, Pilot Officer Greg Lowridge had been waiting for the go order.

"Bulldog 7, cleared for launch," said the CAG, Sunderland, over the commlink. Lowridge punched the engines, and the Bulldog shot out of *Cerberus* into the dark space behind the asteroid. *Cerberus* disappeared again in a jump flare that seemed brighter than normal in the extra dark of the sunless side of a piece of rock far from Sol.

"We're on our own, holding position confirmed, about two billion miles from Earth. Ready for jump," reported Paul Drayson from the rear-seater position over the commlink that was open between Drayson, Lowridge and the Pirate, Cpl. Adrian Longman.

"Corporal, your men buckled up for this?" asked Lowridge, even though he knew Longman would have already triple-checked how securely the insertion was strapped in.

"Aye, as ready as we can be," Longman responded.

Bulldog 7 jumped the next two billion miles in one jump. While that wasn't the sort of distance that would cause any commotion with a Bulldog crew, their destination was. Earth. And it wasn't just some easy jump into orbit. Bulldog 7 reappeared in a jump flare in the dark sky over eastern Russia at a low altitude.

"Jump 1, complete," reported Lowridge, unnecessarily because the Bulldog's violent, fiery arrival in low atmosphere smashed the ship like an angry giant. Lowridge was applying the engines hard to brake themselves before gravity took care of stopping the Bulldog for them. The deceleration briefly pulled nine gravities, and squeezed the breath out of them for the next twenty seconds. Outside the Bulldog, it left a short but impressive flame trail that looked remarkably similar to an incoming meteor except that it began a mere thousand feet above the ground instead of seeming to come down from orbit.

"Gentlemen, we have arrived at our destination. Thank you for flying Bulldog Airlines, where we take you to all the garden spots you would rather not visit," quipped Lowridge over the commlink to Drayson and Longman.

"There! See the landing field?" interrupted Drayson, pointing even though Lowridge had seen it, too. He flew the Bulldog at treetop level over a short distance of the forest to arrive at the landing zone that was marked using a few fires.

"Here we go, landing in three, two, one," announced Lowridge as he guided the Bulldog down into the small clearing. Dark figures could be seen rushing towards the Bulldog with some sort of netting. Before he could grow alarmed, they quickly spread it over the Bulldog and they could see it was a camouflage net that had real pine boughs fitted into it for realism.

"OK, Marines, this is our stop. Debark by the numbers," Longman announced while Lowridge and Paul shut the vessel down. The rear hatch of the Bulldog lowered and formed a ramp.

Longman, looking out at the shadowy figures awaiting their presence, muttered to himself, "Here goes nothing." He led the Marines of Force Omega down the ramp.

One of the shadows stepped forward to Longman.

"Password?" the shadow asked.

"The night is dark and I am far from home," responded Longman.

The shadow approached closer, holding out a hand to shake. "Force Omega? Is good see you," said the man in heavily accented American.

Longman shook the proffered hand. "Corporal Adrian Longman, Omega 1," he replied.

The man motioned for the Marines to follow him. "From here, remain silent until we reach our forward position for briefing," he said. The Marines and several dozen shadows began following the man single file down a very dark trail. Since it was pitch dark and they didn't know the forested and uneven terrain, the Marines turned on their night vision in their exosuits to avoid tripping over anything.

An hour later, the still-silent group arrived at a well-hidden mine tunnel entrance at the base of a large, rolling hill. The leader stepped up to it, popped open a previously unseen retinal scan terminal, and gained entrance after the scan. All of them walked into the lightness tunnel of the old mine and they came to an unremarkable-looking section of wall. Again the leader opened a retinal scan terminal that was hidden in the wall, and scanned. A huge portion of the tunnel swung inwards, revealing a modern-looking tunnel with cement walls and soft lighting. The exosuits compensated for the sudden appearance of light so the Marines weren't blinded.

The man walked in, motioning for the Marines to follow as he did so. The wall swung closed behind them, and it was as if the Marines had never been there as they left no trace of their passing. They followed the man to an elevator, and joined him in it. Riding in silence, they dropped far down into the earth before the elevator came to a stop at the bottom of a long shaft.

When the doors opened, the Marines looked out in surprise at a large cavern that was filled with antiquated looking military equipment. As they walked through the cavern, the man spoke for the first time in quite a while. "Is odd looking equipment, is not?"

Longman nodded as he gawked while they walked. "Yes, I've never seen anything quite like these. What was the purpose of putting the ancient hammer and sickle symbol on them?"

The man replied with a small smile. "Is ancient Soviet military equipment from before The Fall. We are getting them, how you say, reconditioned for combat?"

Longman's eyebrows shot up in surprise. "These are from before The Fall? Seriously?"

As they walked, the man approached a door and opened it with a gesture for the Marines to enter into the well-lit conference room just beyond. "Yes. The Collective knows nothing about this old base. It is forgotten to them long ago. The rebellion has been preparing to use it since we located it a few years ago. We believe the armored vehicles of our ancestors will be useful to overthrow today's rulers and build a new society."

As they sat around the conference table, a mixed contingent of Marines and rebels took up guard positions around the cavern and outside the door.

"OK, we are ready to begin," said the man. "You may call me by name of Dimitri Sokolov, I am one of the *Rabos*."

Longman nodded, thinking to himself it's obviously a fake identity. "The *Rabos*?" asked Longman. "What's a *Rabos*?"

Sokolov thought for a moment, translating the words for Force Omega. "*Rabochiy* are workers in our language. The workers in rebellion call themselves the *Rabos*. Rabos rebel against the *Dvoryanstvo*." Sokolov paused, obviously searching for the proper word to translate *Dvoryanstvo*. "How you say? The nobility? The ruling class? They're *Dvoryanstvo*."

"You said you have a target for Force Omega?" asked Longman.

"Yes, although you might not like where it is. We could not risk openly communicating the target to your Confederacy, which is why you are here now. We wish you to infiltrate the Kremlin and put a stop to the Collective's plan for biological warfare before they create another Fall. This time, it's an engineered Doomsday virus that will kill most of humanity instead of just enough to bring down civilization by creating economic chaos."

Longman had been briefed about the Collective's plan to unleash a virus-based war on the Confederacy in the misguided belief the Collective would be able to contain the spread of the Doomsday virus since there was no trade or travel between the two civilizations this time.

"Tell us about the infectious characteristics of the virus," Longman said, more as a command than a statement.

Sokolov glanced over at Longman as he replied, "It has an asymptomatic and unusually long incubation period of three to four weeks, and extremely high airborne transmission rates that infect nearly everyone. Once symptoms onset, a victim begins to exhibit what appears to be severe bruising before bleeding from eyes and ears sets in. Survival rate is lower than one percent."

"Doomsday virus, indeed," commented Longman as he leaned further onto the conference table and clasped his hands together. "Has the Collective any plans to stop sick people from crossing over a border in Asia? It doesn't seem possible to guard thousands of miles of borders that cross through wilderness and mountains."

Sokolov nodded and replied, "Is not possible, not by any realistic measure. Someone will get through, the Doomsday virus will inevitably infect the Collective, too. Both civilizations will die along with the vast majority of humanity on Earth, and the ruling families of the Collective will eventually return to recolonize the entire planet. They even have several vaults of stored human genetic material scattered about the Collective to help avoid inbreeding. They want to wipe out the populations of the Confederacy in addition to our own overpopulation. Start over on an empty planet."

Longman and Pak looked at each other. "I knew the Collective was an inhuman and evil government, but this is too much," Pak said disgustedly. "Now the Confederacy and the Rabos share a common cause. Our right to survive."

Longman and Sokolov nodded sadly, as Sokolov continued with the briefing. "We have an infiltration route into the Kremlin from deep underground. Another forgotten tunnel from before The Fall. Because the Collective believes the lack of travel and trade also prevents sending infected carriers into the Confederation as a means of disbursing the airborne virus, the delivery vehicle will be via ballistic missiles. Your mission is to upload a computer virus designed by your scientists into the Collective's defense grid to sever government control over its missiles and prevent the Collective from launching its attack two days from now."

"Two DAYS!" exclaimed Longman loudly.

"Yes, two days. That is the attack date we have uncovered at great cost to our people. Unless something major occurs in the interim to change that start date, missile launch is in two days after their preparations are complete. We will create a distraction on the surface while you gain entrance to the facility, but we will have to travel immediately if we are to arrive in time."

Longman and Pak looked at each other. "All right. I'll send a report to the fleet, and then we can get going," said Longman.

THE UNDERWORLD

"It would have been nice if they had provided ground car transportation," Pak quipped to Longman as the fleet Marines from space paradoxically rode horses through ancient underground tunnels. They had been proceeding at a brisk trot for hours through the old tunnel that ran ruler straight far underground.

"Any idea how far we've traveled, Omega 1?" asked Victor Berger, who was designated Omega 4 for this mission.

"Negative. Best guess is we've covered thirty plus miles based on elapsed time and estimated speed," responded Longman. "You getting saddle sore back there, Omega 4?" he asked with an evil grin at Berger's visible discomfort. He received an angry sounding reply in French that Longman was pretty sure included remarks about his parentage and something to do with a goat.

Force Omega collectively roared with spirited laughter over their team commlink. Although Longman felt it was good for the Marines to blow off some steam with the laughs and banter, he was glad the rebels couldn't overhear them outside their exosuit helmets, or they'd start wondering what kind of jokers were posing as Marines from space.

Eventually the horseplay died out as the monotony of underground horseback riding wore on for several more hours. The Rabos had set up several different waypoints with fresh horses to ride and keep the group at speed. Finally, Force Omega and their escorts arrived at an generic-looking underground embarkation platform.

"This is it," announced Dimitri as he dismounted his steed and climbed onto the platform.

Longman looked down the tunnel towards the direction they had traveled. "It is? How can you tell?" he asked, looking around for a sign or some sort of symbol or writing that might identify where they were. There was nothing but white tile for walls, and they had passed multiple such platforms already.

"Based on signage higher up where the exits were blocked many centuries ago, scout teams previously identified this station platform as the one leading into the Kremlin. Fortunately, there was one scout who was conversant with the ancient Russian alphabet called Cyrillic and he recognized the words written in that dead form of writing," Dimitri responded. "Come. We have a long climb ahead of us."

Longman and his team carried the ropes and climbing gear supplied by the rebels, and walked into the exit tunnel heading upwards.

"Uh, Omega 1, you know what happens to guys walking into the dark, scary tunnels in the movies, right?" asked Omega 6, Dale Dannon.

"They always get eaten by the aliens that grab their faces," responded Longman with a grin. "Well, then, in that case, after you, sunshine!" he added.

The lower part of the tunnel was in fine shape, perhaps reflecting the protection provided by the earth when the nukes wrecked the surface during The Fall so long ago. Soon they came to breaks in the ramps leading up. "Time for the mountaineering," muttered Longman as the team began hammering anchor pitons into the walls and climbing past the broken areas. It was slow going.

CHAPTER 27

WAYSIDE STATION

aptain Ronin and Commander Mueller arrived in the same Fleet Intelligence virtual conference room where they originally met with Admiral Rodding and Colonel Hobson. This time, the captains of the Ceres and Cygnus, along with their first officers, join them.

Colonel Hobson spoke first after they were settled. "Sorry for having to do this via holo instead of in person but time is too short to allow for the traveling. As you all have been kept abreast of the deteriorating situation in the Collective back on Earth, none of this may seem shocking. The economy has collapsed, and the political elite have been evacuating their families because they are losing control over their cities due to the rebellion and other troubles.

"We've received a briefing from Omega 1. Force Omega has made contact with the rebels on the ground near Nizhny Novgorod, and they've begun their infiltration of the Collective's defense grid, which is based there. That is the good news. The bad news is the rebels have advised Omega 1 the Collective will attack the Confederation with its highly engineered Doomsday virus in two days. This virus would pretty much wipe out the entire human population of Earth. Because the Collective is unaware we've captured their families out in The Cloud, their government elites still believes all of their families will return from their hideout somewhere in space to repopulate the planet, without the troublesome Confederation to interfere with their scheme to create a new world order and control the overpopulation of their own subjects," concluded Hobson, looking around at the grave faces around the table.

Captain Michelle Rodgers of the Ceres responded first, her dark eyes flashing with anger. "Genocide! That's their Master Plan? It's The Fall all over again!" Angry shouts from the others in the room drowned out the rest of her comments.

Hobson attempted to regain control of the briefing. "Quiet!" he roared, stunning the other officers into silence. "We don't have time to get angry here. We only have time to bring you all up to speed on our next steps. That's it. Admiral?"

At this hand-off, Admiral Rodding began his portion of the briefing. "For months, your three ships have played the spaceship version of guerrilla warfare. Striking hard without warning, and disappearing just as quickly. The purposes, as you all know, were to bleed the enemy's scarce resources, and to force them to expend additional resources to defend everything instead of concentrating their defenses. The strategy has worked brilliantly so far, especially when viewed from the lens of forcing the Collective to divert more of its faltering economy to military spending through higher taxes and redirected government spending. Their people are starving, and revolting because they've had enough and the government has grown too weak to keep suppressing them."

When the Admiral paused to gather his thoughts, Ronin chanced a question. "Sir, while forcing the Collective to crumble earlier than anticipated is a good thing, and we all recognize that the Treaty of Midway is no longer stopping war on Earth, how do we handle the biological weapons if Force Omega can't stop all of them and they actually are deployed against our people?"

Instead of showing anger at the interruption, the Admiral merely nodded. Ronin had framed the very thoughts running through the Admiral's mind.

"That's why you three Captains are here. Welcome to Taskforce 3," said Rodding.

The three captains looked at each, somewhat stunned at their inclusion in a Confederate naval taskforce, because the last time such a taskforce was assembled was 75 years ago. They were powerful groups of warships, but required a huge undertaking in terms of commitment, resources, and war fighting capability. Confederate task forces were also legendary in the lore of the Navy, as Taskforce 1 had wrested control of

Mars away from the Collective, and Taskforce 2 had done the same with Mercury.

As Ronin mulled over the implications of being named a captain in a Navy taskforce, it occurred to him the losses of Mars and Mercury had represented the beginning of the end for the Collective. Losing those planets choked off the Collective's easy access to massive mineral resources and forced them to rely upon the much smaller scale of asteroid mining. *How fitting the third taskforce is here to close that loop and usher in the end of the Collective,* he thought.

As Rodding continued on with his briefing, an image of Earth appeared between their own holo images. "So far in this campaign, your guerrilla warfare style of offensive has featured hit-and-run attacks to simultaneously bleed the Collective and force it to waste dwindling resources by defending everything at the same time instead of massing its forces. Because of the unique firepower and abilities of the Cerberus-class of ships, instead of pinprick guerrilla attacks against minor targets, you've repeatedly wiped out major installations and hard targets instead. And you've done this without leaving behind a footprint or evidence of the existence of jump drives.

"But now this mission is totally different. Cygnus is no longer guarding the *Argos* because the Columbia has joined the fleet and taken over that role, so your three ships will jump to Earth to provide top cover and shoot down any enemy missiles or ships. Detailed orders have been issued to each of you. Questions?"

Alfred Jurgenson, captain of the Cygnus, had the first question and voiced what was also on the minds of the other two captains. With a concerned look, he asked, "Is the Treaty of Midway's proscription against orbital bombardment of ground targets on Earth still in effect?"

Hobson shook his head and responded, "No. We have definite, multiple source confirmations about the enemy's plans to wipe us out with a biological attack. From that point forward, the Treaty of Midway no longer applies."

This caused a few moments of uncomfortable silence as the officers present internalized the implications. Earth has been governed by the Treaty of Midway for three quarters of a millennium, which had allowed civilization to rebuild from The Fall. The only thing surviving from the world before The Fall that had guided humanity for longer than the Treaty of Midway was the Bible.

Jurgenson shook his head slightly, with a highly disturbed look on his face. "Sirs, we can't just disregard the Treaty so casually like that. There are protocols and procedures that must be followed, or we could all hang for violating it!"

The eyebrows of both Hobson and Rodding shot up, and Hobson retorted, "Captain, part of the intel package that is accompanying your mission orders details the procedural steps that were taken to withdraw from the Treaty. They were followed to the letter, and the withdrawal has already been formally communicated to the Collective. As best we could communicate it through the chaos, anyway. We're in a whole new war here."

Ronin asked the next question. "Sirs, by having our ships jump into orbit around Earth, am I to presume we are no longer worried about keeping the jump drives secret?"

Rodding nodded. "That is correct, Captain. Protection of the planet takes top priority over jump drive secrecy."

Rodgers couldn't wait anymore. "Sirs, you referred to the Columbia, and then to the *Argos* in the plural?"

Rodding smiled, and responded "Columbia is the fourth Cerberus-class vessel. She launched several weeks ago and Captain Jurgenson helped with her shakedown cruises. Columbia has become operational, and is guarding both *Argos*, now that there are two of them. The Confederate fleet of new jump ships is just starting to expand exponentially."

The virtual meeting continued for another hour as they discussed situational tactics and the broad brushstrokes of what they might expect to occur. For them, the overarching theme was to be ready for anything because there was no way to predict all the possibilities.

CHAPTER 28

FORCE OMEGA

After hours of sweaty, exhausting climbing, the team had finally reached the end of the tunnel upwards. It was a walled-off platform that clearly looks to have been sealed centuries ago. Thick dust and cobwebs had collected over everything.

Dimitri noted the footprints in the dust. "Our prior scouts left these. They were able to ascertain the location for this platform based on that sign over there," he said pointing his chin towards the wall. A swipe of a hand had previously brushed away the centuries of dirt and grime to reveal a filthy sign with an ancient form of writing that Longman did not recognize.

"That's ancient Cyrillic writing again. Hardly anyone left today who even recognizes it, much less can read it," murmured Pak to Longman.

They glanced at each other, then Longman responded, "It's like we're dealing with ghosts down here."

"Yeah, and practically everything looks the same. A long, dark tunnel extending so far into the distance we can't see either end. A platform. A sign. We take off in the wrong direction and we wouldn't know it for quite a while." Pak stated.

"Da. Old communists were renowned for bland, soul killing uniformity. Here, see this?" Dimitri stated as he brushed off a flat space on the rear wall that Longman hadn't noticed before because it was behind them in orientation.

The thick dust billowed. Obviously, it had completely hidden the bright red and gold marker underneath. "Is in Cyrillic, but it translates into "Forty-three Station, Nizhny Novgorod." The red marker with the stop number and above ground geographic location is the only thing to differentiate stops down in this tunnel. If you cannot read Cyrillic, suggest you not get lost."

They turned around and walked to the wall that sealed-off the platform from whatever was on the other side. "Is unknown what is on other side of wall," Dimitri said as they looked it over. "We did not risk exposure by drilling through."

Longman looked over to Guthrey and said, "Omega 3, job opportunity."

Guthrey, who was carrying what the Marines had informally dubbed a breaking and entering package, was already setting up his equipment to make it happen. He and Omega 4 set up a powerful laser cutting torch while the others stood back to give them room. Soon he announced, "Torch is powered up, beginning test drill."

Minutes later, the test hole was dug and Guthrey snaked a small, rope-like camera into it. "Wall is two FEET thick. Composition is old bricks," he reported with some degree of disbelief at the thickness.

At least the ancient bricks wouldn't be difficult to get through, thought Longman with some relief.

"Appears to be a vacant storage room on the other side," Guthrey added.

Longman nodded. Turning a walled-off departure area into a storage room because it no longer led anywhere useful made sense. The design of the building would render the area relatively useless for most other purposes.

"Good. We'll make our entry here. Launch your Butterfly and Wasp drones through the hole to set up a defensive perimeter on the other side, then let's make a hole we can go through," ordered Longman.

Guthrey quickly launched some of his Butterfly drones and ordered them to keep watch on the other side. He then launched a half-dozen of his armed Wasp drones. The Wasps were similar to a Butterfly, except that they were able to fire a single high-power laser pulse that would burn the drone out and give someone a very bad day at the same time.

Five minutes passed before Guthrey reported the drones were all on station. "We're ready," he said as he monitored his defensive screen.

"Omega 4, begin drilling." ordered Longman. Berger smiled as he began cutting out the grouting around the bricks with the laser torch. His suit helmet provided the necessary targeting guidance since the laser wasn't visible to the naked eye. As he cut out each brick to create an opening large enough to allow a suited Marine to pass through, the team quickly removed the bricks.

Thirty minutes passed as they worked in sweaty silence before Guthrey called out a warning that brought everything to a halt. "Contact! One hostile, entering the room. He's searching for the source of the sounds he heard. Coming closer, target acquired. Firing. Subject is down, life signs negative. Continue with the operation," he said as he talked the team through the steps occurring on the other side of the wall.

One of the Butterfly drones broadcast an optical image to the team's helmets showing an armed guard dressed in the Collective's security service uniform. At the top of his neck where his head used to be, the guard had a smoking stump. The heat had cauterized the wound, so not much blood escaped from the corpse as it collapsed.

Berger resumed his cutting. Two more hours passed uneventfully while the team worked quickly and as quietly as possible. Only two more bodies were added to the tally in the room. One was an administrative flunky who had brought a large box to the room to store it, and never knew what hit her. The other was a guard doing rounds who walked further into the room he had glanced in because there was a burnt smell wafting through the large room that seemed to become stronger the further he walked from the door. Neither survived the Wasp drones.

"We're through, Omega 1," called Berger over the commlink node in his exosuit.

"Roger that. Omega, advance by numbers and cover each other. Dimitri and his unit will guard this location. It's our rally point and exfil route, just like we discussed."

The team flowed through the storeroom like ghosts. "Hallway is clear," Guthrey noted as he watched the feeds from the drones, which were now advancing ahead of Force Omega.

Behind them, Echo 6, Julio Gonzales, and the Rabos were moving the corpses out of the storeroom into the formerly hidden platform and fashioned a makeshift wall of boxes so they wouldn't be spotted by any-one who happened to walk into the room. Gonzales' well-honed camou-flage skills made quick work of the job, and nothing would appear amiss to anyone walking in unless they got close.

The Marines moved out rapidly, maintaining radio silence now that they were inside the building. Longman quickly noted there seemed to be few people as they found a stairway and decided to climb up a few levels. As the stairs only went up from their level and there seemed to be nobody home and no surveillance systems in use, he surmised they obviously were very deep inside the Kremlin.

After they crept up ten levels or so in complete silence, Guthrey's voice over the commlink made everyone jump a little bit even though he didn't speak loudly. "Omega 1, Omega 3. Butterfly drone sensors are reporting high levels of electro-magnetic signals and a heat source on this level. Optics shows multiple armed guards and a kill box down the hall beyond this door."

Longman looked at the data feed sent by the drones to his helmet. "Armed guards, controlled kill box, buried deep for protection. And a certainty of death if we go with a frontal assault. A nice, high value data center and computing core target. Just our kind of place," he commented to the rest of the team.

Guthrey quickly responded, "I sent a Butterfly to the next level up. Two guards on duty, no kill box. They look bored. Want to bet we can tap into the data streams flowing up from the core down on the level below?"

Longman smiled a bit in spite of himself. "Not something I would bet against. Omega 7, you up for a costume party?"

Gonzales nodded affirmative, so he quickly exited his exosuit and donned the security uniform of one of the guards killed by Guthrey's Wasp drone down in the basement.

"Remember, take these guys out quietly. We do any shooting on these levels, and all sorts of alarms will be tripped," Longman cautioned unnecessarily. Gonzales just looked at him with an obvious "don't you know what I do?" expression on his face.

While all the Marines were experts in unarmed combat, they chose Gonzales to wear the guard's uniform by the simple expedient of that it fit him best, and he had a background as a trained assassin. Three minutes later, he was ready.

Pak looked him over carefully. "If they spot the bloodstain on the charcoal gray collar, they'll take you out. Don't give them the chance. Strike swiftly, and incapacitate," he whispered to Gonzales because Julio now didn't have a helmet on. Pak turned to Longman and gave a thumbs up to signal their readiness.

Gonzales walked up to the door, opened it and walked through. He walked with confidence, doing his best to project an authority he knew he didn't have. Anything to keep these two guards from becoming suspicious until he was close enough to try to take them out. Despite the pounding of his heartbeat in his ears, he thought he could hear the faint whisper of a drone following along.

The two guards looked up as he approached, and they held their rifles in a low ready position. *Just my luck these two would be alert enough to be ready for trouble,* thought Julio as he waived away the lead guard's command to halt and identify himself and buy a few more precious feet and seconds.

Appearing as though he were reaching for his identification in a slightly annoyed fashion, Gonzales suddenly lashed out and speared his stiffened fingers into the jugular of the guard who had been reaching out to receive the imaginary credentials. The guard's eyes went wide and he grasped his neck as he choked and fell to the floor in extreme pain. Gonzales' first movement had been to spear hand the first guard before continuing with his turn and spinning into a jumping roundhouse kick aimed at the head of the other guard. It was the best he could do given the distance between the two guards. He got lucky and connected with the head of the second guard on a kick that was powerful enough to smash through a couple inches of oak.

Before he finished raising his rifle, the second guard dropped like a bad habit from the suddenness of an assault that left him completely unconscious. Gonzales continued turning, using the momentum of the kick to again face the first guard, who was still trying to draw a breath of air while simultaneously trying to raise the rifle that had slipped from his hand and hung on a sling. Just as he got it in his hands, the guard made a small, surprised gurgling sound and fell to the floor with both hands clasping his neck while thrashing uncontrollably. He died with frightened, unfocused open eyes. While Force Omega quickly ran in, Gonzales unsheathed his hidden K-Bar knife and slit the throat of the unconscious guard.

"What happened to the first guy?" Gonzales asked as he cleaned the blood off his knife, while glancing at the mask of terror on the first guard's dead face.

"Since he was gasping so much after you throat punched him, I flew a Wasp right into his throat and set it to buzz apart," said Guthrey in a matter-of-fact manner like it was something he did every day. "Ended him in seconds," Guthrey added, only now breaking into a grin.

"Sweet mother of pearl, what a way to go!" muttered Gonzales, grinning like a madman. These lunatics were definitely his kind of Marines.

Longman spoke over the team commlink, but had his outside the helmet speaker reduced to a whisper for Gonzales' benefit, as he was still dressed like a guard from the Collective and was just starting the process of reentering his exosuit. "Omega 3, get eyes on whatever is through this doorway. Omega 2 and 4, rear cover back at the stairs. The countdown clock says we have less than twelve hours remaining until missile launch."

Everyone's eyes flicked to the clock on their helmet screens, slowly counting down the time.

"Omega 1, Omega 3. Drones report a hallway, approximately 25 yards in length, ending in a 'T' intersection. To the left branch at the 'T' there is a maintenance room that is currently unoccupied. To the right is a chamber with a bunch of access panels and nobody around." Guthrey reported.

Longman was surprised for a moment. "How do you know what each chamber is?"

Before Guthrey could reply, Longman's AI responded only on Longman's direct link, "Longman, I'm interpreting the writing spotted by the drones for Guthrey. I can do the same for the entire team if you like."

Longman thought for a moment, then he responded, "Do it. You might need to use pictures. My Marines can't read or write in anything more advanced than in crayons."

The AI unexpectedly responded to Longman's standard quip. "Will do. I'll make it simple enough even for Marines."

Longman wasn't sure if the AI was playing along, or actually insulting them. He made a mental note to find out later.

Switching over to the team commlink, Longman issued a quick command. "Take the 'T' to the right and get us into the room with the access panels. Move out!" The team left Pak and Berger behind as they quickly moved down the hall.

As they moved, Longman discussed the situation with his AI. "How fast can you process that writing you see to help us locate a suitable access to the defense grid?"

The AI responded instantly. "I am already processing using the Butterfly drone video being transmitted right now." The AI projected an image of the room on his screen, then highlighted three different panels. "I recommend hacking into any of these three access points to upload the virus."

Longman nodded to himself, and ordered the AI to update the team as they moved.

When they entered the huge room thirty seconds later, rifles covering all the blind spots, the team knew where to go. The nearest panel was about 40 feet into the room. It didn't take much time before Longman issued the order. "Omega 6, time to upload the package."

Dale Dannon was already moving and breaking out his toolkit. As the AI guided Dannon with recommendations for removing the panel to find a spot to tap into the system, Longman was holding another private conversation with the AI. "Recommendations on other systems we can hack to cause trouble or help us get out of here?"

The AI had anticipated the questions. "I recommend we access the panels that are being highlighted on your screen. They control the Kremlin's communication network, artificial intelligence, internal defense mechanisms, and fire suppression systems."

Longman called Jason Priest over. "Omega 5, job opportunity." He sent the information to Priest and told him to get started.

The next hour and a half passed quickly while the team worked. As they completed uploading various viruses and system taps, there was a call from Pak, who had been quiet until now while guarding the stairwell. "Omega 1, Omega 2. We've got company!" The sudden sound of gunfire punctuating Pak's words was carried over the commlink as well as being audible down the hall.

"Omega 1, I have penetrated their defense grid using the codes we obtained from the *Shanwei* and its command shuttle. I have prevented the alarm from being communicated over their network thanks to the network tap you've placed, but they've already sent a runner to fetch reinforcements. I won't be able to interfere with a face-to-face communication," announced the AI immediately after Pak's message.

Longman reacted quickly. "Force Omega, exfil immediately!" The Marines ran down the hall towards the stairwell where Pak and Berger were fully engaged in a firefight with the still-unseen troops above them.

"Omega 5, you still got that C4?" called Longman as they ran.

"That's affirmative, Omega 1," Priest replied.

"Rig up something to bring down the roof of this hall and block entry to that room with the access panels. You have two minutes to set it up!"

Priest skidded to a stop and scrambled to get it done. "Force Omega, we need to hold them off for two minutes. Hold this location until then!" Priest communicated to Omega.

The stairwell was lit up with intense exchanges of fire, grenades and a few RPGs. Within moments, everyone's vision was obscured due to the smoke that quickly filled the stairway.

"I'm hit!" cried a pain-filled voice. Longman's screen identified the critically wounded man as Omega 6, Dale Dannon. A bouncing grenade had managed to land at his feet undetected, and blew his left leg off. The other leg was shredded. His life signs were failing fast despite the suit's rudimentary medical ministrations and the medical aid being administered by Omega 3.

"Omega 1, Omega 5. Ready for detonation on your command," said Priest after only ninety seconds.

Longman thought fast as he saw Dannon die in Guthrey' arms. They couldn't risk having Dannon discovered as they would figure out the Confederacy had infiltrated the Kremlin and try to shut down everything as a precaution. "Drag Dannon's corpse behind the detonation point and let's get outta Dodge."

In the chaos of the firefight, no one questioned what initially seemed to be a bizarre order, but one that made sense upon reflection because it would hide their identities and not suggest it was a Confederate attack. Instead, the Kremlin would believe it to be a Rabos attack that coincided with the surface assault to distract them.

Guthrey used his suit's strength to hoist Dannon's corpse onto his shoulders and he sprinted back past the bomb planted by Priest. "Sorry buddy, we'll have to let you go out with a bang instead of taking you back with us," muttered Guthrey as he gently lowered Dannon to the floor. Guthrey then loosed his remaining weapons drones to guard the hall and prevent anyone from gaining access before they closed it down. Seconds later he was back with the rest of the team.

"Omega, leapfrog down the stairs!" ordered Longman.

As the team quickly made their way down, there was always one man in rear cover who was expending a lot of ammunition to discourage any chasers from following. As they scrambled, the AI spoke to the Pirate over his commlink. "Longman, I have received notice a large number of missiles launched under manual control before our virus could assert control over the defense grid. They are not responding to self-destruct commands and are flying on auto-programmed coordinates. The remaining missiles will not be launched and self-destruct commands have been accepted. They will be destroyed in four minutes."

Trying not to puff too much from the exertion, Longman asked, "Are there any troops in our exfil route?"

The AI responded instantly. "Coverage of the oldest, lower levels is incomplete, although they also appear to have been little used. Best estimate is to expect light resistance." *As expected*, Longman thought while they ran.

When they reached the lowest floor, there was a massive explosion from the upper levels that could be heard deep down and violently shook the walls and floor. Force Omega was knocked off their feet by the power of the blast, and thick clouds of dust billowed everywhere.

"Longman, I have prevented the activation of the fire suppression system to allow the fires to grow and prevent more troops from accessing your location. The stairwell on the level where the detonation occurred was shattered for two levels, and is impassable." said the AI over the team commlink.

Longman and the team slowly picked themselves off the floor. As soon as they could see a little bit, Longman ordered them to move out again.

"Boss, I don't like the looks of the ceiling," called Pak as they ran through falling dust and small chunks of rocks that we're steadily breaking loose.

"Me either. Run like you stole something," Longman commanded over the team commlink.

Soon they reached the storeroom containing their now hidden entry point. The Rabos lookout had alerted the rest of them that Force Omega was hauling arse back to the entry point.

"We've set the detonators for ten minutes, and the clock starts running when we get to the tunnel down below. The cave-in will block the entire access tunnel to the platform down below. Hurry!" yelled Dimitri as the Marines swiftly crawled through the hole in the wall to the rappelling ropes they would use to quickly get back to the bottom.

Their horses had been fed and watered while they were playing commando in the Kremlin. As the team leapt onto them using their powered exosuits, Dimitri yelled, "The clock is now running! Let's go!" and they galloped away down the tunnel.

CHAPTER 29

TASKFORCE 3

As Captain Ronin and Commander Mueller left the virtual strategy meeting, Ronin removed the holographic visor from his head and thought about how he felt disconcerted to suddenly return to reality onboard his own ship following virtual meetings.

"I hate those virtual meetings," commented Mueller, as though she were reading Ronin's mind.

"Yeah, me too. I'd rather do it in person, or not at all," replied Ronin as he stood and stretched. They had been sitting in his ready room for hours while *Cerberus* lurked unseen among the asteroids in the belt.

His collar node commlink buzzed. "Captain, Bulldog 7 has returned from delivering Force Omega to the rebels for insertion. Chief Taylor has them on landing approach to the landing bay now."

Ronin tapped his link and replied, "Acknowledged. Contact the CAG and tell him we need his presence in my ready room asap."

He looked at Mueller. "The clock is ticking already. We'll loop Sunderland into the plans when he gets here so his pilots will be ready."

They didn't have to wait long, as Sunderland arrived simultaneously with the coffee Ronin had also summoned. "It's a coffee kind of meeting, Captain?" asked Sunderland as he ushered the steward in ahead of him.

"Yes, it is, CAG. We have a job opportunity for you." At hearing the Captain's use of the ever-cynical phrase "job opportunity" and "CAG," Sunderland clicked on. There was serious work to be done when those were used together.

Hours later, Mueller sat in the Captain's chair while Ronin got his kids into bed before catching a few precious hours of shut-eye himself. LeCroy broke the silence on the bridge when a new ship jumped into their vicinity. "Commander, sensors indicate a new ship has jumped in. It's not a Cerberus-class vessel, though. It's squawking Confed ID for the Kitty Hawk!"

Before Mueller could respond, Lieutenant Delgado said, "Commander, we're receiving a communication from Kitty Hawk Actual."

Mueller looked over at Delgado. "Put it on the forward view screen, Lieutenant," he ordered.

The screen shifted to show an image of Capt. Hu Nagun. "Commander, good to see you again. Ronin getting his beauty sleep?"

Mueller smirked slightly at Captain Nagun's irreverence and disregard of commlink protocols. "That he is, Captain Nagun. We weren't aware Kitty Hawk had any jump engines, is that a new upgrade?"

Nagun smiled broadly. "Yes, it is, Commander. We don't have a lot of range yet due to our smaller power plants, but I do appreciate having any kind of jump capacity. And it answered all my questions as to how Cerberus seemed to be everywhere when it defied the known laws of physics. I understand you have a package for us?"

It was Mueller's turn to smile. "We have some toys to send your way, because Cerberus plays nice with others and we share our toys. Are you ready to receive them? Time is running short."

Nagun nodded with a slight laugh at Mueller's choice of words and her emphasis on the word "share." "We are. I promise to return as many of them unbroken as I can when we're done playing with them."

Mueller looked over at LeCroy. "Lieutenant, notify Chief Taylor to begin the transfer."

LeCroy nodded and began issuing the orders. When they were done, *Cerberus* and *Kitty Hawk* continued with their preparations.

After five precious hours of sleep, a still-exhausted Ronin stumbled out of bed. The kids would still be sleeping for hours yet. After stretching and a shower, he brewed a cup of coffee. It was going to be a long day.

The door chimed. It was Dahlia, smiling as she loved spending time with Ronin's kids. "Dahlia, are you ready to ride cowboy over my herd?" Ronin asked.

"Yes, Captain, I'll rope 'em and wrangle 'em as needed."

Ronin got a small laugh from the mental image conjured up by Dahlia's words. "You're welcome to them! You know where I am if you need me," Ronin replied as he grabbed his coffee mug and walked out.

Moments later, Ronin walked on to the bridge and made eye contact with Mueller.

"Morning, Captain," she said, somewhat envious of the few hours of sleep Ronin clocked in, even if it was at her insistence to keep him from becoming too tired.

"Everything coming along?" Ronin asked in response.

"Yes-sir. We're as prepared as we can be." Mueller replied, saying the two words as one, as she stood to exit the Captain's chair.

Ronin nodded. "Good. Go grab some sleep while you can. We'll wake you when things start to heat up."

As Mueller walked back to her quarters, it occurred to her she should wear her duty uniform to bed to save time after she woke up. So, she did.

While Mueller went to get some rest, Ronin rotated the bridge crews with their backups and settled in to read the latest reports and get up to speed on the past few hours.

***

"Action stations, action stations! All hands, man your action stations!"

Mueller awoke with a terrible start as the ship-wide call to man their battle stations sounded. She was running down the hall to the bridge by the time her mind woke up enough to even realize where she was or what she was doing. As she entered the bridge, she saw it was a beehive of activity.

"Commander, we're jumping into action momentarily," Ronin said, catching sight of her out of the corner of his eye.

"Captain, Kitty Hawk reports their jump drive is synced with ours. Both ships are at Action Station and ready for combat," said LeCroy, from his tactical station.

"Ships are ready to jump," added Perez quickly as he plotted the coordinates.

"Lieutenant Perez, jump the ships," ordered Ronin without delay.

Both *Cerberus* and *Kitty Hawk* appeared in Earth orbit with simultaneous jump flares. Seconds later, they were joined in orbit by Cygnus and Ceres from the location they had also been awaiting their own orders to jump.

"Captain, the full complement of Task Force 3 has arrived," reported Delacroix from his scanning station.

"Bandits! Multiple squadrons. Three enemy destroyers have taken up position behind their fighter screen!" yelled LeCroy from his tactical station.

"Are they in Grasshopper range?" asked Ronin.

"Negative, they're too far," LeCroy replied after taking a second to confirm the range.

As he was commander of Taskforce 3, Ronin quickly issued more commands. "Order Kitty Hawk to draw off the fighter screen, and task Ceres to jump behind the destroyers to launch a hit-and-run, jump bomb strike."

While Ronin issued the strike order, LeCroy and Delacroix were rapidly scanning to develop a more complete tactical picture. Delacroix spoke first. "Captain, scanners are receiving intermittent readings coming from low orbit below the destroyers. There's a blanket of electro-magnetic interference being generated down there to mask sensor readings, but optical resolution shows three satellites. AI presumes they're anti-sensor platforms."

Ronin wasted no time. "Plot them on Tacnet. Any other threats, friendly or otherwise?"

LeCroy shook his head. "No sir, nothing on screens at this time."

Ronin thought for a moment. "Launch Grasshoppers at those satellites. Hostilities have begun, and we need better sensor coverage of the planet."

LeCroy nodded and immediately launched the missiles. "Satellites destroyed," he said moments later.

Ronin nodded before moving on to the next thing.

KITTY HAШK

"Captain Nagun, message from *Cerberus*. They're ordering Kitty Hawk to draw off the fighter screen."

Nagun smiled a cold half-smile. "Looks like we're doing business right away! Navigation, plot a course to take us close enough to get them to come after us. I want to pass by close enough to get off a few shots at them and kick the hornet's nest."

As Nagun spoke, Ronin stepped over to the tactical station to get eyes on the Tacnet plot with his tactical officer. "Benton, can we get the fighters to slew over to this area?" Ronin asked Tactical Officer Mary Benton, pointing his finger to a spot that was located over the Pacific Ocean.

"With pleasure, Captain. If the helmsman can get the fighters to commit with a reasonable sized space buffer, I recommend our velocity be just below the max speeds of the fighters to keep them interested so they stay committed," Benton responded with an evil smile.

"I like it. You're thinking along the same lines I am. Lead 'em on and keep their heads in the game thinking they have a chance by slowly catching up. Hopefully they're not terribly disciplined or experienced enough to catch on to what we're doing and break contact," Nagun said.

He turned his head to the helmsman, who was seated next to Benton on the small bridge. "Thatcher, you catch all that?" asked Nagun.

"Yes-sir, we'll play hard to get and be the rabbit for the dogs to chase!" responded Helmsman Ned Thatcher, who was already plotting the course and speeds based on the known acceleration of the enemy fighters. Seconds later, Thatcher added, "Captain, we're ready."

With a nod over to Benton, Ronin simply said, "Rotate the ship, and open fire."

Both Thatcher and Benton reacted instantly. Benton initially fired the forward rail guns, followed by a few high-speed, anti-fighter missiles. "Captain, initial salvo away. Our chosen attack profile should indicate to the fighter screen we are intending to stick around and slug it out. Missiles are tracking and should arrive in five minutes."

The minutes passed slowly, because everyone was glued to the Tacnet plot. "No change in fighter posture yet. Rail gun slugs passed harmlessly. One minute until the missiles arrive." Benton commented, somewhat distractedly sounding. "Targets acquired by the missiles. They're homing in. Fighters now reacting, at last."

Nagun wondered why the fighters were so slow to react. Their sensor net should have alerted them to the incoming threats much earlier.

"Impact! Now multiple impacts. Six fighters destroyed." reported Benton. "Fighters are splitting off. Looks like we finally got their attention. Some of them, anyway. Only two groups coming after us."

"Helm, we still on our approach?" Nagun asked with a perplexed look on his face.

Thatcher nodded, without fully turning his head to look. "Yes-sir. We are rapidly closing. I don't understand why they aren't already chasing the big, juicy looking spacecraft that's coming so tantalizingly close."

Neither did anybody else on the bridge.

THE PEOPLE'S FIGHTER SQUADRON 254

"Comrade-Commander, where did those missiles come from?" yelled Pllot Wu, the squadron's second in command. "My scopes aren't showing anything, but I can see the enemy corvette right there!" His garbled communication was just barely discernible through the static on the channel.

"I don't know. Calm yourself, comrade. We can attack what we can see, so let's attack." said Squadron Leader, Alexander Kasparov.

"Squadron 254, attack pattern bravo. Attack the corvette. Confirm," Kasparov said over the squadron's channel, adding "confirm" as was their protocol when communications weren't reliable. Only some of the pilots confirmed, and followed him.

Kasparov couldn't understand what was happening because they hadn't detected any enemy broadcasts to interfere with their communications. Why were all their defense systems suddenly so wonky? He even had to eyeball an approach vector to the incoming corvette because his nav system crashed.

KITTY HAWK

"Fire some more missiles at the other squadrons. Get their attention," ordered Captain Nagun. Tactical Officer Benton launched the birds, and they waited some more minutes.

"Captain, the partial squadrons that have turned to attack us won't even come close. They took approach vectors that look like someone eyeballed it instead of calculating anything. There's still room for us to close with the main body. Show the flag and get their attention if we want." reported the XO, Steve Fisher.

Nagun concentrated on that report and recommendation for a few moments while he slowly nodded his head slightly. "Yeah, I think that's prudent at this point. I'm not sure what the story is over there. Helm, make it happen."

Thatcher laid in a new course. One that was guaranteed to get some attention.

CERBERUS

LeCroy looked hard at what Tacnet was telling him. He could hardly believe what he was seeing. "Captain, Kitty Hawk reports only a few scattered fighters are giving chase, even after the missiles destroyed some of them. And we can hear the enemy communications! They're not encrypted for some reason, but they're filled with static and fading out from time to time. They seem very discombobulated over there," he reported.

Ronin half-smiled as he looked at Mueller and she did the same while looking back. They knew why.

"We can only surmise that our Marines operating as Force Omega were successful," Ronin responded cryptically.

Mueller nodded. "I wonder why they haven't reported in?"

FORCE OMEGA

"Argh!" yelled Longman in surprise, as a piece of shrapnel pinged off the back of his helmet while the ground shook violently and making their horses stumble a bit while they galloped down the tunnel deep underground.

"Tunnel is sealed, Omega 1," commented Pak, catching his breath. The shockwave from the demolition charge was stronger than they expected.

"Looks like Omega 5 followed the Marines P for Plenty formula," Longman commented dryly as he glanced to the smoke and dust billowing from their rear.

"We still too deep for commlinks to *Cerberus*?" asked Pak.

"Yep. They'll have to figure out whether we were successful on their own until we reestablish contact."

They galloped on down the long, dark tunnel. They could clearly see where they were going because the dark tunnel was displayed in a ghostly green night vision projected on the inside of their helmet screens.

THE PEOPLE'S FIGHTER SQUADRON 254

Alexander Kasparov was pretty frustrated at his squadron's lack of responsiveness, and at his fighter's systems, and at the world in general. Their preflight briefing had said today was the day they went to war in the skies over Earth and to expect the Confederacy to respond in kind. They'd been assured that everything was in place, and all their systems were manned and responsive. Two hours later, the only part of that briefing to come true was the going to war part. He craned his neck from side to side to visually check where his fighters were. Looks like ten, with maybe another partial squadron bringing up the rear where he couldn't see.

Great. A suicide run at a modern Confed corvette that suddenly appeared out of nowhere, with about a dozen or so fighters. Not how I pictured my day when I woke up this morning, Kasparov thought. About that time, he realized they were going to miss the corvette because he had misjudged their relative speeds. Pulling hard, he made a sharp course correction and hoped the others could follow along.

KITTY HAWK

"Incoming fighters making a course correction. They're still shallowing," said LeCroy as he stared hard at his Tacnet readout. Ronin nodded suddenly. *That was perfect.* "Helm, execute new course. Time to leave these guys in the dust."

The helm responded to Ronin's commands immediately. "Coming on to new heading now, Captain. We're coming in hard on the main body," Thatcher said. Kitty Hawk suddenly sprinted ahead, using her powerful drives to rapidly accelerate.

Benton squinted at her Tacnet readout. "Captain, still no reaction from the enemy formations. It's like they still don't see us or something!"

THE PEOPLE'S FIGHTER SQUADRON 254

Kasparov helplessly watched the enemy corvette change course. It was a nimble spacecraft for a large ship, and he couldn't help but admire its sleek lines as the main engines fired. *She's a sprinter, that one. I would love to helm one of those. Just to see what she handles like!* he thought wistfully. As they watched the enemy ship accelerate away, Kasparov and Wu couldn't help but feel a strange mix of frustration and relief because they were now out of position to take part in the engagement, which was not going well from their perspective because the Collective's defense systems had glitched so badly.

KITTY HAWK

"Rotate the ship, and launch several broadside missile salvos," ordered Nagun. He was getting annoyed at the lack of responsiveness by the enemy fighters.

"Hard to play the rabbit when we can't get the attention of the hounds," commented Fisher as he stepped to stand next to Nagun in the command chair.

"No kidding. Who would've thought we had to get so close we could kick down the doors just to get their attention!" replied Nagun.

Fisher smiled a crooked smile. "Maybe you should've dabbed perfume behind our ears and dressed the ship up real cute as we sashay past them?" he quipped. Neither of them had an explanation for what was going on here.

"Captain, Tacnet plots show the fighter formations are slowly breaking up, but only because they appear to be drifting!" Benton announced with more than a touch of surprise in her voice. "Salvo one, away," she added.

"Keep firing until they react," ordered Nagun.

Minutes passed. Finally, Benton noted, "Our birds are tracking and have locked on to individual targets. Tacnet is keeping them from double targeting enemy fighters for maximum dispersal. Still no reaction from the main body."

CERBERUS

"Kitty Hawk has changed course. Tacnet plot has them angling closer to the main body. The first group of breakaway fighters has been left in the dust by them," LeCroy reported.

"Still no organized reaction from the main body." Ronin took a deep breath and continued, "Keep Ceres on standby. Those fighters need to be drawn off and out of position before they jump behind the destroyers so they can't protect those ships."

As they watched Tacnet, the enemy failed to react until the missiles started destroying dozens of the fighters. "Fighters slowly dispersing. There's still nothing coordinated about their movements. There have been at least fifteen collisions between their birds so far. And Kitty Hawk is still firing missile salvos." LeCroy reported.

THE PEOPLE'S FIGHTER SQUADRON 254

Wu sat in his fighter. He had partial control over his flight systems, which meant by experimenting he retained spotty forward thrust and inconsistent maneuvering thrusters for yaw, pitch and longitudinal control. His fighter had already received slight damage in a collision with a nearby fighter from one of the Russian squadrons, based on the markings. He couldn't tell which, because his tactical information was nil and he only saw the markings briefly enough to identify the squadron origin.

He was also frustrated that his squadron leaders went after a ship somewhere. He couldn't see it, and didn't know where it was. Nor had they said what they were doing, or so it seemed, because his commlink systems were down.

While Pilot Wu hadn't vented his frustrations, he craned his neck and looked around using his Mark I optics (his eyeballs). Space is vast, and even an engagement in Earth orbit takes up a huge amount of area. Accordingly, Mark I optics weren't going to tell him much. As he looked for other fighters, he was shocked to see small, distant explosions suddenly start appearing all around. There were dozens and dozens of them.

"We're under attack!" he called into the commlink system from his helmet mic. There was no response of any kind, and he could see dozens of other pilots dying in short, fiery deaths. Wu clicked his commlink transmit button again. Then several more times, before he figured out the thing was totally dead.

Oh no! I thought it was quiet from radio silence procedures! he thought to himself worriedly. Breaking against all the Collective's training that quashed individual initiative, which is something the Collective drilled into its subjects from birth as a means of control and to prevent them from getting big ideas about rebellion, Wu panicked and he hit the forward thrusters to build up speed and start maneuvering.

"Wha? Huh? Umph…" he managed to sputter when the fighter failed to respond. It was the last thing he ever uttered as a missile from Kitty Hawk's next salvo slammed into his fighter and ended his part in the war.

CƎRBƎRUS

Ronin was watching the Tacnet plot closely, waiting for the proper moment to unleash Ceres on the destroyers, when his collar node commlink chimed with an incoming message from Nagun.

"*Cerberus* Actual, go ahead." Ronin said after opening the link.

"*Cerberus* Actual, *Kitty Hawk* Actual." Nagun said, all business now. "We're changing our attack vector to drive right at the main body. They seem to be shut down for some reason and I want to take as much advantage as we can."

Ronin responded, "Acknowledged. We thought you were doing exactly that. Keep exercising initiative as you see fit and be advised, we'll begin Stage 2 on this end. *Cerberus* Actual, out."

As he closed the commlink, Ronin looked over at LeCroy and Mueller, who were waiting at the tactical station. "Tell Ceres it's go time," he said.

LeCroy and Mueller nodded, and LeCroy issued the order.

C≡R≡S

"Captain Rogers, *Cerberus* Actual has issued us a go order," reported the ship's tactical officer, Terry Ignatius.

From the Captain's seat, Rodgers smiled broadly at that report. *Finally!* she thought. She pursed her lips for a moment and nodded slightly. "Helm, initiate jump on my command. Tactical, launch Grasshoppers as soon as you're able after the jump."

"Aye, aye, Captain," came the simultaneous replies. "Helm, keep our FTL drive spun up for an emergency jump in case our LZ gets too hot. Initiate the jump, helmsman," said Rogers.

Ceres disappeared in a jump flash that was all but invisible to the naked eye because of the distance to the destroyers. The arrival flash was a different matter entirely.

"Jump 2, complete," reported the helmsman as soon as they arrived.

Navigation took their bearings, while the Tactical Officer, Terry Ignatius, busily updated the Tacnet plot. "We're only 100 miles behind the destroyers. No response yet. Launching Grasshoppers now," he reported. "Missile launch!" he suddenly yelled. "Multiple contacts, inbound! Time on target, thirty seconds."

The jump bombs went FTL with a flurry of jump flares, and announced their arrival with devastating effect.

"Helm, emergency jump. Take us above this whole mess, and we'll launch a few more from there," ordered Rodgers. She was a few seconds too late, and Ceres shook with multiple hits that had overwhelmed the ship's point defense batteries.

"Captain, jump drive has been hit, we can't jump!" reported Ignatius with a worried look. "Damage control teams are on the way." he added.

Rodgers issued a swift series of orders. "Helm, evasive maneuvers! Tactical, open fire with whatever is still working. Alert the medical bay to expect incoming. Launch our fighters, now!"

CΞRBΞRUS

"Commander, we've received a message from Force Omega. One KIA, some minor injuries. They're reporting success with their objective," said the communications officer, Lt. Maria Delgado.

"Acknowledged. Tell them to hole up in a safe spot for the time being and someone will be along to retrieve them when things cool off up here," Mueller ordered. She was interrupted by a message from the ship's AI.

"Ballistic missile launch detected. Reading multiple heat blooms from thirty-seven different locations around the Collective. Missiles rapidly accelerating. Trajectory analysis has been uploaded to Tacnet." said the AI.

"There's too many birds!" cried LeCroy after he surveyed the missile plots.

"AI, can we shoot down all the missiles?" Mueller quickly asked.

"If all Taskforce 3 ships respond to the command within the next thirty seconds, but Tacnet was just updated to indicate Ceres' jump drive is damaged and they've no choice but to further engage the destroyers at close range. Best case scenario leaves between six and eight missile strikes against Confederate civilian targets."

Ronin had to make a terrible decision, and he had to make it swiftly. What he and others thought about the decision to abandon Ceres and try to protect civilian cities would just have to wait until later. "All available Taskforce ships to engage the missiles immediately," he ordered.

Within seconds of each other, *Cerberus*, *Cygnus* and *Kitty Hawk* jumped into lower orbit and they began shooting immediately. "Captain, Kitty Hawk is launching the fighters we transferred. The remaining Tomcats on Cerberus are still waiting in the tubes. AI needs them launched." LeCroy reported.

"Launch immediately!" Ronin responded.

The ship's rail guns continued to launch salvo after salvo of anti-ship ordinance, while the anti-ship missiles did likewise. The fighters were chasing down any strays so the ships could concentrate on the main body of missiles. At least any misses would splash into the Pacific or the Atlantic, and the ordinance was the much smaller anti-ship shot.

The next fifteen minutes would forever be a blur to Ronin and the bridge crews of Taskforce 3. Dozens of coordinated micro-jumps around the planet by each of the ships, each of which was prodigiously burning their fuel reserves. Jump and fire, then repeat. It had never occurred to Confederation scientists to even test out the effects of repeated micro-jumps on the human body, because no one had imagined a scenario where that might become necessary.

"Jumps complete. Remaining missile impacts beginning in twenty seconds," announced the AI.

Ronin looked around the bridge crew woozily. They all appeared to be drunk out of their minds, as they moved slowly and unsteadily. "Report," he said, which caused his sudden headache to pound even harder.

"Ship is secure, ordinance is low, fuel is low, no damage. Medical bay is reporting a huge rush of disoriented crew calling for assistance," replied Mueller as she gripped the rail by the tactical station while LeCroy was updating the tactical situation on Tacnet.

"Ceres still locked in combat with the destroyers. One is no longer maneuvering but still firing, one is destroyed, and one is attacking hard," LeCroy reported.

"Tell Cygnus to jump in to maximum Grasshopper range and give Ceres a hand with her remaining jump bombs," Ronin ordered, as his eyes fell on the main view screen. There he could see the wildly separated cities that were highlighted. The AI had placed red highlights on the screen over six cities around the globe.

"Missiles have released their biological payloads over the following cities," announced the AI. "Old St. Louis, North America. Formosa, Argentina. Kyoto, Honshu Island, Japan. Albany, Western Australia. Juarez, Mexico. Cambridge, British Isles. Konin, Poland. And Satura, India," added the AI.

Ronin's console node commlink chimed for attention. In his current state of shock and disorientation, he was pretty inclined to ignore the evil device until he noticed the origin of the call. The Citadel. More than the very capital of the Confederacy itself, The Citadel was the residence of the President of the Confederacy.

"Cerberus Actual, go ahead," Ronin said after he opened the commlink.

"Captain Ronin, this is President Wellington Harrison," said the voice on the other end of the line. Harrison carried a strong northern Midwest accent from Wisconsin. "I'm sorry we have to meet under these circumstances, but you have to act immediately if we are to save the planet."

In his current state, the overly dramatic phrasing of "save the planet" still wasn't enough to faze Ronin. He had already reached the same conclusion President Harrison and his defense counsel had when they all had gamed out different missile scenarios before the battle.

"Yes, Mr. President. I presume you are authorizing the first orbital strikes by the West since The Fall?" Ronin replied.

Harrison responded after a few seconds, his voice strained and sounding a bit choked. "Yes. You are authorized to release rail gun orbital strikes and nuclear weapons as necessary to destroy the virus."

Ronin said nothing for a few seconds, the weight of the moment overwhelming him for a moment or two. "Sir, let me clarify. You are authorizing orbital and nuclear strikes...against our own cities?" he asked, the horror in his voice unmistakable. Everyone on the bridge stared at him during this exchange. No one moved or spoke; they were frozen in shock.

"Yes, you are so authorized. We have to sacrifice millions now, to save billions. If you don't, the contagion will overwhelm our ability to constrain it and become a worldwide pandemic. It is elegantly designed, nearly always lethal, and extraordinarily contagious with a long, asymptomatic incubation period. That, in combination with the current dispersal, will prevent any chance for us to stop its spread."

Ronin nodded slowly, appreciating that Harrison articulated what Ronin already knew for the benefit of the bridge crew and for posterity.

"May God have mercy on their souls," he said, acknowledging the decision to act had been made.

After a few seconds of silence, Harrison responded, "Agreed. Harrison out."

Ronin looked over at LeCroy and Mueller. "Lieutenant, advise Kitty Hawk to destroy the missile launch sites with her rail guns," he ordered.

LeCroy nodded, and send the instruction to Kitty Hawk. Nagun quickly acknowledged and jumped his ship away to make it happen.

Ronin let a few more seconds of shocked silence pass before he could bring himself to continue. "Lieutenant, transfer control of the nukes to my station."

A second later, his screen lit up showing he had control. The bridge crew still couldn't figure out if they were more shocked by the order to bomb their own cities with nukes, or the fact the ship had been secretly armed with nukes.

"AI, this is the Captain. Launching a nuclear strike is authorized against the following cities. Old St. Louis, North America. Formosa, Argentina. Kyoto, Japan. Albany, Australia. Juarez, Mexico. Cambridge, Britain. Konin, Poland. Satura, India. Command code Ronin, alpha, 1A."

Ronin looked over to Mueller, and the remaining color drained from her face. "Commander, it's millions now, or billions over the next few months. We are out of time here, and I don't believe rail guns will adequately purge the contamination," Ronin said. She nodded slowly with a slight flinch, her eyes reflecting her near disbelief about the situation they found themselves in. *She doesn't balk at doing what must be done, not anymore*, Dan thought as he saw the emotions and resignation in Mueller's face.

"AI, this is the Commander. Authorization code Mueller, bravo, 2B."

The AI wasted little time on the import of the moment or how heavily it would forever weigh on the officers present. "Voice authentication and codes accepted. Identified cities targeted. Missile launch imminent. Initial launch in thirty seconds."

No one spoke. The bridge crew stared off in different directions. Some were looking at their screens without seeing a thing. Others blankly looked at the forward view screen. A few looked at each other in disbelief of the moment. The past few hours had been filed with repeated shocks. Biological weapons. Disabled enemy fleets. Orbital bombardment. Nuclear weapons, and the surprise that they were already onboard. And now, nuking their own cities.

"Missile one, away. Coming about on new course," announced the AI in response to Perez's helm commands. "Reaching next launch window in two minutes."

The AI repeated its launch, course change, and launch window procedure several more times until they were approaching the final launch window for Old St. Louis in Missouri.

"Captain, is there anyone who even lives in Old St. Louis? It's already a bad-luck ghost town because it's been destroyed several times," asked LeCroy.

The question broke through Ronin's quiet reverie. "Yes, I believe there's a small colony there again," he replied after a moment's thought. "I saw it somewhere in a briefing that there was a group who didn't believe the old city was cursed, and that it would not be destroyed again."

The bridge crew didn't need to ask about the luck of Old St. Louis. The city had originally been known just as St. Louis, Missouri. When it was ravaged by The Fall, the population mostly died or fled from the original flu virus. Originally, the city had developed into a major transportation hub for the country, and that traffic brought in the virus before anyone was aware there was a problem. It wasn't a pretty death, and the city struggled to get back on its feet when the nuclear weapons were exchanged before the Treaty of Midway had been signed.

Then a year later, a one-megaton warhead that slipped through the western air defenses reduced the city to rubble. For a few centuries after The Fall, it effectively didn't exist as an urban center. But, due to its location on two of the continent's major shipping rivers, St. Louis was eventually rebuilt in more primitive fashion, only to be wiped out once more when the old prewar Oahe Dam in South Dakota failed after a particularly wet couple of years. Billions of gallons of water roared down the Missouri River and crashed into St. Louis. Since then, the ruins had been renamed Old St. Louis and the site was avoided as a dead, repeatedly unlucky place.

"Missile six, away," announced the AI.

There were no more course changes, and the mushroom cloud of their final nuclear strike became visible on the forward view screen. Ronin's console node commlink chimed with an incoming message from Nagun.

"Kitty Hawk Actual to Cerberus Actual. Launch sites destroyed. Their defense grid is smashed," he said soberly.

"Captain, Cygnus reports the enemy destroyers have been disabled, and their fighters scattered around the planet and out of fuel," LeCroy added, intruding on Ronin's conversation with Nagun.

"Acknowledged. Let's mop up the skies and I'll tell the ground pounders to start Phase 3," Ronin replied to both of them.

Weeks later, the Battle of Earth was over.

CHAPTER 30

THE END OF THE BEGINNING

Cerberus jumped into the designated arrival point for incoming jump capable ships at Wayside Station, something the traffic controllers at Wayside had realized was needed now that jump ships had joined the fleet.

"Jump complete, Captain." announced Perez tiredly. They were all exhausted. Circles were visible under their baggy eyes.

"Captain, incoming message from Wayside. Admiral Rodding and Colonel Hobson are waiting for you and Commander Mueller for debriefing." Delgado said.

Ronin merely nodded. "Begin docking when you're ready, Perez," he said.

All too quickly, Ronin and Mueller were soon ushered into Rodding's office.

"Captain. Commander. Welcome back. We've a lot to discuss." Ronin had been dreading this discussion. Every night he had awoken from a nightmare where he nuked the planet, then used rail guns to bombard lesser targets for weeks.

Hobson took the glasses from Rodding's private bar without seeking his permission, and placed one in front of each of them. Hobson solemnly filled them with several fingers of the precious bourbon.

"Before we begin, I would offer the following toast. Not to victory, but to honor the memory of those who can no longer be with us," Hobson said, raising his glass. "To our fallen. May our people never suffer from war again."

They all raised their glasses and took a sip. It was the same high-quality bourbon Rodding always had on hand, which made the sipping easier.

"Sir, has the enemy resistance been mopped up already?" Mueller asked.

"Mostly. There are pockets of resistance, but the ground troops have been cleaning them out one by one. We're about to enter a period of consolidating our victory, which means you and your crew will start to get some leave time to rest and recuperate."

Ronin nodded wearily. He needed a vacation.

"Captain, we have a new mission for you, should you choose to accept," Hobson said, staring intently at Ronin.

"Sir, I'm sure worn down now. I don't think I would be mission effective," Ronin began to respond as Rodding interrupted him.

"Agreed, Captain. Now. But later you won't be. And your ship needs a refit after we finish repairing the battle damage to the Ceres," he said.

Something about the way Rodding mentioned "refit" tickled Ronin's internal warning lights. "Sir, a refit? Cerberus is still a fairly new ship."

Rodding and Hobson exchanged knowing glances, before Hobson responded. "Captain, while you were fighting the Battle of Earth, the science division made multiple dark matter breakthroughs out at Ninebase. Cerberus is to be refit with a new, dark matter power plant."

Ronin was speechless for a moment before he erupted. "What! Why? What's wrong with our fusion plant?"

Rodding took the opening. "Nothing, except that your jump range is far too limited. Captain, with a dark matter power plant Cerberus can skip the need for an interstellar gas station and jump out to the Baidam constellation and search for our former colonies or explore new worlds.

"Ronin, we need to start finding out more about our galactic neighborhood, and Cerberus is the key to doing so. Besides, it's not like you can just return to Earth and relax at your family's cottage in the north woods without drawing attention to yourself," Rodding concluded.

Ronin flinched a bit involuntarily as the Admiral just nixed exactly what Ronin had in mind. "Sir, I don't understand. Why couldn't I just take the kids camping out in the north woods or go to my folk's cottage? No one would recognize us."

The cluelessness of THAT statement nearly shocked Rodding for a moment, until he remembered that the Cerberus crew was busy fighting a war in space, and really hadn't been planet side to watch the news for a long time.

Rodding's eyes softened as his face broke into somewhat of a sad visage. Dispensing with formalities, he continued, "Dan, I hate to be the one to break this to you, but you, and to a lesser extent, Commander Mueller, are the two most famous people on the planet. And you've been the most famous for quite some time, but neither of you have been made aware of the true extent of your worldwide fame.

"You've found secrets possibly leading to the legendary lost colonies. You found a hidden planet and base. You've destroyed many enemy vessels. You led the Battle of Earth and defeated our ancient enemy. You nuked our own cities to stop a worldwide pandemic from wiping us out.

"There have been multiple television programs about the two of you, and about certain members of your crew. Your Marines have been especially popular subjects of the cinema. There have been hit movies about all these exploits. There isn't anywhere you can hide on that planet where someone won't find out and draw unwanted attention."

Ronin and Mueller were speechless as they both turned to look at each other in horror. Both of them hated fame, the media, and anything to do with either. "Uh, I guess, perhaps, leaving the solar system is a good way to avoid all that," stuttered Mueller, speaking for both herself and Ronin.

"Agreed. Maybe it's time to get away while we can."

Rodding smiled broadly, knowing his two highly perceptive officers would quickly reach the same conclusion he and Hobson already had reached. "Good. Excellent, in fact. We took the liberty to already cut the orders for you. In the meanwhile, I want the both of you to get as much downtime aboard Wayside as you can. The refit will commence in a few weeks at *Argo 1*, who is already expecting Cerberus after they launch their next vessel.

"Also, regarding the Marines from Force Omega. We have arranged a little publicity tour for them, so they will be detached for that duty for a few months. Omega's exploits have been featured in a new hit movie that is drawing massive crowds, and the people want to see the crazy Marines who brought down the Collective's defense grid. We understand the Marines 'P' for Plenty formula plays a key role in both the actual events and the show."

Despite his weariness, Ronin couldn't help but smile at the thought of his combat Marines being paraded around in a public relations role for a while. "Sir, they're quite the characters. I can't guarantee they'll behave or even enjoy the duty. Best I can tell, they'll either end up killing someone in boredom, or ham it up and have far more fun than is appropriate."

Both Rodding and Hobson smiled, having worked closely with Marines earlier in their respective careers. "Understood, Captain, and not unexpected. We have already assigned Fleet Intelligence Security to ride herd on them, which both the Marines and the Security personnel will mutually hate. Those sort of folks are notoriously unforgiving in the humor department." Hobson noted.

Ronin smiled broadly at the mental image of Fleet Intelligence Security trying to corral Marines bent on a good time. "I wish them the best of luck, sir," Ronin said, making them all laugh somewhat maliciously.

Still chuckling a bit, Rodding continued where Hobson left off. "We can certainly celebrate a great victory for now, but we all know of greater problems than honoring our dead, and corralling Marines on a PR tour await us in the future."

That might be the understatement of the millennium, thought Ronin as he and Mueller just glanced at each other with raised eyebrows, and took another sip of bourbon.

ABOUT THE AUTHOR

John Filcher is an avid sci-fi reader who enjoyed writing *Cerberus*. Due to his tragically, some would say comically, bad skills with all things math, after an exceptionally misspent youth he went to law school instead of medical school.

Despite all that, he has been trying to write like a normal human being ever since. Someday, he has high hopes to master coherent sentence structure in addition to proper punctuation and stuff, but for now just makes do like everyone else.